To end a war, he must free a spirit.

Ronin Toshi Umezawa has captured the Taken One:
the prize over which humans and kami have fought
for decades. But now, as moonfolk, foxfolk, Princess
Michiko, and the daimyo all converge on him, he must
make a fateful decision: Should he release the
imprisoned spirit and risk her wrath?

**Scott McGough concludes the epic story of a ronin
and a princess and their battle to save a kingdom from
war and destruction.**

EXPERIENCE THE MAGIC™

MAGIC: The Gathering™

Kamigawa Cycle · Book III

GUARDIAN
SAVIORS of kamigawa

Scott McGough

Wizards OF THE COAST™

GUARDIAN: SAVIORS OF KAMIGAWA

©2005 Wizards of the Coast, Inc.

Distributed in the United States by Holtzbrinck Publishing. Distributed in Canada by Fenn Ltd.

Distributed to the hobby, toy, and comic trade in the United States and Canada by regional distributors.

Distributed worldwide by Wizards of the Coast, Inc. and regional distributors.

Cover art by Donato Giancola
First Printing: May 2005
Library of Congress Catalog Card Number: 2004116895

9 8 7 6 5 4 3 2 1

US ISBN: 0-7869-3786-6
ISBN-13: 978-0-7869-3786-8
620-96884-001-EN

U.S., CANADA,
ASIA, PACIFIC, & LATIN AMERICA
Wizards of the Coast, Inc.
P.O. Box 707
Renton, WA 98057-0707
+1-800-324-6496

EUROPEAN HEADQUARTERS
Wizards of the Coast, Belgium
T Hofveld 6d
1702 Groot-Bijgaarden
Belgium
+322 467 3360

Visit our web site at www.wizards.com

Dedication

This book is dedicated to my grandmothers: Katherine Teeny Schiro and Kitty McGough.

Acknowledgments

This book would not have been possible without contributions from the following exceptional individuals:

Elena K. McGough, who makes the real world worth living in Tim Kreider, for his excellent internet comic The Pain—When Will It End?; The Venture Brothers Hank and Dean; plus Brock, Rusty, the Monarch, and even H.E.L.P.E.R.

Princess Michiko stood among the ancient cedars of the Jukai forest, staring patiently up through the thick canopy of leaves. Though the horrors and strife of the Kami War had spread to every corner of her nation, here at least was one place where the wind was soft and pale yellow light streamed placidly through the trees. The war would find her again, she was sure of that. The serenity of the forest's edge would not last, but while it did she meant to come here often to appreciate this one tranquil place left in all the world.

Michiko continued to watch the canopy overhead, gracefully balanced atop a small grassy mound. Beside her stood her friend Riko, a slight young woman who wore a student's robe and carried a short bow with all the confidence of a professional soldier. Riko's eyes continuously scanned the surrounding area, but they also passed over Michiko herself as often as possible.

Four kitsune warriors also accompanied Michiko and Riko. The foxmen blended into their surroundings so well they were almost invisible, but Michiko always knew they were there. She had been a frequent target for attacks and abductions lately, and her kitsune hosts back in the village were not about to let her come to more harm while she was their guest.

Michiko was grateful for the escorts, but there had been no further attacks on her since they had escaped the massacre at Minamo Academy. She welcomed the kitsune's protection, but it was maddening to sit idle while her nation and the entire world tore itself apart. The elders were keeping her safe, but they were also keeping her from doing any good.

Riko shifted her weight and flexed the fingers on her bow hand. "Any sign, Michiko-hime?"

The princess slowly closed her eyes. She shook her head. "Not yet."

Riko's voice betrayed the archer's scowl. "He won't answer. And I'm glad of it."

Michiko opened her eyes. The kitsune were treating her as a gifted child, but a child nonetheless. They included her in their council meetings and they listened politely when she spoke, but her arguments rarely held sway.

So Michiko had called upon her allies outside the forest. After taking her mentors' dire warnings into account, Michiko had sent a messenger to Toshi Umezawa in the Takenuma Swamp. She had retained the ochimusha's services, and he had proven himself both reliable and effective. The kitsune who had met him didn't object to his abilities, however, but his character. Indeed, when he and Michiko first met, Toshi had impulsively kidnapped her and held her against her will. Fortunately, he had seen working for the princess as more valuable than ransoming her. Toshi was an opportunist and a mercenary, but he was at least a competent one.

In her message, Michiko requested that Toshi provide some general information about the situation in the marsh lands and requested that he to come to her for a new assignment. It had been several weeks since she sent it, and so far Toshi had not replied.

Michiko was anxious to see him, but not for his report on the criminal goings-on in Takenuma. Toshi had laid his hands on the great prize her father had stolen from the spirit world, the Taken One, whose abduction sparked twenty years of Kami War. When she had seen Toshi with it in his arms, she had longed to reach out and touch it herself, to feel its power and perhaps finally understand the spell it had cast on her father.

But the Taken One was too powerful and too unpredictable. Her guardians and Toshi himself had cautioned her to keep away, and Michiko never came within arm's reach of the prize. Since then her thoughts had often returned to the rough-hewn disk with the etched figure of a serpent across its face. She felt it was the key to ending the conflict that had erupted between the spirit world and the physical one. It was the key, and she herself was somehow tied to it.

So she waited for Toshi's reply, or better still, Toshi himself. Only he could tell her what she needed to know, and she could feel their time running out. Toshi was cunning, so she expected he was still alive. She had also worked diligently to improve her skill with the messenger kanji, so she was sure that it had reached him.

He would have to reply soon. When she pictured the world, Michiko saw waves of violence and conflict all rolling toward her and her peaceful patch of forest. Not even the kitsune could keep her safe forever.

Something rustled in the trees, then a strange black symbol burst through the canopy. Michiko's heart raced. She recognized the same messenger kanji she had sent to the swamp and felt a small rush of pride. It had returned just as she had intended. And if it had found Toshi, it might also bear his response.

The queer black bird fluttered through the beams of sunlight toward the princess. The kitsune warriors and Riko all tensed as they prepared for a fight. Two of the fox samurai stepped between Michiko and the symbol with their swords drawn.

Well clear of the kitsune blades, the messenger kanji stopped and hovered in place.

"Deliver your message," Michiko called.

The thick, inky strokes of the kanji pulsated as purple light twinkled along their edges. A clear voice rang out, its words tinged with a touch of amusement.

"Princess," Toshi's voice said. "Nice work with the kanji. Unable to visit you at present, but I promise I'll see you soon. As for general information . . . it's a complete nightmare out here. But don't worry. I'm working on it."

The kanji deflated back to its original size and began to crumble. The light breeze blew ash and grit back into the thicker reaches of the forest, where they disappeared into the gloom.

"He's working on it," Riko sneered. "We can all relax. Toshi's working on it."

Michiko frowned. "Riko," she said. "Toshi rescued all of us from Minamo, and from the forest myojin before that. Surely you appreciate just how much Toshi is capable of."

Riko held Michiko's stern eyes. "I do, Michiko-hime. I'm not scoffing at his abilities. I'm afraid of what he can do, not what he can't."

"I have paid for his services," Michiko said. "So whatever he is or isn't capable of, he will do as I ask him. That's why I wanted him here."

"And I'm sure he'll come. You asked him for help . . . that's like a delicious smell to Toshi. He'll show up when we need him least and profit from it, like he always does."

Michiko did not reply, but turned back toward the village. The kitsune samurai spread out before her, gliding through the forest without disturbing a single twig.

Riko was underestimating Toshi. Michiko had seen him confront the most powerful adversaries and win through guile instead of force. He was capable of great deeds, and not just in scope. If she could just talk to him, he could help her understand the Taken One, and she could help him understand the rewards of working for the common good. He was a criminal, but he was a learned and loyal criminal. He could yet be redeemed.

Michiko sighed as she headed back to the village. There were so many dangers on the road ahead that redemption was a remote possibility for any of them. Survival was a far more pressing concern.

Behind her, a great bank of clouds covered the sun, and the princess's bright, quiet haven descended into shadow.

PART ONE

THE ICEBERG BREAKS

Toshi Umezawa stood facing the thundering waters of Kami-taki Falls. It was one of the most magnificent sights in all the world, where the mighty Yumegawa River plunged over five hundred feet to the lake below. It was a place of scintillating beauty and raw elemental force that drew pilgrims, seekers, and students alike to its mysteries.

Toshi was resting on the rail at the edge of a city-sized platform that served as the foundation for Minamo Academy's main building. The massive hall was a grand and opulent structure of blue steel and glass spires that rested on a magical column of water hundreds of feet above the surface of the lake.

Overhead, the soratami capital Oboro peeked through the clouds. The city was not clearly visible from where Toshi stood, but he had been there once before so he knew that it was even more lavish and visually stunning than the academy grounds. Where Minamo was designed to mimic natural forms found in the rocks and water, Oboro was all sharp, clean edges and proud, almost arrogant towers that stood draped with gleaming, crystalline wire that glistened in the moonlight.

Toshi glanced up at Oboro one last time and then spit on the ground. He hated this place. Despite all the natural beauty and architectural splendor (and in some ways, because of it), Toshi resented the snobbery and elitism that dripped from both Oboro and Minamo like spray from the river.

Toshi's vivid green eyes darted across the entrance to the academy, and he shook his long black hair from his face. When he left the academy, it had been under an all-out attack, but now it was as still and as quiet as a tomb. The somber mood around the academy clung to the place like thick fog. The school was supposed to be a place of learning and enlightenment, but it felt like one of the daimyo's prisons after a plague wiped out all the inmates: empty, foreboding, and dead. There was bad magic here—raw emotions and violent death permeated the air like incense.

Still, if there were no one left alive inside the school, his job would be significantly easier. Toshi didn't let his hopes rise too high; nothing he had done lately had been easy or gone according to plan. He placed one foot on the bottom step of the Minamo entrance and waited. When nothing happened, he climbed another step. Nothing.

On the fifth step, two lean, muscular people sprang from inside the open doors, tumbling and spinning as they came. The male was bald and dressed in bleached skins, the female in tight braids and a red wool wrap that covered her from breastbone to mid-thigh. Both were armed with swords and the man carried a staff. Each warrior wore a black phylactery strapped to their head and bore a circular symbol with a jagged line through it—the man carried the standard on the end of his staff with a series of metal rings looped through it and the woman wore the symbol as a necklace.

Though their leaps carried them twenty feet into the air, they both landed soundlessly a few paces from Toshi. He glanced at one, then the other, and shrugged.

"Well?" he said. "You either recognize me or you don't. If you do, take me to see the ogre now. If not, draw your swords."

Toshi smiled. The two warriors did not. They stared at him, vacant as sleepwalkers. They did not react to his words, his smile, or even his presence on the grounds.

The ochimusha sighed. He waved a hand in front of the glassy-eyed woman, and then snapped his fingers in front of the man.

"Hi-de-tsu-gu," he said slowly. "Your boss. My partner. You helped him wreck this place awhile ago. Is he still here?"

The sound of the ogre's name made the man flinch, but the woman remained expressionless. Toshi paused, winked at her, and then stepped up into the man's face.

"Hidetsugu," he said again, enjoying the ripple of fear that crossed those otherwise inscrutable features. He turned back to the woman and gestured at the man. "I can keep this up all day, you know." He turned back to the man. "Hidetsugu."

The man snarled. The woman's blade appeared in her hand and Toshi yelped. Before he could backpedal, the man's staff thumped solidly into Toshi's back and he clamped on to the ochimusha's sword arm.

Gingerly, with the tip of the woman's blade inches from his nose, Toshi pushed the sword aside with one finger. He slid his left wrist free of his sleeve and showed them the triangle-shaped symbol there.

"*Hyozan*," he said. "This symbol is the kanji for iceberg. Your master has a similar mark on his chest. It signifies membership, brotherhood. We're members of the same group. You two should recognize me, we've met before."

Toshi took a moment to study his fingernails. Casually, he added, "And if you don't say something useful soon, we're going to have to fight." He put his hands on his hips. "And Hidetsugu won't like that. He'll probably bite your heads off just for making me explain this much. If you're lucky." He smiled a wicked smile and cocked his head. "Think about it. You know I'm not exaggerating."

The man's grip on his shoulder softened. The woman lowered her sword.

"Good," Toshi said. "Now, you don't have to announce me and you don't have to escort me. Just let me pass and I'll find him myself."

The woman sheathed her sword. She stared at Toshi through her dead eyes, then pointed up the stairs into the academy interior. With a soft grunt, she sprang high into the air and landed on the lintel above the main doorway. Toshi heard feet scuffling the ground behind him, and then the man joined his fellow sentry on top of the door.

Toshi waved pleasantly as he strode up the staircase. These two were *yamabushi*, feared and powerful warrior-priests from the mountains. They were notoriously reclusive and highly trained in the art of killing, especially effective against opponents from the spirit world. Toshi almost chuckled. Getting past them was the easy part.

His gallows-humor mirth dissolved when he approached the door, as Toshi saw dried bloodstains and sword slashes carved deep into the marble stairs. He paused for a moment to wonder what would have happened had circumstances been different, and if he hadn't shown the yamabushi his hyozan mark. Such thoughts were extremely unpleasant and unhelpful as he prepared to face

Hidetsugu once again, so he shoved them to the back of his mind. Outwardly confident, Toshi slipped inside the building.

Inside, the academy was just as still and lifeless as the outside. Toshi could see high water marks on some of the walls as if a flash flood had swept through the halls, but there were no people, no bodies, and no signs of a struggle. He knew what Hidetsugu was capable of and he had seen the aftermath of the o-bakemono's rage many times, but the academy was not at all like Toshi expected.

That made him nervous. Hidetsugu was at his most dangerous when he was deliberate, and the conspicuous lack of trophy corpses meant he was being especially precise. If there weren't heads decorating the academy gates, Hidetsugu must have found another use for them. Toshi shuddered at the thought.

The layout of the school was unfamiliar, but Toshi knew that Hidetsugu would be in the largest centrally located chamber. He followed the entrance hallway into the center of the building and then climbed a set of stairs to a mezzanine-style reception area. Opposite the stairs on this level, he saw two yamabushi standing guard outside a wide doorway.

The yamabushi barely noticed him as he approached. After pausing to make sure they did not intend to prevent him from passing, Toshi swept into the great hall. Without looking for Hidetsugu, Toshi bowed deeply and said, "Greetings, oath-brother," as jauntily as he could.

Toshi stood staring at the floor for a few moments. He heard a deep, stentorian growl and the clatter of falling stones. The ochi-musha waited until the first drop of sweat fell from his forehead to the stone floor, and then he raised his head.

Hidetsugu the ogre sat on a mound of white, polished bones

piled higher than Toshi's chest. The massive figure was smiling slightly as he stared down at Toshi, his eyes glowing dull red like embers in a blacksmith's forge.

"Hello, old friend." Hidetsugu's grin widened and he cocked his broad flat head in a disturbing parody of Toshi's own quizzical expression. Each of his gnarled, twisted teeth was as big as Toshi's hand.

Toshi felt a familiar chill. An ogre's smile was never something to be taken lightly. A cunning, learned, and patient ogre was still an ogre, and while Hidetsugu was always scrupulous in observing the terms of their shared hyozan oath, he also seemed amused by the dread vow they had sworn.

Toshi kept his tone respectful but looked the ogre unflinchingly in the eye. "We were supposed to meet here and take down the school together, oath-brother," he said. "Remember?" Toshi opened his arms, indicating the vast empty space around them. "You didn't wait, so now I'm not sure if the plan is still intact." He smiled. "Or if I'm even welcome. I know how much you hate guests."

The o-bakemono stood, sending a cascade of bones rattling down the mound. "Nonsense, Toshi. You are always welcome to visit me." Hidetsugu tilted his head back and drew a long stream of air into his nostrils.

The uneasiness in Toshi's stomach hardened into a cold, hard ball. It was said that o-bakemono can smell powerful magic, and Toshi knew it was true. If Hidetsugu guessed Toshi's latest secret, this little errand would be over before it began. Everything hinged on the next few moments, in a contest between Hidetsugu's instinct and Toshi's preparations to deflect that instinct.

Hidetsugu finished his breath and smiled down at Toshi once

more. "You stink of your myojin and the dead of winter," he said.

Relief swept through Toshi and he almost smiled. Calmly, he said, "Why shouldn't I? I am an acolyte of Night's Reach. In her name I took on the blessing of lethal cold, of frigid darkness."

The ogre nodded. "And the longer you contain that cold, the more it consumes you. Like your newfound religion. I wonder if you realize how much they are taking from you, old friend."

"I'm getting the best of the bargain so far." Toshi grinned wickedly, hoping to disarm Hidetsugu's suspicion with an open display of greed and ego. The ogre would expect that of Toshi.

But Hidetsugu's expression grew sharp. The bulging muscles in his arms and legs twitched, launching the ogre high into the air over the throne of bones. Toshi held very still as Hidetsugu landed heavily beside him, sending a web of cracks across the thick stone floor.

Toshi waited as the ogre inspected him. When Hidetsugu had stalked a complete circle around him, Toshi said, "If you're done appraising me, oath-brother, I'd like to discuss business. This reckoning," he gestured at the academy around them, "seems complete. Our next step should be—"

"Our work here," Hidetsugu interrupted, "is far from complete. The wizards and the soratami crossed us, the hyozan reckoners. Their suffering has only begun." The ogre's great nostrils flared as he snorted angrily. "We are sworn to it."

Hidetsugu was wearing a mantle of black silk across his shoulders, so Toshi could clearly see the hyozan mark branded into the ogre's chest. In the shadows behind the mound of bone, Toshi also saw more yamabushi lurking in the darkness, edging closer to their master and his guest.

"Well, I hate to argue," Toshi said. "But there's no one left to reckon with, is there?" He pointed to the white mound. "I mean, their suffering is over, right? What's left to accomplish?"

Hidetsugu smiled, his tongue lolling grotesquely across his lips. Toshi swallowed hard.

"No, my friend," the ogre said. "Their lives have ended and their bones have been picked clean, but their souls are still being savored and digested. According to the terms of our oath, which you created, the reckoning is not complete until tenfold vengeance has been taken."

He crouched, bringing his wild eyes and carrion breath directly into Toshi's face. "The ones who ordered our brother Kobo's death are here. My apprentice's reckoning is already upon the wizards and the moonfolk, but it will not end until it reaches their patron kami. I swore I would feed every one of them, everything they owned, and everything they loved to the All-Consuming Oni of Chaos. For him, this," he pointed to the mound, "is barely a mouthful."

Toshi felt his eyes go glassy. "I see." He smiled weakly and, fearing the answer, asked, "And where is your oni now?"

Hidetsugu rose. Laughing, he spread his arms. "Here. Everywhere. He gorges himself on all Minamo has to offer. The wizards had amassed a remarkable collection of powerful artifacts and spells. When I last saw my god, he was devouring the central library one scroll at a time."

Toshi swore inwardly. If the oni was consuming inanimate objects of great power, it was unlikely to overlook Daimyo Konda's prize, which Toshi had left in the depths of the academy's maze of offices and passageways, hundreds of feet below where he now stood.

Hidetsugu's manic mirth subsided. He strode past Toshi toward his makeshift throne. "And you, ochimusha?" he called over his shoulder. "If you have not come to honor our oath to Kobo, why have you come?"

Toshi abandoned the truth—it had never served him that well anyway. He had hoped that Hidetsugu and his demonic spirit would be too caught up in the ongoing carnage to care about the disk. If they didn't know what it was, or how powerful, they might have let him have it for the asking . . . after all, he was the one who brought it here.

He swore again. Now he would have to find a way to convince the o-bakemono to relinquish the prize instead of feeding it to his oni. Toshi didn't relish the task. He was a newcomer to the idea of spirit worship, but Hidetsugu had been a true believer for a long time. If his oni had any interest in the disk, the ogre would never let it leave here.

"I have come," Toshi said, "On behalf of the Myojin of Night's Reach. I am her acolyte and her interests are mine. Currently, she wishes to protect the Takenuma Swamp. Now that Konda's tower has fallen and the daimyo himself has gone missing, she sees a chance to confront her enemies and expand her influence."

Hidetsugu cocked his head again. "And this affects me how?"

"Look," Toshi said, exasperation overwhelming fear, "you've managed to combine our oath with spirit worship. Why can't I?"

The ogre chuckled. "Oni and myojin are both spirits in the same way butterflies and hornets are both insects. You should never confuse the two while picnicking."

"Point taken. But you're not listening to me. What if I say I'll help you finish here then you come with me to the swamp. You can even bring your team of mind-raped yamabushi killers.

Slaughtering things in the bog will seem like a vacation from slaughtering things on the water or in the air.

"Look around, oath-brother. The wizards are all dead or gone, and your oni is eating whatever they left behind. Kobo's reckoning will continue. The next step was always going to be the soratami, correct? Well, the soratami are in the swamp, and if we kill them there, we'll be honoring the oath and my myojin."

Hidetsugu's smile evaporated. His eyes flared. His voice was low and husky. "The soratami *are* next. And we don't need to travel to kill them, my friend. They are close by." The ogre glanced upward and his yamabushi let out a hollow, mournful moan.

Toshi smelled an opening. "I've heard that the soratami only left a small force to defend their city. Most of them are in the swamps, trying to muscle in."

"Most are in the forest of Jukai," Hidetsugu corrected. "But the hyozan will find them and deal with them all, in time."

"So why haven't you?" Toshi said. "Oboro is protected by a token force, and surely the taste of moonfolk flesh is more exotic to an oni than old books or human meat. Don't tell me a great and powerful o-bakemono and a half-dozen yamabushi are stymied by some skinny aristos with swords."

The ogre grinned again, raising a cold sweat on Toshi's neck. He had seen Hidetsugu rampant in battle, swinging a spiked club in one hand and a dead foe in the other as he roared with laughter and spat sparks. Compared to his current expression, that wild mask of malevolence and bloodlust seemed like the warmth in a doting mother's eyes.

"I won't tell you that, Toshi," Hidetsugu said. "But I will tell you that I have visited Oboro. Recently, in fact. Things there are currently quite to my liking. Care to see?"

"No," Toshi said quickly. "I was just—"

But Hidetsugu scooped him up and tucked Toshi under his arm like a log for the fire. The ogre raised his other hand and snapped his fingers.

"Take us to Oboro," he boomed. "I want Toshi to see how fares the city in the clouds."

Toshi was unable to protest with his lungs compressed in Hidetsugu's grip. Five yamabushi emerged from the darkness, including the two that had greeted Toshi at the gate. They linked hands and formed a circle around their master and his burden, and then the warrior-priests began to chant.

A series of circular platforms made of dull amber light formed between the floor and the highest exterior window. Toshi craned his eyes to follow the series of steps as it extended out the window and up into the evening sky.

The female yamabushi from the front gate bounded onto the first platform. She hopped like nimble spider from step to step, pausing after each landing to cushion the impact and gather her strength for the next jump. As soon as she cleared the window, another yamabushi started from the bottom.

When he went outside, Hidetsugu leaped. Toshi tried to yelp as the world twisted around him, but his lungs were still too shallow. The ogre's grip tightened as he hit the first platform. Toshi gritted his teeth and concentrated on not being crushed.

Outside, the sky had cleared and the soratami city Oboro glowed gold in the setting sun. Through tear-clouded eyes, Toshi could see the amber platforms of light reaching up to the edge of the city itself. The first yamabushi was almost there; Toshi and Hidetsugu would soon catch up.

Toshi closed his eyes and said a quick prayer to his myojin.

O Night, he thought. *I am still your faithful servant, and true. But it may be awhile before I can complete the task you've set for me.*

After a moment, he mentally added, *You too, Michiko.*

Helpless in the grip of his former oath-brother, Toshi wondered what he would find at the top of this peculiar staircase.

CHAPTER 2

High over the gemstone streets of Oboro, Hidetsugu and his yamabushi ended their journey. The ogre still held Toshi tucked under his arm while his warriors formed and occupied platforms of light arranged in a wide semicircle. The streets below them converged into a wide public quadrangle, half of which lay draped in shadows from the towering spires and gleaming domes of the soratami capital.

"Oath-brother," Toshi spat through clenched teeth, "if we have arrived, I prefer to stand on my own."

Hidetsugu did not reply, but turned to inspect the arc of yamabushi curling around to his left. With a shrug, he loosened his grip so that Toshi fell to the platform.

Toshi paused while down on all fours to inspect his perch. The amber light felt as solid as stone, rough and cool to the touch, but it also pushed back against his hands as if surrounded by a layer of invisible springs. It was clearly sturdy, though he couldn't actually touch it.

Toshi glanced down at the quadrangle as he rose. They were far too high for him to simply jump and hope for the best unless he landed among the shadows. One of the blessings he had taken from

Night's Reach was the ability to travel from shadow to shadow, so all he had to do was make contact with the silhouettes of the soratami buildings and he'd be free to go where he pleased.

Eyeing the distance he'd have to cover, Toshi decided to wait. Things would have to grow far more desperate before he pursued that particular option.

"So." Toshi straightened his sword belt. "You've dragged me all the way up here to show me . . . this? I'll say it again, oath-brother. It looks to me like the show's long over and the crowd's gone home."

Indeed, there were no signs of people at all in Oboro. The streets were silent and still, and the buildings seemed empty, forgotten, and almost lonely in the gathering dusk.

"Wait for it." Hidetsugu's voice was low and calm. He did not take his eyes off the quadrangle. "You know how to wait, don't you? It's a skill worth practicing."

The ochimusha crossed his arms and huffed. The longer this took, the more likely something horrible would happen. There was no way he could compel Hidetsugu to hurry, however, so he forced himself to relax and let the o-bakemono have his demonstration. One of the first lessons Toshi had learned about dealing with ogres was not to rush into things.

* * * * *

Toshi's first glimpse of Hidetsugu had come almost a decade earlier, when the ochimusha was still an indentured reckoner working for Boss Uramon. The sallow-faced crime lord was one of Takenuma Swamp's most powerful figures, and she had been trying to clear a new route for her black-market caravans. Along a crucial part of the route was Shinka, Hidetsugu's home. The boss had sent messengers, gifts, and offers of friendship to Shinka, but none of her envoys ever returned. When she sent one of her toughest negotiators and a team of hatchet-men to force the issue, Hidetsugu sent their mangled bodies back in one large sack. He also sent a mocking note telling Uramon the missing heads were now decorating his pathway, and that she could come view them any time she liked.

Uramon was an even-tempered boss, but such insults are bad for business in Takenuma. Following time-honored criminal tradition, Uramon had organized her most dangerous thugs into revenge gangs called reckoners, whose job it was to make very public, very painful examples of anyone who crossed the boss. She assigned to her most reliable reckoners the task of chastising Hidetsugu.

The boss was no fool, and she was determined not to underestimate the ogre's power, especially in his own stronghold. Toshi was part of the largest team of reckoners ever assembled for Uramon, almost thirty of the most experienced mages, strong-arm experts, and killers-for-hire Takenuma had to offer.

They were led by a heavyset assassin called One-Eye who wore a thick wooden eye patch. One-Eye was a notoriously indiscriminate killer, even in Takenuma. They said he had traded his eye for a cursed gem that would kill anyone who looked upon it, and he was quick to lift his eye patch and show the gem over the most minor disagreements.

One-Eye was the only man who could have led such a large group against such a target. He was part drill instructor, part brutal taskmaster who insisted the entire gang follow his lead and act like seasoned professionals. He even killed two of them before the job started to hammer his point home: he would not die because of someone else's mistake.

They made the long trek to the Sokenzan Mountains quickly and quietly. When they reached Shinka, One-Eye positioned them all around the ogre's hut where they could ambush him as he emerged.

It was Toshi's bad luck that One-Eye simultaneously respected his skill with kanji magic and hated his smart mouth. Since One-Eye's plan required someone to anger the ogre and lure him into the ambush, he sent Toshi. There was no one more suited to stand openly in front of Shinka and provoke the ogre until he attacked. And if the jaws of the trap didn't slam shut fast enough, well, the bait could defend itself.

"So I'm bait?" Toshi complained.

One-Eye was trying to signal two of the more monstrous reckoners that they were out of position. Preoccupied with keeping the poisonous *acuba* and nightmarish, grasping *gaki* in check until the attack began, the assassin hardly noticed Toshi.

"You're a kanji mage, right? You've got paper and ink. If he comes too close, make one of those characters that freezes people solid and throw it in his face."

"That's no good. All-purpose stuff like that won't work on something as powerful as—"

The burly assassin's hand twitched toward his eye patch, but he stopped halfway and made a fist instead. "Get down there and bait the ogre." One-Eye crossed his arms. "Why else do you think I brought you?"

So Toshi marched up to the hut's door and stood, just out of view for anyone inside. As One-Eye quickly made the rounds and prepared everyone for the all-out attack, Toshi did take out a thin roll of parchment and a small ink bottle with a built-in brush. These were the basic tools of kanji magic, used in the art of infusing symbols with magic and willpower. Toshi had been beyond ink-and-paper casting for months, but he kept his true abilities hidden while he worked for Uramon. If the boss knew all that he could do, she'd just make him do it on command with no benefit to him.

Toshi pretended to fumble with the scroll, but instead of the paralysis kanji that One-Eye had suggested, Toshi carefully eased his sword an inch out of its scabbard and ran his index finger along the blade. Dripping crimson, he quickly traced quite a different symbol across his own face. When it was complete, the mark crackled like water on a hot pan and let out a puff of red smoke.

Feeling slightly more confident, Toshi then used the ink to draw One-Eye's paralysis kanji on the roll of parchment and tore it off. He didn't expect it would work—didn't even expect to get a chance to use it—but it couldn't actually hurt. One-Eye was competent and he had some of Uramon's toughest muscle ready to go. The ambush might succeed, and if it did, Toshi wanted to be able to say he'd done his part.

His own blood drying on his face, Toshi stood and listened to his heart pound as he waited for the signal and the wild melee that would surely follow.

* * * * *

"There," Hidetsugu said. The sun had almost set behind Oboro's highest tower. The ogre pointed down, into the corner of the field of sapphire paving stones.

Toshi looked. "I don't see . . ." His voice trailed off as a small, whirling cloud of black smoke formed on the edge of the lengthening shadows. The tiny cyclone expanded, then dispersed into a drab cloud dotted with orange sparks. Even from a distance Toshi could see monstrous, humanoid forms shambling inside the cloud.

The first oni stepped out onto the quadrangle, hissing like a furious cat. It was roughly the same size and shape as a man, but its frame was larger, broader, and heavier. Its hide was thick and leathery, angry red in color, and its muscles bulged grotesquely whenever it moved.

Its face was a skull-like mask of naked bones, blistered calluses, and jutting teeth. Two savage, red eyes gleamed in the dim light, with a third blinking its vertical lids higher up in the center of its forehead. Two long, jagged horns swept up from its forehead and curved back over its crown, and bony spikes erupted from its knees and elbows. Something dark and oily dripped from its sharp claws, searing through the matted fur that covered its waist, hips, and legs. As it emerged completely into the light its barbed tail swished menacingly through the air.

Most disturbingly, the oni wore skillfully carved rings on some of its fingers and sported ceremonial bindings that ran up both forearms. It also wore a handcrafted necklace that was strung alternately with unidentifiable red orbs and human finger bones, which Toshi recognized all too well.

The oni emerged from the cloud of smoke into the last bright rays of sun. There was something awful and alien about the way it moved, and as more humanoid demons formed and shambled into the quadrangle, Toshi realized what it was.

Their bodies looked human, but their outlines stretched and bulged like a thick, boiling liquid. Their arms stretched farther than their bones should have allowed, and their legs expanded and collapsed like a partially blocked hose. Though they moved quickly and smoothly across the quad, it was as if each bone, each finger, forearm, vertebrae, and thigh were not attached to its neighbors. Instead, each steel-hard bone floated free inside a sinewy cushion of muscle, bound tight by the oni's tough crimson hide.

Toshi's guess was vindicated when the first oni sprang onto the nearest wall. He had seen soratami float on magical clouds, mighty birds that soared under the power of their own wings, and spirits who sailed on the wind itself. Some, like Hidetsugu's yamabushi, made prodigious, magically assisted leaps to take the high ground whenever they chose.

Watching the first oni scale up the walls of Oboro like a suction-toed lizard, Toshi knew that it was not magic or air that kept the monster moving upward; it was sheer muscle power. The oni dug fingers and toes deeply into the stone wall, repositioning each individual bone to exert however much pressure was required. The oni would spring, dig into the wall, gather its strength, and then spring again. It all happened so quickly that it seemed like one continuous, fluid motion instead of a brutal tug-of-war between the oni's muscles and the forces of gravity. In fact, if he didn't concentrate so hard, the oni slithering up the quadrangle walls almost resembled misshapen drops of red rain flowing up the wall, back to the sky.

"While the All-Consuming feasts on the academy," Hidetsugu sneered, "these lesser oni prey upon Oboro. And in many ways," the ogre paused to nod down at Toshi, "you made this possible. Watch now, and enjoy the view."

Toshi was about to speak when the first soratami rose up over the quadrangle. They were tall, lean, willowy creatures with silver-white skin and indistinct features. Their faces were all uniformly thin, pinched, and stoic, their long ears wrapped or pinned tight around their heads. There were almost a dozen in all, each bearing katanas, each borne up by a small white cloud that completely enveloped their feet. Among all the tribes of Kamigawa, the soratami were feared and respected as warriors and scholars, and some even considered them semi-divine beings. Before he had been thrown into conflict with them, Toshi himself had been awed by their reputation from afar and by their presence up close. He didn't like the soratami, but he knew to take them seriously.

Counting up the numbers as the oni and soratami converged on each other, Toshi noted, "Your demons are outnumbered two-to-one, Hidetsugu. Against the moonfolk, I wouldn't choose those odds."

"That's because you're a soft little human who still bleats and moans to the kami for protection," the ogre replied without taking his eyes off the impending battle. "Ogres and oni are made of sterner stuff. Be silent and watch."

Toshi swallowed his next thoughts and watched. From the sky, the largest and fiercest soratami warrior descended like a bird of prey. From below, the first oni clamored up the wall, its sharp-toothed jaw distended and dripping caustic foam.

The soratami drew his sword. The oni widened its jaws. Above them both, Toshi winced, anticipating the terrible meeting of these two savage forces.

* * * * *

One-Eye gave the signal. All around the entrance to Shinka, monsters prepared to pounce, mages prepared to cast, and hatchet-men drew their weapons. It was time to reckon with Hidetsugu.

One-Eye gestured impatiently at Toshi, who nodded. The ochimusha turned to face the entrance to the ogre's hut, the paralysis kanji clutched in his hand. The other character on his face still tingled, but it had not yet dried.

"Hoy," Toshi called. "You there, in the hut. O-bakemono! Boss Uramon demands satisfaction."

Though a dull buzzing roar continued unabated, no new sounds came from inside Shinka. Toshi waited, and before One-Eye could prod him with another gesture, he shouted again.

"Ogre!" Toshi cupped his hands around his mouth. "You hung Uramon's last party in your garden. Now she will use your hide for a rug in her dining hall. Her reckoners are here to burn Shinka down around your ears and defile the ashes."

The wind shifted. Toshi caught a foul, smoky smell wafting from inside the hut. He could not see through the darkness inside, but he felt something massive moving closer to him. And was that a low, sinister chuckle he heard? The ochimusha swallowed.

"Last chance," he shouted. "Face us and fall with as much honor as you have left. There will be none once you die. Face us, or cower there in the dark until we drag you out for Uramon's justice."

The chuckle was unmistakable this time. Toshi wasn't sure there was an ogre inside the hut, but whatever was in there was amused by what it heard. Toshi shrugged. He knew he was not doing his best work as a provocateur, and he was sure One-Eye would make him suffer for it. Until he had some sort of idea how formidable the o-bakemono was, however, Toshi had no intention of singling himself out for special attention any more than he had to.

Two red eyes suddenly shined from the entrance to Shinka. Toshi stood rock-still as Hidetsugu squeezed out of the hut, hauling his burly body forward with his massive arms alone.

Once his hips cleared the doorway, Hidetsugu drew his legs under him and rose to his full height.

He wore a simple wrap around his waist and carried a thick, studded *tetsubo* club. His wild, red eyes were crinkled in something like mirth, and his long, pointed tongue flashed eagerly across his terrible teeth. Hidetsugu opened his arms wide, exposing his broad, muscular chest, and roared defiant laughter.

The ogre's size and confidence momentarily startled the assembled reckoners, including One-Eye. The assassin recovered quickly and shouted for the attack to begin.

Toshi blinked as the reckoners began to chant and charge. When he opened his eyes, Hidetsugu was standing directly in front of him.

The ogre's violent joy swept over Toshi like a hot wind. Hidetsugu was smiling down at Toshi, his lips spread wide over interlocking teeth. He squinted slightly, scanning the mark on the ochimusha's face.

"Hah!" Hidetsugu laughed. He reached forward with a finger as thick as Toshi's wrist and playfully nudged the kanji mage.

Toshi blinked again, and when he opened his eyes the ogre was gone. The space between himself and the entrance to Shinka was completely empty. If he'd wanted to, he could have taken refuge inside the ogre's own hut.

Instead, Toshi stood completely still. He didn't know if he was able to move and he didn't want to be embarrassed by trying and failing. His heart pounded and cold sweat stuck his linen shirt to his back.

Behind him, he heard screams intermingled with wet, ripping sounds. Though his life probably depended on doing so, Toshi could not bring himself to turn and see how the ambush was progressing.

* * * * *

The soratami made only one mistake in engaging the lead oni: he delivered a mortal blow as his first attack.

The moonfolk's gleaming sword sliced down through the top of the oni's head, bisecting its third eye and cleaving the demon's skull from crown to nose. Driven by momentum and malice, the oni's body pressed forward, bringing its shattered face into contact with the soratami's chest and throat. Reflexively, the dead oni's teeth clamped shut around the warrior's windpipe. Its grasping claws ripped through the soratami's torso and then punched through his back. For a moment, the combatants hung in midair with the oni's body stuck clean through the soratami's like a living spear. Then the entire grisly mess fell tumbling to the quadrangle below.

It was a study in the contrasts of combat. The soratami were disciplined, graceful, even elegant with their gleaming blades and razor-sharp throwing spikes. The oni were no less fast or powerful, but they were wild, savage, and unrestrained in their bloodlust. For the first few moments of the brutal skirmish Toshi thought the sides seemed evenly matched, even with the soratami's superior numbers.

The tide quickly turned in favor of the oni, however. The demons could still fight after losing an arm, a leg, or as their leader had proved, their head. Maimed or mortally wounded, the oni continued to attack, to tear at the soratami with their teeth, claws, and horns.

The soratami, on the other hand, felt the impact of their wounds far more keenly. When the moonfolk suffered a deep wound or a broken bone, they hesitated, even faltered. They seemed as pained by the fact that they had been wounded as they did by the wounds themselves. Toshi saw one warrior die with an oni's horns punched clean through his back, and as the twin points of bone erupted from his chest, the soratami looked down at them with distaste. Toshi looked twice to confirm what he saw, and yes, the moonfolk's expression was not one of pain or shock, but of outrage. How dare such base creatures draw blood from one of the moon's favored children?

To a warrior, the soratami were more focused, more disciplined, and more efficient than the oni. But the oni were creatures born of chaos and they did not fight in single combat. Instead, they bounded, slithered, and leaped from enemy to enemy, ripping a throat here and plucking an eye there. They seemed completely unfocused on anything but spilling as much soratami blood as possible, but as the battle progressed their tactics proved superior. When the last soratami retreated into the sky on their cloud platforms, there were an identical number of oni in the quadrangle. Hidetsugu's demons had lost over half their number since the battle started, but they had inflicted far worse on the soratami defenders.

Now unchallenged, the remaining oni moved across the sapphire paving stones, out of the quadrangle and onto the streets of Oboro. Toshi had very limited experience with oni and hoped to keep it that way, but he knew that these feral brutes would continue to kill whatever they found until they themselves were dispatched.

"You see, Toshi?" Hidetsugu's face was alight with joyful

malevolence. "There is no need to rush Kobo's reckoning. While the All-Consuming feasts on Minamo's secrets, we are teaching Oboro the true meaning of terror. They cannot stop us. They cannot resist us. They cannot retreat, and they cannot avoid us. Soon the entire city will be full of oni."

The ogre scooped up Toshi in one hand, bringing the ochimusha close to his broad, flat head. "Then and only then will our work here be done."

Toshi struggled in Hidetsugu's grip. "You've made your point, oath-brother. But I am becoming very tired of being hoisted and toted like a jug of wine."

The ogre's fingers relaxed, but he did not let Toshi down. "You raise an interesting point, my friend. After our long history together, you think I owe you more respect."

Toshi drew as deep a breath as he could; one could never be sure when Hidetsugu would decide to clench his fist again.

"Yes, oath-brother," he said. "I think you owe me a bit more consideration, at least."

The ogre's lip twitched, showing Toshi a flash of gleaming sharp fang.

"Do I, now?" Hidetsugu's voice was barely above a growl. "Perhaps I do. Perhaps we should both remember what it is we owe each other."

Toshi fought to remain calm. Around them on platforms of amber light, the yamabushi waited for their master's orders. Below, savage nightmares stalked the streets of the soratami capital.

And in the center of it all, the founding members of the hyozan reckoners held each other's eyes without blinking.

CHAPTER 3

Outside Shinka, Toshi still stood where he had started. He had not moved at all while the battle raged behind him, and he didn't move now as Hidetsugu began to heap mangled and headless corpses in front of the ochimusha. He was barely willing to adjust his eyes, but Toshi did see the parchment with the paralysis kanji hanging from the back of Hidetsugu's clothing. He had slipped it onto the ogre's wrap just as Hidetsugu leaped away from him. Now the parchment fluttered as the ogre went about his grisly work, its symbol whole, complete, and utterly without effect.

If he dared to move at all, Toshi would have shrugged. He had warned One-Eye it wouldn't work.

Judging from the remains, One-Eye and the rest of the magic-using reckoners had all been burned to death in the ambush's opening seconds. The heavyset assassin's eye patch was still in place, but the thick wooden square was smoking and seared into his blackened flesh, the cursed eye forever closed behind it.

Much later, Hidetsugu ambled up to Toshi and sat facing the last of Uramon's reckoners. He seemed calmer but still dangerous, like a bear after a huge meal. He inspected Toshi standing there with something quite like amusement, and then Hidetsugu gestured at the mark on Toshi's face.

"Little kanji mage," he said, "why did you put that symbol on your face where I could see it? Did you think I wouldn't recognize it and attack you anyway?"

Toshi fought to keep his voice calm and his body from trembling. "It was a calculated risk. I don't really feel the need to die for Uramon, but I wasn't in a position to refuse her, either. I figured this was the safest way to make you understand: I can't hurt you, I don't even want to hurt you . . . but I will if you hurt me. I just hoped that you'd recognize the reflection kanji and leave me be. It's not as if there weren't plenty of other targets, plenty of other reckoners who were actually out to get you."

"And if I didn't recognize it," Hidetsugu said, "whatever I tried to do to you would come straight back to me. Either way, you win." The ogre grinned, displaying bloodstained teeth. "In the short term."

"Uh, yes," Toshi said uncomfortably. "I'd be lying if I said that hadn't crossed my mind."

Hidetsugu reached around and plucked the parchment from his wrap. "And this?"

"That . . . was his idea." He gestured to One-Eye near the bottom of the corpse pile. "I advised against it."

"But you did it anyway."

"I did. You see, I'm nothing if not loyal."

The o-bakemono laughed loudly. "That's the biggest lie you've told me yet," he said. "And yet somehow, I believe it." The light in Hidetsugu's eyes darkened, becoming more ominous. "But what am I to do with you now, little reckoner?"

"Well, I've given that some thought, too. I can't go back

home—Uramon will demand to know what happened, and why I was the only survivor. I'm still indentured to her, so technically she owns me."

The ogre nodded as he considered Toshi's position. "Might as well let me devour you now," he offered.

"Or," Toshi said smoothly, "we could come to an arrangement. I'm bound to Uramon, but I don't want to be. You're going to keep getting visits from the boss until she's satisfied, and I bet you don't want that. I don't think you're in any danger," he nodded toward the corpse pile, "but it could become quite a nuisance."

Hidetsugu perched his chin on his clenched fist, hanging on Toshi's every word. He seemed honestly and thoroughly amused.

"I've been looking into forming my own gang of reckoners," Toshi said. "The idea came to me when I realized that there's no way to break a reckoner oath, but you can swear a new one. I figure, why should I put my life on the line for someone just because they own me? If I could get some . . . serious fellows like yourself to join me, we could get out from under the bosses altogether."

"A reckoner gang," Hidetsugu mused. "Without a boss? That's almost novel."

"Thank you. I figure we'd look out for each other rather than some crimelord's reputation. And if we were demonstrably . . . serious, all of the bosses would soon see the value of leaving us alone. They're all businessmen in the end, and they don't do things without some form of profit. If it were ruinously expensive to cross us, eventually they wouldn't bother."

"This is an admirable idea you've had. What is your name?"

"Toshi Umezawa," he said.

"An admirable idea, Toshi Umezawa. But I see several flaws." The ochimusha swallowed. "Fatal flaws?"

"Perhaps. First, you are not . . . serious enough on your own to make the kind of impression a new reckoner gang needs. And more, I doubt someone so young has learned the fine art of a truly binding blood oath."

Toshi smiled his most winning smile. "That's where you come in, noble o-bakemono."

Hidetsugu's nostrils flared. "That's another flaw. You interest me, ochimusha, but as soon as I no longer feel full, I'm going to bite off your head and swallow it whole." The ogre's eyes sparkled and cast out tiny sparks.

"Oh." Toshi sagged where he stood. "That's not good for me."

"No. It is not." Hidetsugu rocked back and placed his hands palm-up on his knees. He closed his eyes and fell totally still as if meditating.

Toshi decided to stake everything on one last throw of the dice. "All right," he said. "What if you take me on as your pupil? I know the o-bakemono train apprentices to maintain their influence. Ogre magic is some of the strongest and most feared in all Kamigawa, but it's worthless if no one practices it. Teach me, and your name will still be spoken in fearful whispers for generations after you're dead."

Hidetsugu's eyes remained closed, but he smiled. "You are not as well-informed as you think, my friend. That would also kill you, only it would be much more protracted and painful. None of my last four would-be apprentices survived more than a month."

Toshi decided to risk a bit of bravado, hoping it would impress the ogre. "Give me a try. You won't be disappointed."

The o-bakemono's lids snapped open and he fixed Toshi with a withering stare. "No, ochimusha," he said. "You are too clever, too independent to be a proper student. And I already have my next two apprentices selected. No, I can save myself a lot of time by killing you now."

He extended his hand as if to grab Toshi, but the ochimusha yelled, "Wait! Make me an offer. There must be something that you need or want. Put me to work and we'll both profit."

The ogre's hand stopped just a few feet from Toshi. He could not see Hidetsugu behind the rough palm and thick, clawed fingers, but he heard the ogre's voice clearly.

"You seem remarkably dedicated to striking a bargain with me. Do you appreciate how dangerous that is?"

"Maybe I don't," Toshi said. "But I don't have many options, do I?"

Hidetsugu lowered his hand. "All right, ochimusha. I will set a task for you, something to prove yourself useful. In ten days I go collect my next student. It will take me years to train him."

"If he survives."

"If he survives. I would prefer not to be disturbed by any more of Uramon's lackeys while I test him. It only draws the process out.

"Convince Uramon to leave me be until next spring. I will know by then if I have a new apprentice or another failure. In return, I will join your gang of freelance reckoners." The ogre's eyes flared bright red. "I may even help you craft the spell that binds us."

"Deal," Toshi said instantly. "Though I would be stunned if you simply let me walk away with only my word to bring me back."

"That is because you are a quick thinker. No, Toshi Umezawa, I am not willing to trust your good nature. But I do trust blood magic."

Hidetsugu lashed out and lifted Toshi into the air. Before he could scream, Toshi felt his arm disappear into the ogre's mouth up past the elbow. Hidetsugu simultaneously bit down and squeezed with his hand, crushing the air from Toshi's lungs as the ochimusha's blood dripped from the ogre's jaw.

Hidetsugu dropped Toshi and licked his chops. Toshi quickly touch-inspected his wound, which was shallow but bleeding freely.

"Blood," Hidetsugu said through crimson-stained lips. "Blood is the key to all ogre rituals. Now I have tasted yours, ochimusha. I can find you anywhere. And if more of Uramon's reckoners come here before spring to interrupt my student's training, I will blame you. After I mount their heads on stakes I will come and find you in your bed. I will drag you back here and take sublime joy in your suffering for as long as I care to before feeding you to the All-Consuming Oni of Chaos."

Toshi tore off the bottom of his sleeve and wrapped it tightly around his wounded arm. The pain felt far away, and he almost swooned as his stomach knotted and unknotted.

"Done," Toshi said again, though he could barely hear his own voice.

"Good," Hidetsugu replied. He stood and turned his back on his guest.

"I am becoming hungry again. Go now, ochimusha, before I change my mind."

Still dazed, Toshi turned and woodenly began to run. The last thing he saw was Hidetsugu bending over the pile of corpses, sinking his arms into the mound to gather as many as possible in his broad, powerful arms.

*   *   *   *   *

"Put me down, oath-brother," Toshi said. "We have been bound for too long to squabble."

Hidetsugu shook Toshi in his fist like a child's rattle. "The bond between us is stretched too thin at present, Toshi. Find a more compelling argument."

Toshi was ready. "There is a stone disk hidden in a chamber deep within the academy. The same creature that almost leveled the daimyo's tower will follow wherever that disk goes and will crush anything that stands in its way. Let me take the disk to where the soratami are. Let them die in battle with the great spirit beast, and we will have engineered a fine reckoning for your lost apprentice."

Hidetsugu seemed impressed, but he shook his head. "An intriguing idea," he said. "But if the daimyo's prize is here, my oni has already laid claim to it. Only a fool would try to take something off the All-Consuming's plate.

"But more to the point, Toshi, I've had my fill of your bargains and plans. What I need now is a straight declaration of your loyalties. Are you working for the hyozan? The Myojin of Night's Reach? Or are you merely doing what you've always done, playing both ends against each other so you can capitalize in the confusion?"

"My loyalties are unchanged," Toshi said sharply.

"And that is what concerns me." Hidetsugu placed two fingers in his wide mouth and blew a piercing whistle. "I cannot harm you, Toshi, because of the oath we share. But I can have you monitored. I can keep you in check." He glanced down into the quadrangle. "Behold, ochimusha. Your newest companion has arrived."

The massive, four-legged brute was unlike the other bipedal oni, but it had the same three eyes and the same curved horns. It was covered in tough leathery skin and thick plates of bony armor. It walked on all fours, and its head was as broad as a man's chest.

Toshi's throat almost closed when he recognized the demon dog—it was the same oni that Kobo had summoned in the forest weeks ago, the same one Toshi himself had released to run rampant on the streets of Oboro. Earlier, Hidetsugu had insisted he carry the dog's summoning token, promising it would fade after a few hours of blood frenzy. Yet here the same dog was, almost a week after Toshi had released it.

"Wherever you go," Hidetsugu said, leering, "the dog of bloodlust and slaughter will accompany you. If you run, it will chase you down. If you hide, it will sniff you out. If you fight, it will cripple you and drag your broken body to me. Our oath prevents us from harming each other directly, or causing each other harm, but you summoned this demon. Whatever it does to you now is your burden, not mine."

Toshi was surprised to find himself growing angry. Hidetsugu had tricked him, had connived to get Toshi to place himself in danger so that the ogre could threaten him without risking the hyozan oath's retribution. If Toshi hadn't already planned something similar for Hidetsugu, he would have been truly offended by the ogre's lack of trust.

Toshi decided to take his leave. The trip to Minamo had been a complete failure: he hadn't secured the Taken One, he was once more on bad terms with Hidetsugu, and he had not determined if the ogre knew his secret—that Toshi had already found a way out of the hyozan oath. The tattoo on Toshi's arm was a decoy, one that looked and felt like a real reckoner's mark but had absolutely no connection to the oath they had sworn almost ten years ago.

Toshi turned his thoughts inward, focusing on the power of his myojin. Night's Reach had bestowed many blessings upon him, but one that he had manufactured for himself was the killing power of intense cold. He had bested an elemental spirit and bound her power to his own, and he called upon that power now as he hung from the ogre's fist.

Ice formed across Hidetsugu's fist, and Toshi felt the pressure on his torso ease. His breath blew out in great white clouds of fog and he felt a cold, tingling shape emerge on his forehead. The glowing, purple-white kanji was the symbol for the *yuki-onna*, the snow woman of legend who lured the unwary to a frozen doom in the darkest hours of winter.

The yamabushi sensed their master was under attack and converged on Toshi. Below, the oni dog howled and sprang into the air, bounding from wall to wall on his own path to the platform.

Toshi summoned another of Night's blessings and began to fade from sight. With the myojin's help, he could become formless, weightless, and intangible. So far nothing had been able to interfere with him in this state, not the most powerful spirit or the keenest animal instinct.

As he disappeared from Hidetsugu's frozen fist, Toshi locked eyes with his former oath-brother. There was anger in the ogre's face, and grim determination. But most of all, Toshi saw sadness, disappointment, even if it were only because they had come so far without turning on each other. But now they had, as they had always known they would.

Toshi recognized the complicated emotions on Hidetsugu's face because he shared them. For many reasons, he had sincerely hoped either he or the ogre would die before they had to face each other. But now that hope was dead and Toshi had to find a way to overcome the single most terrifying creature he had ever known.

Toshi nodded as he faded away. To his lasting joy and eternal regret, Hidetsugu nodded back. For one final time, they were partners, peers, warriors with a common bond.

And then Toshi was gone, leaving Hidetsugu to stoke his anger for the inevitable day when one of them would destroy the other.

* * * * *

Toshi drifted down from Oboro until he fell under the shadow of the cloud city itself. Like a sinking ship, Toshi slid into the great patch of black until he was completely engulfed by it. After a moment's disorientation he turned toward the palpable presence of the Taken One and urged himself toward Minamo Academy.

It was still here. Toshi could feel it. Between the giant serpent in the sky and the mad, immortal daimyo, there was no shortage of very powerful entities who were willing to kill to recover the prize.

Then, Toshi had hoped they would destroy each other, the academy, and the soratami city overhead in the process. Now, he had to find some way of removing it before they arrived and then keep it from their continued pursuit.

Toshi's phantom body emerged in the deepest recesses of the academy. He had been to this space before, though he did not know what the room was for. It was some administrator's office or private library with walls covered by scroll racks. Scattered around the room were a series of glass display cases featuring strange, arcane objects that Toshi couldn't recognize and didn't care about. He glanced around to verify he was in the right place and nodded, satisfied.

The Taken One was lying faceup where he left it. The disk was roughly six feet across and about a foot thick. It gave off a constant pale white glow and a steady flow of wispy steam as if it had just been taken from a boiling pot. He knew from experience that it was cool to the touch, but it somehow delivered a jolt of strange, unnerving force to anyone who made bare-skin contact.

Toshi peered at the Taken One's face. It was as he remembered it, with the etched serpent facing right and its tail circled under it. Somehow it also looked different, more detailed and substantial.

He shook his head and blinked. The stone was hypnotic, he reminded himself. He had seen how crazy it had made Konda. Toshi forced himself to look away from the Taken One so that it could not enthrall him as it had the daimyo, and that's when he noticed the people.

They crouched behind tables and across chairs, they slumped against naked walls, and they slept fitfully in clusters on the cold stone floor. Shaking his head in disbelief, Toshi counted almost thirty live bodies in the room, breathing softly and barely moving. There were students in blue robes, Konda's soldiers in full uniform, and even a handful of kitsune fox-warriors. Most appeared to be asleep or at least resting while four alert guardians watched over them from the far corners of the room.

Toshi wanted to shout, "What in the cold gray hell are you people doing here?" but he could imagine the answer. When Hidetsugu and his yamabushi came to the academy, they came for slaughter. It was hard to believe that the ogre or his patron oni hadn't sniffed them out in their hiding place, even this far down.

Hard to believe but not impossible. Somehow, they had managed to stay alive and remain undiscovered for almost a week. From the looks of things, they wouldn't last much longer.

A sentry hissed at the far end of the room, raising an urgent but understated warning. To Toshi's growing horror, a pair of black, razor-toothed jaws materialized near the opposite wall. The disembodied teeth snapped lightly, testing the air like a snake's tongue. A second pair of jaws appeared and the sentry backed away with his sword drawn.

Toshi fought back a wave of dread and panic. This was Hidetsugu's oni manifest, the All-Consuming Oni of Chaos. Toshi recognized the voracious mouths as part of the great demonic spirit's body, like the scales of a fish or the hairs on a spider's leg. From what he had seen, the All-Consuming was nothing but a thick cloud of hungry mouths and snapping teeth crowned by gigantic oni horns and three malevolent eyes.

The other guardians quietly crossed the room, nudging and shaking people awake as they went. Weary and resigned, the survivors quickly withdrew from the now growing number of jaws floating and snapping at the other end of the room.

Safely hidden and immaterial, Toshi watched as he pondered his next move.

The warriors all waited with their hands on their weapons, watching the jaws. The flying teeth drifted deeper into the room, but they never strayed far from the interior wall where they appeared. After a long, agonizing minute, the jaws turned and began to fade. If they were searching for something good to eat, they hadn't found it here. Toshi wondered if the oni had missed the Taken One, or if it just didn't recognize the disk as a gourmet meal.

Moments later, the library was completely still and silent once more, though now everyone in it was wide awake. Toshi watched the group until he sorted out who was in charge, then silently approached a sturdy-looking officer wearing the daimyo's standard. One step away from the soldier, Toshi faded in and tapped him on the shoulder.

"Captain?" Toshi read the man's rank from his shoulder insignia. "How much longer can we last?"

The officer looked Toshi over suspiciously. "As long as it takes."

"Oh, good. Very good, thanks for that. But you know what? That's not really an answer, is it?"

The captain scowled. "Who are you? I don't recognize you."

Toshi leaned in and hissed, "I'm the guy who can get you out of here if you keep your wits about you." He faded from sight, maneuvered around the captain, and reappeared behind the soldier. "Interested?"

The officer slowly turned and faced Toshi. "Keep talking," he said, his own voice pitched low. "I'm Nagao." He gestured over Toshi's shoulder. "That's Silver-Foot."

Toshi croaked as a huge gray kitsune samurai startled him. The fox-warrior nodded his short muzzle to acknowledge Toshi then stood by with his hand on his sword.

Nagao, the human captain, leaned closer to Toshi. "I'll ask you again, friend. Who are you?"

"Call me Toshi." Thinking quickly, Toshi said, "I'm a thief. I'm here to loot the place. But I'm good at getting in and out of places, so I might be able to help you. How often does that thing come sniffing around?" He pointed to the wall where the oni mouths had appeared.

Nagao still looked suspicious, but Silver-Foot said, "Tell him, Captain. I don't believe him either, but he wasn't here an hour ago and he is here now. He might know something that we can use."

Nagao nodded. "It comes about once a day. Its visits are growing more frequent."

"Has it gotten anyone?"

"Not yet. Tonight was typical . . . it shows up, then suddenly seems to lose interest. But it'll be back."

"Good," Toshi said. "That's good."

Nagao glowered. "I don't see how that's good, friend."

Toshi smiled. "That's because you're not me. Listen, if that thing were going to eat you, it would have by now. I think you're safe in here for the time being."

"Thanks for the vote of confidence," Nagao said dryly. "But if you can't offer us anything more than that, I think you've wasted enough of my time."

Toshi cocked his head. "Just stay here. And don't let anyone touch that big stone disk. It's dangerous."

"I needed you to tell me that," Nagao muttered. Then, slightly louder, he said, "And where will you be? If you can leave, you're taking at least one of us with you."

Toshi smiled and winked. "Sorry, Captain. I refuse. But do as I say and I'll be back in a day or two."

Silver-Foot's sword slid out of its sheath like a whisper. The blade gleamed in the dim light and the kitsune said, "Don't move, Toshi. Nagao is quite right—you must take someone with you if you can."

Still smiling, Toshi faded from sight. Both officers grabbed for him as he went, but their hands passed through him.

"Trust me," he said, his voice hollow and distant. "I just need to call in a few favors. Two days, three at the most—I'll be back with help."

The good captains continued to search their immediate

surroundings for any sign of the stranger. Toshi maneuvered himself into the nearby shadows, already planning a series of jaunts through the shadow realm that would eventually allow him to return to Minamo and collect his prize.

Though the hyozan reckoners were broken and in turmoil, there was one last job they needed to do together.

CHAPTER 4

Home again for the first time in weeks, Toshi stood in the Numai district of Takenuma Swamp. No matter what the old ones said, he would never believe the fen had ever been anything but a greasy, bubbling cauldron of muck and rotten bamboo. If you wanted to build a house or a business in the swamp, you had to do it on twenty-foot stilts, high above the surface of the bog. Everything rested on sturdy bamboo legs: every building, every walkway, every structure that might conceivably be used by nontoxic, non-amphibious life forms.

Toshi hated the swamp. If the quicksand-like filth didn't drag you down and the swamp insects didn't infect you with bleeding fever, there were larger, crueler dangers waiting for the unwary who braved the bog. Numai's entire human population, for one. Here, the only things more malevolent than the cursed ground were the people who thrived on it. For as long as Toshi could remember his district had been the crossroads where the criminal-minded and the bloodthirsty met and mingled. Those with shady work could sit down with those who didn't mind doing it for cash.

There was precious little foot traffic now, which Toshi suspected was due to more than the swamp's bad reputation. There was a heaviness in the air, the kind of damp, oppressive stillness that usually precedes a major storm. It was similar to the dread he had felt hovering over Kamitaki Falls, but the swamp's mood was even darker, wetter, and more oppressive. After two decades of the Kami War, Toshi was all too familiar with the signs of a spirit crossing into the physical world, but that sensation was usually limited to a small area. Now, the pressure and sense of impending attack was everywhere.

He hadn't actually seen any spirits yet, but he had seen their wake. Mangled and partially consumed corpses left hanging in trees, temples smashed and painted over in blood, and charred, smoking ruins where great manors once stood.

Toshi heard a distant scream that echoed across the surface of the swamp. He waited for a moment to listen for the sequel, but no further sound came. He resumed walking. Just as well, he thought. He had no time for new adventures. He had already mortgaged too much of his future to powerful beings and made enemies of still more, so there was simply no chance for anyone else to make demands on him. The screamer would have to save himself.

Ahead, the end of the walkway materialized through the haze. From there he had a short climb and a long wade through the swamp until he reached his goal.

Toshi smiled thinly as he strode on. His patrons and foes were all lined up to greet him. He would face them as soon as he mustered his allies.

Toshi's smile faded. He decided not to think too far ahead with this plan for the time being. He couldn't worry about what happened after he recruited his partners until he had actually recruited them. Just because they considered themselves oath-bound to avenge his death didn't mean they were willing to prevent it beforehand.

He emerged onto solid ground less than an hour later. The small hill rose up out of the fen, and as he climbed it Toshi stamped mud and leeches from his feet. He was now on the outskirts of Numai district, along the western edge of Takenuma. Apart from the odd fugitive or hermit, the only humans who lived this far out were the Numai *jushi*, a close-knit clan of *mahotsukai*, or dark wizards. The mahotsukai delved more deeply into the black arts than was safe or sane, but they were powerful casters and exerted significant influence over the swamp's criminal society.

He had never met any of the mahotsukai elders but he had heard the rumors: they drank the blood of their apprentices, they took them as wives and forced them to bear monstrous children, and they were not living men at all but vampiric spirits who corrupted human souls with black magic then consumed them like some exquisite delicacy.

None of this truly mattered to Toshi. Residents of the swamp liked to exaggerate their power and their dark reputations as much as they liked to spread pointless gossip. Whatever those twisted old men did to their charges, they also taught them powerful magic. Kiku, one of the most dangerous people he had ever met, was a mahotsukai from the Numai jushi. All Toshi had to do was find her and convince her that helping him was in her own best interest.

He broke through the hedgerow of thorn bushes and stinging nettles to a clearing at the top of the rise. The ground was dry here, almost sandy, and the hilltop was dotted with clumps of gray-green grass that swayed hypnotically in the fetid air. In the center of this field of swamp grass stood a large, one-room building made of mud bricks and straw. It was round with a circular chimney in the center of the mud-thatch roof. No smoke rose from the hardened clay pipe, and no sound came from the building's interior.

Toshi's gut shifted and he knew something was wrong. The mahotsukai were not gregarious folk, but they always sent someone to meet visitors. If no one had come out to greet him by now, that meant either no one was here to do so . . . or no one was alive to do so.

He went closer, and a clearer view of the building confirmed his fears. The front door was hanging off one hinge, the thick clay of the doorway cracked and crumbling. There was a rough hole punched through the ceiling on the south end. A pale and lifeless hand dangled from one of the front windows, a thin stream of blood dripping slowly from its index finger.

Toshi drew his jitte in one hand and his long sword in the other. As he ran to the mahotsukai dwelling, he turned over the possibilities in his mind. Kami attack? Clan warfare? Had the daimyo's troops begun cracking down on black magicians while their lord and master was away?

He stepped up to the ruined front door and peered inside. A foul, stale odor hung in the air. Two small fires burned inside the building, one in the fireplace at the center of the room and one on a pile of debris nearer the door.

Toshi stopped when he saw the scene inside, and then he grimaced. Unlike the post-massacre scene at Minamo, the floor of the mahotsukai hut was nearly covered with broken and twisted bodies.

A young man was lying facedown just inside the doorway. From the huge slick of blood beneath him, Toshi guessed his throat had been cut. More students littered the rest of the residence, young and old alike, their torsos displaying neat, precise holes surrounded by crimson blooms. The pale hand that extended out through the window belonged to a girl, but she was too small and too slight to be Kiku.

Toshi sheathed his long sword but held onto his jitte. Whatever had happened here was long over, but that didn't mean there wasn't still danger. He quietly moved across the crowded floor and opened the large ornamental door at the far end of the room.

It was much worse inside. The bodies were crammed together and piled two-deep between Toshi and the altar at the center of the room. Toshi recognized sword wounds and dagger thrusts on every body he saw, the terrible evidence of a sharp blade and a skilled hand at work. Whoever did this did so with weapons of steel, not tooth and claw. Armed warriors had attacked the mahotsukai in their home and slaughtered them to a man.

Near the altar, Toshi stopped. This was more than a simple massacre—it was a message. Some of the older students had been killed and then hung from the walls. Toshi peered closer at the mangled body of a bearded man with one long, dangling earring and a tattoo that covered most of his face. His eyes were still wide-open in shock.

Correction, Toshi thought. Some had been hung from the walls and *then* killed. That ruled out the daimyo's troops. He had seen Konda's soldiers on punitive missions first-hand, and they would never have displayed such cruelty or taken the time to stage the corpses—they would have simply lined the mahotsukai up and decapitated them with swords, one by one and with great ceremony. Toshi grimaced and went on to the door that led deeper into the building.

The next room was the smallest, so it was fortunate that it held the fewest corpses. Toshi did not enter the room at first, but stood outside, gazing down at the half-dozen humanoid bodies scattered around the chamber.

These were different from the other victims. These bodies were all tall, thin, and elegantly dressed. Most wore black silk with their heads and faces concealed beneath scarves. The others wore cobalt-blue chain mail and carried katanas. What flesh Toshi could see was pale, gleaming white, like the reflection of moonlight on bleached bone. These new corpses were those of soratami, and their presence proved the battle was not one-sided.

Toshi was impressed. He allowed himself a moment of pure, cruel joy at the soratami's expense. Most of Toshi's current problems could be laid squarely at the feet of the soratami and their patron kami. Since Konda had vanished, the soratami had been openly working to take control of the entire swamp region. They killed those they couldn't intimidate or bribe, and he had to assume the mahotsukai were targeted because they would not knuckle under. It hadn't saved them and it wouldn't bring them back, but Toshi was glad the Numai jushi made the moonfolk pay for this night's work.

Toshi blinked. The soratami warriors were exceptional and their shinobi were as silent and invisible as leaves falling on a moonless night. They were far too proud to leave proof that mere ground-dwellers had defeated some of their tribe. Why then, had they left these bodies behind?

He looked again, noting that the soratami corpses were all equidistant from a central spot at the far side of the room. He puzzled for a moment, then nodded to himself. They had attempted to gang up on someone and been brutally killed and hurled backwards by their intended victim. Did this small victory take place away from the main body of invaders, so that they didn't realize their loss?

Or, more incredibly, did the last surviving mahotsukai defeat or scare off all of the attacking soratami so that none were left to carry off their dead?

Toshi hoped that was the case. He also hoped whoever it was could still shake hands—he wanted to congratulate him.

A woman sighed from the other side of the wall at the far end of the room. Toshi crept forward, peering past the altar, until he saw a loose seam in the wall itself. If the secret door hadn't been slightly sprung open, he would never have found it. Now, he nudged it open with his toe and crouched as he carefully picked his way through.

The secret door fell shut behind him, but the inner chamber was lit by a pair of black candles atop another, smaller altar. In the soft sphere of yellow light, Toshi saw the back of a woman's head rustling rhythmically back and forth. He tightened his grip on his jitte, but relaxed when the woman started singing softly. Her voice was soft, sweet, and clear.

"Kiku," Toshi called. He couldn't see clearly in the dim light, but he recognized the voice and the silky head of purple-black hair. "It's Toshi. I've come to help."

"Toshi." Kiku's voice was dreamy and somehow sad. "No work for you here, oath-brother. Nothing for the hyozan to avenge. I'm the only one they didn't kill."

Toshi stood rooted in place. He was not about to approach Kiku until he was sure of her mind. She might be wounded, or dying, or . . .

Kiku stood, rising into the flickering candlelight. Her head was tilted forward so that her exotic hair hung down past her chin, hiding her features. She steadied herself on the altar with one hand as she carelessly clutched the neck of a ceramic jug in the other.

"Join me in a drink, oath-brother?" She did not lift her face, but did wave the jug. "The masters were saving this for a special occasion. I think this qualifies. The mahotsukai have survived another night."

Toshi swallowed. "Sure, Kiku." He stepped forward with one hand extended for the jug and the other ready with his jitte. Kiku was mercurial on her best days, and she was devastating with her short-handled throwing hatchet. If she were intoxicated, she might remember she hated Toshi for binding her to the hyozan.

But Kiku simply stood, singing softly with her head tilted down while Toshi carefully approached. She was not dressed in her traditional outfit of lavish purple silk and leather armor, but in a sheer white linen shift that left her arms and shoulders bare. The fabric was so delicate it was nearly transparent in the soft light, and though Kiku was a beautiful woman, Toshi kept his attention firmly focused on her hands, where the threat would come from.

Toshi reached out and took hold of the jug. Kiku held on for a moment, resisting him, and then released it. From its heft Toshi guessed Kiku had consumed half of its contents. From its smell Toshi guessed that if you lit a match after taking a sip, your breath would catch fire.

He raised the jug to his lips, keeping his eyes on Kiku. After he was through wincing, Toshi handed the bottle back, but pulled it away when Kiku reached for it.

"Mahotsukai," he said. "What happened here?"

Kiku let her free hand fall to the altar so that she was leaning on both arms. "Soratami," she said. "Sent word. We were a threat, unsanctioned magic. We were to vacate, or else." She lifted her face and smiled wickedly at Toshi. "The elders chose 'or else.'"

Toshi almost coughed as he met Kiku's eyes, but his face remained calm. The flesh on Kiku's forehead, cheeks, and nose was covered in a dark, shifting stain that crawled across her face like oil on the surface of steaming hot tea. Rounded blobs and thin, spiky tendrils oozed and fluttered across her features, forming currents and eddies that alternately encircled and engulfed the topography of her fine-boned face.

It was horrifying to see such a strong person so fractured, to behold such beauty marred by magic. Worse was the undeniable sense of familiarity Toshi got from Kiku's new appearance. He was not a mahotsukai, so he did not practice their craft, but as an acolyte of Night's Reach he recognized shadow magic when he saw it.

Still jarred by Kiku's wild eyes and transformed face, Toshi said evenly, "Listen, Kiku. Tell me what happened."

Kiku motioned for the jug and Toshi handed it over. She tossed back a long draught and shuddered. Then, blinking her eyes rapidly, she focused on Toshi, and the dreamy, singsong quality to her voice disappeared.

"The masters did this." She made as if caressing her own face, but her palm never made contact. "Just as the soratami arrived." Kiku shook her head clear and went on. "You were right about them, oath-brother. The soratami. They are not to be taken lightly. Most of us were dead before the masters finished the ritual."

"What ritual? What did it do?"

Kiku steadied herself on the altar and then stood up straight. She swayed for a moment. Then she straightened her shift and brushed it clean in two long strokes. She focused on Toshi again, and her eyes glittered like hard, sharp gems behind narrowed lids.

"You use kanji magic," she said. "Characters, symbols as your weapon. The masters," she waved aimlessly behind Toshi, where the old men lay dead, "didn't use symbols. They used me." She set her jaw, suddenly serious and sober. "I was the tool of my masters' vengeance. I am their weapon. When they saw they would die, they turned to me. Cursed me, made me more dangerous."

Toshi took the bottle and sipped. "Did it work?"

"Killed the raiders all at once, in a single heartbeat." The mahotsukai's cruel mouth twisted into a sharp smile, then sagged. "But not fast enough. Couldn't control the power when I needed it. Self-preservation only. You should understand that." She croaked a hag's laugh and her eyelids fluttered. Kiku almost swooned, but Toshi caught her shoulder and she clutched the altar before she toppled.

"They'll be back," she continued. "And I'll be ready. All I have to do is sit here and keep killing them. The more they send, the more I'll get, and the more efficient the masters' tool shall become."

"How, Kiku?" Toshi came around the altar and stood beside the mahotsukai. He took her by the shoulders and guided her toward the altar. "How did you kill the soratami?"

Kiku allowed Toshi to turn her around and help her up onto the altar. She sat with her feet swinging freely for a moment and then crossed one leg over the other, the very picture of an elegant lady at a prominent social function. She even tossed her head.

"Solid shadows," she said. "Something else you understand. You may have direct contact with your myojin, but she's not the only one who commands the darkness." Her eyes lost focus as her thoughts turned inward. "Just as ochimusha and ogres aren't the only ones who knows how to craft revenge magic. Here, I'll show you—"

Toshi quickly grabbed Kiku's chin and turned her face to his. "Please don't," he said.

The oily shadow on Kiku's face had begun to churn. Tiny crested ridges of liquid darkness had started to form around her features, like waves made choppy by driving winds.

Kiku held Toshi's gaze for a moment, then looked away and exhaled. The motion on her face slowed, but it did not stop.

"Kiku," he said. "We are both bound by the oath. I have work for us to do." After all she had been through tonight, he didn't think he could hold Kiku to any promises she had made before, but he had to get her out of this abattoir. As long as there were corpses and mahotsukai liquor to sustain her melancholy, she would probably just sit here going madder and madder until the next group of soratami sneaked in and killed her.

"Can't go," she said firmly. "I am an instrument of vengeance. My entire clan is gone. I am the only bearer of the mahotsukai's wisdom. The last of the Numai jushi. If I do not avenge them—"

"We can avenge them together," Toshi said. "That's what I'm trying to tell you."

Kiku blinked, her eyes suddenly clouded once more. "You can help me?"

"I can. The soratami and their kami have been on my list for months now. I was just talking with Hidetsugu about finishing things with them once and for all. But I'd go out of my way to hurt them for the sheer fun of it. If getting them helps you, well, that's just a bonus."

Kiku's eyes opened wider. She turned to Toshi and said, "You can do it, too, can't you? You're crafty." She held up her hand, showing Toshi the triangular hyozan symbol on her palm. "You tricked me into joining your gang. If you can trick the moonfolk and get me close enough, I can release the full power of the masters' ritual and wipe them all out." She smiled dreamily. "Again."

Toshi nodded. This was going to be easier than he thought. "And do right by the memory of your clan. Your masters—"

"My masters can starve in the cold gray hell," Kiku flared, and for a second she was very much like her old self. "This." She circled her own face with her hands. "I need to be free of this. I can't think with this. I'm not me with this." She sagged, sad and defeated. "Take this from me, Toshi. I don't want it. Please, oath-brother. Help me."

Kiku's eyes closed and she lurched forward. Toshi caught her in his arms, her face pressed against his neck.

"I'll help you, Kiku. We'll help each other."

Kiku did not withdraw from Toshi's chest. "Thank you, oath-brother."

"We . . . uh, Kiku? What are you doing?"

The mahotsukai's lips were leaving delicate trails along Toshi's throat. Was she kissing him? He felt the hard, straight edges of her teeth as she seized his flesh between them, and squawked as she bit down.

Kiku lifted her head, fixing the ochimusha with a fierce glare. "Shut up, stupid Toshi." She grabbed the back of his head with both hands and pressed his face into her, mashing their lips together. She leaned back as she kissed him, pulling him partially up onto the altar beside her.

"Ah, Kiku, I—"

She pulled back, her eyes wild. "As you said, oath-brother, we can help each other." She pushed Toshi back and slid off the altar. In the blink of an eye she tossed the thin shift over her head and let it flutter forgotten to the floor. Kiku wore a silver chain around her waist and a golden one around her left ankle. There was a brilliant purple flower tattooed on her right hip.

She kept her eyes on Toshi and extended a delicate hand, beckoning him. "Now," she said. "Come here."

Toshi stared goggle-eyed. Kiku was in shock. She must be in shock, or drunk, or overwhelmed by grief and the power of her masters' spell. At the very least she was doing this to bind Toshi to her cause, using him to achieve her own goals.

Kiku stood, watching him, waiting for him. "Well?"

Toshi took her hand, drew her to him, and kissed her. They stood embracing for an endless moment before Toshi remembered something and pushed her away.

"Two things, mahotsukai."

Kiku stepped back, demurely crossing her arms. "I'm not used to accepting conditions at this stage."

"Two simple things, easily addressed. One, we agree to talk more in the morning."

"Of course. And the second?"

Toshi grimaced. "Stop calling me 'oath-brother.' It's making me queasy."

Kiku laughed lightly, a short crystalline sound that carried beauty and sharp edges alike. Once more, Toshi was given a glimpse of Kiku the way he knew her, confident, beautiful, strong, and more than a little bit frightening.

"Done," she said. She opened her arms once more, and Toshi leaned forward, bearing her back up onto the altar.

CHAPTER 5

The moon shone down on the fortress of Eiganjo. For the first time in over a decade, the glowing half-orb hung from a clear and cloudless sky, surrounded by pinpoints of clean, white starlight. Fat, lazy clouds drifted across the night sky, but even they curved around the moon as if unwilling to spoil the view from below.

Far beneath the waxing moon stood the tower-fortress of Eiganjo, a massive white-stone edifice that stretched proud and strong up to the very clouds themselves. Moonlight cast the tower's shadow far across the lowlands to the south, with only its ragged tip to spoil the smooth and solid wall of black. The tower's uppermost level was an irregular line of broken rock, and its shadow passed through a similar jagged gap in the mighty walls around Eiganjo. There were no signs of life from the tower or the courtyard within the fortress walls. From a distance, Eiganjo appeared as silent as a tomb, as pale as a spirit, and as lonely as a headstone.

The hooded figure of Toshi Umezawa stepped from the shadows at the northwest corner of the walls. He adjusted his finest acolyte's robe (or, at least, the finest robe he could steal that looked like an acolyte's robe) and stole a quick glance around the deserted parade grounds. With his head bowed, he began to shuffle across the courtyard toward a two-story outbuilding on the west side of the tower.

His journey continued in complete silence until he approached the door to the outbuilding. From just outside the wide double doors, he heard a strange burbling sound. It was a clean, flowing sound like the tone from some fabulously exquisite musical instrument. The hooded figure tilted his head up to the second floor, the source of the sound.

The lush, soothing song was interrupted by a ferocious barking from inside the building. Toshi stepped back as a huge pale dog erupted from the double doors, its gruff voice both alarm and threat.

Oh, good, the ochimusha thought. He drew a hook-shaped weapon from beneath his robes and held it point-first toward the dog. The hook had been hammered from dull, gray metal and shaped so that the shorter, blunt tine stood below the thicker tapering spike above. The dog stopped just outside the double doors, still barking at top volume.

Toshi peered from beneath his cowl. "I know you," he said to the dog. "Why are you always so loud when you see me?"

"You may know Isamaru," a thin but steady voice said. "However, he does not know you. Stand very still, sir. I would regret it if you were bitten accidentally."

"Isamaru," Toshi said, memorizing the name. The next time he saw this dog he wanted to be able to order it around by name. He nodded to Isamaru and dropped his jitte to his side but did not sheathe it. He called out over the dog's barking, "This is Princess Michiko's dog."

"Sir. That dog belongs to Daimyo Konda himself." An elderly man in a rumpled white uniform stepped out of the building. His skin was like translucent paper stretched tight over his bones. Wisps of silver hair peeked out from under his helmet and his left hand trembled. In his right he carried a long pole with a paper lantern strung to the end. Shuddering slightly, the old man lit the lantern and extended it out over the newcomer's head.

"I am Acting Constable Aoyama," the old man said. He peered at the robed man, scanning him from head to toe. Isamaru stopped barking but stood alert and ready within springing distance of the new arrival.

Constable Aoyama's lamp shook as he spoke. "What are you doing near the stables, priest?"

Toshi shook his head, more amused than he expected to be. "I'm no priest."

The constable grunted. "You wear the robes of a seeker. Are you a monk?"

"I am a seeker, but not a monk. I'm more of an acolyte, a follower. I aspire to spiritual greatness, but aspiration is a long way from achievement."

The old man lowered the lantern. "Well, whatever you are, don't try to preach strange religious beliefs in Eiganjo. The spirits have brought great hardship upon us lately."

Toshi tilted his head toward the broken walls and the damaged tower. "So I see," he said. "But rest easy, constable. I'm not one for preaching, though I do feel much safer knowing you're on the job."

Aoyama laughed. "Don't be too confident," he said. "All of our able-bodied men are dead or fighting on the frontier. That leaves patrols and other mundane duties to old men like me. I'm really just a groomsman with a uniform." He lowered the pole to the ground to steady the lantern and drew his own weapon, a metal truncheon similar to Toshi's.

"They told me the jitte was a constable's tool," Aoyama said. He absently turned the hooked truncheon over in his hand, letting the moonlight play across its surface. "But you wield one too."

Toshi slowly lifted his jitte, extended his index finger, and let the hook dangle from it. "I didn't realize the Daimyo was so specific about who can carry what weapons."

Aoyama straightened. "In Eiganjo," he said sternly, "the constable's hook is like the samurai's sword. It is a badge of office as well as an essential tool for performing the duties of that office."

"Of course, Acting Constable. Please know that I respect that office and those duties." Toshi twirled his own jitte around his finger and then caught it by the handle. "But I mainly use mine to keep people from stabbing me."

Aoyama laughed. "It's good for that, too." He sheathed his jitte and relaxed. Isamaru also sat, but his eyes were wide and he panted, showing the hooded figure his large white teeth.

The constable gestured with the pole. "Why aren't you fighting with the other young men?"

"I am not a citizen of Eiganjo. But that doesn't mean I haven't been fighting the Kami War elsewhere, in my own way."

"Forgive me, acolyte. I meant no disrespect," Aoyama said. "But you should know there is danger here. An akki horde not half a day's march to the north. They have been trying to mount an offensive against the fortress since . . . since . . ."

The old man faltered. Isamaru whined.

The visitor spoke up. "Since the walls were breached?"

"Yes."

The hooded head cocked to one side. "A terrible day. But still . . . goblins on the plains of Towabara?"

"Unbelievable, I know. But true. They were led here by sanzoku bandits and they breed like maggots. Isamaru here accompanies the soldiers to and from the battle. Captain Okazawa himself made him an honorary soldier for the duration." He leaned forward and ruffled the fur on the dog's head with a palsied hand. "Without Isamaru here, and Yosei, the fortress would have been overwhelmed in a matter of hours."

"Yosei?"

"The spirit dragon who protects Eiganjo. He could not stop the destruction of the tower and he suffered terrible wounds, but he still kept the goblins from our door." Aoyama moved the lantern aside and looked up into the night sky. "There," he said. "That streak of light to the north. Can you see it?"

Toshi followed Aoyama's gaze. "I see it." Indeed, a thin stream of light etched a glowing spear to the left the moon. It could have been a large comet or shooting star, but it was uniformly bright along the length of its streamlined body. As it streaked over the broken tower, its serpentine features stood out clearly against the dark sky. This was Yosei, the Morning Star, guardian beast from the spirit world who served Eiganjo when most of his fellow spirits turned against the world of flesh and substance.

As majestic and awe-inspiring as Yosei was, he was clearly diminished from his full glory. His proud, whiskered head indicated he should be a long, sinuous creature, but his body seemed to be only half of what it should be. Yosei shone with a bright white light, but the mangled end of his body left a trail of glittering purple haze and thick pink vapor.

"He is awesome indeed, Constable. But is he well?"

Aoyama's chest swelled. "He has borne that terrible wound you see for many days now. Any lesser creature would have died on the spot, but Yosei continues to fight. The soldiers say he will not die until the last goblin has been scoured from the plains."

"Magnificent. Between the great spirit dragon and the daimyo's glorious battle-moths, Eiganjo rules the sky. The akki cannot hope to prevail."

Aoyama's face soured. "Forgive me, acolyte. I never did get your name."

The green-eyed man turned to the constable. "Toshi," he said. "You can call me Toshi."

"I am the keeper of the moth stables, Toshi. It is my sworn duty to care for these great beasts and to protect them from harm." Aoyama drew his jitte. "What is your interest in them?"

Toshi smiled. "You may be old, Acting Constable Aoyama, but you are still keen. I had heard that the moths were all but wiped out in the recent battle here. I wanted to see them with my own eyes before they are gone for good."

Aoyama lowered his weapon. "I see. You're almost too late, Acolyte Toshi. There are barely a dozen of the great moths left, and even that is too many for us to feed."

"How tragic," Toshi said. "Will you let them starve, or will you release them to fend for themselves?"

Aoyama shifted uncomfortably on his feet. "I am a loyal servant of the daimyo," he said stiffly.

"But also the moth's only caretaker. I'm told they are magnificent creatures. Surely you wouldn't just let them wither? Gossip around the fortress says Konda and the bulk of his army were slain, but survive as spirits to fight for your freedom. If the moths die, will they go on fighting? Will they join Konda's spirit army? Or will they simply be dead?"

"Konda was not slain," Aoyama said angrily. "And as for

what happens to these moths when they die, I have no intention of finding out."

"Ah, but you already have, constable. Because there are less than a dozen moths now, but a week ago there were more. As the food stocks dwindle, you've been letting some of them go." Toshi's eyes twinkled. "Haven't you?"

Aoyama thumped his lantern pole on the ground. "I think you should move along, acolyte." Isamaru stood, his eyes on Toshi, waiting for a command.

Toshi clasped his hands together and bowed lightly. "I understand your concerns, Aoyama, and you should not feel ashamed. I must be honest with you now: I have ridden the daimyo's moths before. I hold them in the highest esteem, and I support your efforts to save them, no matter what Daimyo Konda or anyone else may think. You are a hero, sir, a kind friend to these noble creatures."

Aoyama stared at Toshi, his paper lantern swaying on the end of its string.

"Please," the constable said. "I'm old, not feeble. Every warlord and minor daimyo across Kamigawa would do anything to acquire one of Konda's battle-moths. I may have . . . relocated some of my charges, but I would burn them all alive in their stables before I would turn them over to Eiganjo's enemies. A priest's robe and a flowery speech will not convince me otherwise."

His growls rising with the new tension between the two men, Isamaru barked.

Toshi's open, guileless face did not change. Through bright eyes and a slight smile, he said, "So, there's no chance of convincing you to turn away for a few moments and overlook the loss of one more moth?"

Aoyama pointed his jitte at Toshi. "None." Keeping his eyes on Toshi, Aoyama said, "Isamaru!"

In response, the dog's eyes narrowed and his claws dug into the ground.

"I ask you to reconsider, Constable." Still smiling slightly, Toshi tossed his head back. The cowl fell back and settled around his neck and shoulders.

The symbol inscribed across the flesh of Toshi's forehead glowed softly, casting a light purple sheen over the rest of his face. A cold wind whipped up around him, swirling his robe around his body.

He turned to the dog. "Isamaru," he said, "stay back."

The dog's growling trailed into an uncertain whine. As Toshi spoke, his breath came in great clouds of white fog. The mist from his lungs hardened into crystals before him and fell like snowflakes to the dusty ground.

Aoyama gasped, his lantern making the shadows dance crazily across the ground. The old man held his jitte out in front of him, backing away and praying furiously under his breath.

Toshi pointed to the symbol on his brow. "I bear the mark of the yuki-onna. Just as the akki goblins from the frozen wastes have come to Eiganjo, so does this, the curse of lethal cold, the primordial fury of winter. Stand aside, old man, or feel the icy touch of death."

Aoyama blinked. "Hang on. The yuki-onna is a female spirit. Snow-*woman*. How did you . . ."

Toshi frowned. "Don't dodder, Constable." He gestured at the symbol again. "This is the kanji for yuki-onna. I bear her power as well as her symbol."

Aoyama simply stared, his jitte trembling in his hand. Isamaru advanced a pace and began growling again.

Toshi sighed. "What does it take to frighten you and that damned dog away for ten seconds?"

"More than you possess, false acolyte. You're no seeker, you're just a lowlife."

Toshi shrugged. "I mean well."

Aoyama steadied his lantern. "Go on now, Toshi. You've had your jest."

"I'm afraid I can't, Constable. I really am an acolyte, even if you can't believe it. My myojin has given me a very clear mission in life, and I can't accomplish it without one of Konda's moths."

"You're lucky your patron spirit just gives orders instead of tearing you to pieces. It's not even safe to worship most spirits anymore."

"My point exactly. We don't want to make the spirits any angrier than they already are, right? Give me what my myojin demands and you'll never see me again."

"Never. Leave this place, now. I won't give you another chance."

"You don't have any chances to give, my friend. It's not up to you."

The old man trembled. "I have but to raise my voice—"

"—to cause a great echo. Come on, Constable. Now who's blowing smoke?" Toshi smiled and then puffed another cloud of snow through pursed lips. "There's no one here to answer your call. And even if there were, Isamaru here is the only real fighter left in the fortress."

"That may be true," Aoyama said. "But at least he is already here."

"Not for long."

"Longer than you. Isamaru! Attack!"

The big dog was well trained. He snarled as he leaped for Toshi's arm, his powerful jaws capable of crushing bone to powder in a single bite.

As he stepped back, Toshi wondered why he seemed to be having so much trouble with dogs lately. Isamaru did not allow him time to find the answer, so the ochimusha waved his arm in a circle as Isamaru hit him, tangling the dog's teeth in the folds of his sleeve. He wrapped the loose-fitting fabric around the top of Isamaru's nose as he caught the heavy dog against his chest and shoulder. Quick as a mousetrap, Toshi slammed the dog's jaws shut and kept them closed by pulling the fabric tight around Isamaru's face like a muzzle.

Toshi's foot plunged into a shadow cast by Aoyama's lantern, and the foot plunged into it. Isamaru's weight seemed to bear Toshi down into the shadow more quickly than normal, and in less than a second they were both gone.

Aoyama stood blinking in the lantern light. He moved the paper globe closer to the spot where Toshi and Isamaru had vanished, but the pale light revealed only cold, hard ground. The old man hesitated.

"Isamaru?" he said.

"Safe and happy," Toshi's voice replied. Aoyama spun in place, swinging the lantern as he went, but there was no sign of the intruder. In the cold glow of the paper globe there were no shadows to conceal him, either.

"He's probably confused right now," Toshi continued, still unseen. "But once he stops to sniff around, he'll find a friendly scent or two. He'll be fine. Is there anywhere you'd like to go, Constable? I can freeze you like an icicle and leave you here, but I'd be willing to deposit you somewhere comfortable and warm to sit out the rest of the war. It's up to you."

"You have taken Eiganjo's hope," Aoyama said miserably. "Yosei is like a god, but Isamaru was our own defender, born and bred in the fortress. Return him at once!"

"Trust me," Toshi's voice said. "He's much happier where he is now."

Aoyama dropped his lantern and drew a short sword. The lantern light flickered, then expired, leaving only the moon's silver-blue tint. With his jitte in one hand and a blade in the other, the old man said, "I will not abandon my duty to the daimyo."

Toshi's voice was unperturbed. "Fair enough." He materialized like a ghost one step behind Aoyama, strode forward, and then tapped the handle of his jitte behind the constable's left ear. The old man groaned softly, and as he crumpled to the ground his eyes rolled back in his head.

Toshi stood silently for a moment, listening for any other sentries and spinning his jitte. Finally, he turned to face the constable.

"You're a brave man," he said to Aoyama's supine form, "but a dismal constable."

Then Toshi turned and went quickly into the building. The first floor was some kind of warehouse. It was built for storage, but these days there was barely a cartload of grain in heavy sacks and a small supply of fresh water in clay jars. Toshi searched until he found a stack of small wooden boxes piled neatly at the foot of the stairway. Each box was filled with what appeared to be soft grayish bricks. He pulled one of the bricks out, inspected it, and nodded. With a grunt, Toshi hauled a box onto his shoulder and climbed the staircase in the center of the room.

The strange musical sound was louder and clearer on the second floor. Toshi put the wooden box down as he waited for his eyes to adjust to the moonlight streaming in between the ceiling slats overhead.

Roughly a dozen gigantic moths were here, housed in individual stalls twenty feet wide. Their broad, flat wings sparkled eerily in the gloom, leaving faint trails of iridescent powder in the air. Each was large enough to carry three grown men and strong enough to bear a month's worth of rations for each. As they raised and lowered their wings, a glittering breeze swirled around the stable and the air echoed with their burbling song.

Toshi walked along the row of stables, appraising each moth in turn. He had ridden such great beasts before and knew how to spot the strong ones. In the second to last stall, he found one to his liking.

It was one of the largest, and its wings were covered in a colorful collage of pale yellow, brilliant orange, and gleaming white. Its body was thick and sturdy, its movements solid and strong. Here was a steed that could carry the burden Toshi had in mind.

He went back to the wooden box and brought it into the moth's stall. Toshi tore off a piece from one of the gray bricks, thinking once again of how the soft and spongy material reminded him of moist bread. The moths were intelligent creatures, as much as dogs and horses, but they still responded best to food.

Toshi held the gray mass in front of the moth's head. It inspected the stuff for a moment before plunging its sharp proboscis in. Within a few seconds, it had sucked all the moisture out of the material, leaving only a thin membrane in Toshi's hand.

Toshi patted the great moth and it trilled happily. He unlatched the stall door and opened it, revealing the clear, calm courtyard below. Then he retrieved a bridle and reins from a hook on the wall and slipped them over the moth's head. He lashed a saddle to the moth's back and tied the wooden box full of moth food into a leather harness that fit behind the saddle.

"Steady, now," Toshi said. He climbed onto the moth and eased into the saddle. Without being prodded, the moth rose on its legs and began to beat its wings more forcefully. It skittered forward and hopped out of its stall. Toshi's stomach dropped.

Before they could fall, the moth's great wings caught the air, and it swooped, skimming the ground. Toshi pulled up on the reins, and the moth burbled again, picking up speed and height as it soared silently through the huge hole in Eiganjo's stone walls.

For a moment, Toshi watched the moth's shadow on the ground far below. To someone down there, he and his steed would be silhouetted against the gleaming half-moon. He wondered if the daimyo's people would be heartened by such a majestic sight or frightened by the strangeness of it.

Toshi glanced up at the great half-circle glowing so brightly in the skies over Eiganjo.

"Soon," he whispered. "Your turn will come soon."

CHAPTER 6

Toshi kneeled outside the mahotsukai stronghold in the early-morning sun. He was dressed once more in his standard outfit of nondescript black cloth and leather armor, and he meditated as he traced simple kanji characters in the sandy soil, sorting through the next stages of his plan. He had left the moth securely tethered with three days' supply of the gray bricks. He would be back to collect the great beast long before it ran out of food or grew bored enough to wriggle free of its harness. Kiku was with him, so he just needed to collect Marrow-Gnawer to complete the current roster of hyozan reckoners and get this grand enterprise underway.

"Toshi!" Kiku's voice was furious from within the building.

Quickly, Toshi stood and faced the door. Kiku came storming out, her hard eyes blazing with rage and her soft mouth twisted into a grimace. She was fully dressed once more, decked out in fine purple satin and silk and bearing her colorful *tessen* fan that was as much a weapon as it was an accessory. She also wore two *fuetsu* throwing axes on her belt and a vivid purple camellia flower on her high-collared blouse.

"Good morning," Toshi said. "How did you—?"

Kiku grabbed Toshi by the shirtfront and slammed her forearm into his chest. Toshi grunted as the air left his lungs. Kiku continued to push him backward.

"What happened to my face?" she seethed. "Where is the masters' spell?"

Indeed, the shadowy black sheen that had been crawling across her face was gone. Toshi had hoped it would take Kiku longer to notice its absence.

He gagged as Kiku tightened his shirt around his throat. "You asked me to get rid of it," he choked. "Remember? 'I'm not me with this'? Last night, you asked me last night . . ."

"I said and did a lot of things last night that I'm regretting right now," Kiku said. She shoved Toshi back, releasing him to stumble and fall on his backside. "In fact, I'm seeing things quite clearly." Smoothly, her hand slid up to the flower on her blouse and picked it off.

"Stop," Toshi said urgently. "We are both hyozan. We can't turn on each other."

Kiku held the camellia gingerly between two fingers. This was Kiku's chosen form of killing magic. Her blooms could poison an entire village's water supply or devour a man from the inside out. Once the flower touched its intended target, it grew and lashed out according to its nature, its roots digging into flesh and its perfume overwhelming anything it touched.

"Funny," she said. "But I recall you telling me not to invoke the oath last night."

"That's not how it works," Toshi said curtly. "We're meant to protect each other, and, if that's not possible, avenge. If we harm each other, the oath itself will destroy us." Toshi cursed inwardly. He had abandoned the hyozan oath when Night's Reach demanded it, so Kiku could in fact kill him with impunity right now. The only reason she hadn't that was she didn't know she could.

So instead Kiku stood, flower at the ready, her gaze sharp enough to cut glass. "Give me back the masters' curse. It was their will and is my duty."

"I didn't take it," Toshi said. "At least, I didn't take it for myself. I only did what you asked. After you fell asleep. Look." He pointed.

Kiku did not take her eyes from Toshi. "No," she said. "Show me."

Toshi marched slowly to edge of the kanji he had drawn in the dirt. He bent and retrieved a small clay tablet and showed the dull brown plate's face to Kiku. Etched into the surface of the hardened clay was a kanji, a magical symbol formed from the combined characters for "solid" and "shadow."

"It's here," Toshi said. "Ready when you want it. The masters' spell was hasty and rough, Kiku. The power it gave you would have consumed you inside of a week. Now you can hold it in your hands, keep it in check until you decide to use it. You know I can contain power this way. You've seen me do it with the yuki-onna. You have to trust me." He spread his arms out wide, exposing his chest and throat.

"I did what you asked me to do. I did it because we're partners. If you still think I'm playing you, then strike. Kill me, crack the tablet, and reclaim the power. If you survive breaking our oath . . . which you won't . . . I guarantee you'll be cackling and drooling and singing to yourself in a matter of days."

Kiku's eyes were clear. Toshi watched her jaw work as she considered his explanation.

"We're still headed for the waterfall? Where the soratami are?"

"Absolutely. As soon as we collect Marrow-Gnawer, we can be there in no time."

Kiku sniffed, turned away, and then reattached the flower to her collar. "I don't see why we need the nezumi."

"Because he's part of the hyozan as well. Because he's tougher, smarter, and braver than any other ratfolk in Takenuma."

Kiku turned. Her face was beautiful but brittle, like a china doll cast in a perpetual sneer. "Forget it, ochimusha. The deal's off." She scooped up the clay tablet and tucked it into her belt. "I suppose I should thank you. I am thinking far more clearly without the masters' curse."

Toshi cocked his head. "If you're thanking me, why are you—?"

"Because I no longer need you, now that I have this." She patted the plate on her hip. "I can pursue my own path to vengeance. When I get the soratami where I want them, I'll invoke it and kill them all."

"But you'll never—"

"Maybe not," Kiku interrupted. "But now I might never have to. I will deal with this in my own way, in my own time. Thank you, oath-brother. Now piss off."

Kiku turned away, and Toshi's brain fairly whirred as the thoughts assembled themselves. He had to act quickly and speak carefully. He hadn't wanted to do this, but he absolutely needed Kiku and Marrow to make his plans work.

"I will release you from the hyozan oath," he said.

Kiku stopped. Slowly, she turned, a sly grin forming at the corners of her mouth.

"Say that again."

"I'll let you go," Toshi said. "Do this one last thing with me.

One last go-round for the hyozan reckoners. Work with me and Marrow to take down the soratami. You'll be entirely free. No gang, no masters, no shadow curse, nothing to stop you from doing exactly as you like, whenever you like."

Kiku stepped up to Toshi. She looked him full in the face, her maddening, enticing scent wafting up to his nostrils.

"Say it again," she said. "Once more, and plainly. Toy with me and I'll plant a bloom in your throat before you can breathe."

"Once last job," Toshi said. "Be a reckoner with Marrow and me one last time, and then the hyozan will cease to exist."

Kiku shook her head, still smiling. "I knew you were lying. What about the ogre?"

"He's still around, still a central pillar that supports the oath," Toshi said. "And that's how you know you can trust me."

The gorgeous mahotsukai's eyebrows raised, but she said nothing.

"Our first stop," he said, "is Minamo Academy. That's where the soratami are. And that is where Hidetsugu is, actively and enthusiastically pursuing his own grudge against the moonfolk and their patron kami. With our help, he will very likely succeed."

Kiku toyed with her flower. "And if he can't?"

Toshi held her eyes. "If he can't or won't, we go on without him. If he tries to stop us, we destroy him."

Realization flashed across Kiku's face. "Which you cannot do if the oath is still in place. But as long as he thinks it's in place, he won't attack us." She grinned mirthlessly. "I like it."

"Told you I was crafty."

"No, I told *you* you were crafty. And I was drunk when I said it." She paused. "All right, ochimusha, you win. But let me out of your little gang now, before we take another step."

"Bad idea," Toshi said. "Without the oath, Hidetsugu can hurt you. He hasn't been the most rational being lately, and I wouldn't trust him to restrain himself. He might suffer for killing us, but we'd still be dead."

Kiku looked at him icily.

"Also," Toshi added, "if I let you off the hook now, there's no guarantee that you'll come with me . . . or leave me alive, for that matter. I need your help and I want to stay alive, so I'm going to wait a little while longer."

Kiku stood and stared for a while. Slowly, she started to nod, and the gesture grew stronger until she was shaking her purple-black hair vigorously up and down.

"All right. I know there's a lot you're not telling me, but that's just you. Even so, you make a compelling case. It will be nice to be free of certain . . . entanglements for a change." Kiku pressed her palms together and bowed slightly. "You win, Toshi. Let's go."

"You won't regret it." Toshi was careful not to let the relief show on his face. He needed Kiku's power, even without her masters' curse enhancing it. He hoped convincing Marrow-Gnawer would be easier, because even though the ratman was far less useful in a fight, he was ultimately as important to the job as Kiku or even Toshi himself.

Kiku straightened up and took a step closer to Toshi. She trailed a finger up his throat and touched his lips.

"Do you remember last night?" she cooed. "Every thing we did, every sound we made, every sensation we felt?"

Toshi nodded, enthusiastically earnest for the first time in a long time. "Every second, Kiku."

She chucked him gently under the chin. "Good," she said. "Because it's never going to happen again."

The mahotsukai turned and wafted into the dwelling. Toshi

waited until she was completely out of sight, then blew a long, thin stream of relief between his pursed lips.

So far, so good, he thought.

* * * * *

They found Marrow-Gnawer in the western quadrant of Takenuma. The *nezumi-bito* ratfolk were everywhere in the swamp, but most of them made their homes as far from human society as they could. They were generally vicious and filthy creatures, but they were tough and cunning and could follow orders. Marrow was a leader among his people due to his size, his smarts, and his long history of working with humans. There was no job too dirty for a nezumi, but Marrow brought a bit of competence and common sense to his criminal endeavors.

As Kiku and Toshi approached the huge nest Marrow's people had excavated into the side of a hill, they noticed hundreds of yellow pinpricks staring at them. Fiery rat eyes shined from the brush, from behind trees, from holes in the ground. Usually, a crowded nezumi den would be a noisy, chattering mess, but despite so many ratfolk being nearby, the hillside was eerily silent.

Marrow emerged from the nest and motioned for Toshi and Kiku to stop. They waited as the ratman dropped to all fours and scurried toward them.

He was big for a nezumi, almost four and a half feet tall, and he was armed with a rusting but viciously sharp short sword. His rough-woven clothes were caked with grime and threadbare, but he had covered his chest with a piece of someone else's shield and fashioned a leather harness into crude protective headgear.

Marrow stopped a few feet away and tentatively sniffed the air.

Satisfied, he rose and offered a cringing little bow. "Fellow reckoners," he said, "it's not safe here."

Toshi looked around. "Soratami?"

Marrow shook his head. "Kami," he said. "The spirits have been very restless for the past few days. We've got nowhere else to go, so we're digging in until things settle down."

Toshi pulled back his sleeve and showed Marrow the false hyozan mark there. "We've got reckoner business, oath-brother. The nest will have to manage without you for a little while longer."

Marrow glanced back at the yellow eyes watching him from the tunnel entrance. His voice suddenly rose, echoing off the hillside. "I can't possibly leave now, oath-brother," he declared. "As the pack elder, my place is here." Marrow's voice dropped to a whisper. "I'm in," he hissed. "Take me with you."

Toshi cocked his head, confused.

"No, don't argue." Marrow's voice rang out loud and clear. "My people need me." Whispering again, he said, "Come on, Toshi. Get me out of here. We're crammed in there six-deep, and I don't know how much longer I can take it."

Toshi opened his mouth, but before he could say anything, Marrow bawled, "All right, then. An oath is an oath." He winked at the ochimusha.

A concerned chattering began to rise inside the hill. The other nezumi didn't seem happy about their new elder leaving them to fend for themselves.

"Do you need to get anything?" Toshi muttered. "Maybe you should say goodbye, soften the blow a bit. They seem upset."

Marrow-Gnawer stared at Toshi for a long moment, and the ochimusha could almost see the thoughts assembling in the nezumi's brain. When everything fit, the little brute's eyes snapped open and he flashed a devilish grin.

"Good idea, oath-brother. Soften the blow." He turned to Kiku and his smile widened. "That's why he's in charge." Marrow turned back to the nest, where the most anxious of his fellows was just starting to emerge from the tunnel entrance. They blinked in the evening gloom and waited expectantly for him to speak.

"You're on your own," Marrow called happily. "Goodbye." He waved, his tail swishing in the grass behind him. He stopped, tightened his belt, and turned to Toshi. "All done. Let's go."

As their new leader walked away without looking back, the hidden nezumi began to wail. Toshi stood uncomfortably for a moment in the growing chorus of mournful groans and gnashing teeth. He turned to Kiku and shrugged.

"That was easier than I expected," he said.

Kiku had always hated working with the ratfolk. She spoke through a fine silk handkerchief she was holding over her mouth and nose to blunt the stench wafting from the hillside. "Quite. Very easy. In fact, extremely easy." She sniffed. "Almost worth the effort."

"True." Toshi started after Marrow. "I still feel like I got off light. I didn't even have to kiss him to get him on board.

"Don't hit me," he said without turning. "We're still oath-bound." Toshi tried not to smirk as he walked away from the rats' nest. He could almost hear Kiku's rage mounting. "And don't take it out on the nezumi, either."

Marrow stood waiting just out of sight of the hill. Toshi stopped on the path just before he himself would have dropped out of sight and looked back. Kiku was still seething outside the tunnel entrance, so Toshi waved for her to catch up.

Instead, the mahotsukai said something sharp to the rats in the tunnel and beckoned them closer. Still speaking through her handkerchief, Kiku gestured with her free hand until the rats nodded enthusiastically. Then she reached into her purse and tossed a few silver coins onto the ground. As the nezumi scrambled for the cash, Kiku turned and marched toward Toshi.

Toshi smiled, but Kiku stormed past him without speaking. Still grinning, he fell in behind her and kept pace as she went down the path.

"I hope you didn't hire them to kill me after the oath is broken," he called. "You'd still have to answer for it."

"I did no such thing." Kiku did not turn. She strode past Marrow without acknowledging him and continued on her way.

"So what was the cash for? Charity?"

"I told them how to spell your name. I gave them more than they could earn in a year." The mahotsukai stopped, planted her hands on her hips, and tossed her hair from her eyes. "And in exchange, they're going to write your name at the bottom of every nezumi latrine, chamber-pot, and cesspool in the area. Just in case we don't survive this, oath-brother, I wanted to make sure that I left a fitting tribute to you behind." She smiled coldly, her eyes daring Toshi to respond.

After a moment's consideration, Toshi said, "Hmm. Okay, that is a good one." He raised his hands. "I surrender, mahotsukai. For now."

Kiku rolled her eyes and turned back down the path. Once she was clear, Marrow sniggered and pointed at Toshi.

"Let's move, oath-brother," Toshi said. "I'll explain what we're up to on the way."

Still tickled, Marrow darted off after Kiku. Toshi waited for a moment, fought back the laugh he felt building in his own throat, and then followed. He'd have to remember the nezumi latrine treatment the next time someone annoyed him. That was, in fact, a good one. But that wasn't the only reason he'd decided to let Kiku have the last word.

The hyozan was all but over, its two founders openly declared against each other. The future of the group and everyone in it now depended on Kiku and Marrow, though they did not have the slightest idea what that meant or what impact it would have. And the reason they had no idea was because Toshi hadn't told them, would never tell them, and would in fact keep them ignorant for as long as he could. Because if they knew, Marrow and Kiku both would surely turn and tear him to pieces before he took another step.

Toshi unsheathed his jitte, spun it around his index finger, and then jogged to catch up to the others.

CHAPTER 7

Outside Minamo Academy once more, Toshi stood with his allies. Behind him, the borrowed battle-moth still burbled happily, securely lashed to its tree. Kiku and Marrow both faced Toshi, listening closely as he spoke.

"And that's it," he said. "If we can get in and get out quietly, we don't have to worry about Hidetsugu and his yamabushi. Once we've got the disk, we can leave. I can dissolve the hyozan oath from anywhere once we're done here. But we need it in place until we're done, in case Hidetsugu finds us."

Marrow looked in annoyance at the glorious moth. "I still don't see why you don't just go in there and carry the thing off yourself. You brought it here alone, didn't you?"

Toshi nodded. "I did. But that particular avenue is closed. My myojin doesn't want this thing in her domain."

"Then why doesn't she leave it here?" Kiku had been especially sharp and penetrating with her questions during Toshi's little briefing. She was also supporting Marrow whenever possible, which Toshi guessed was a way to force more information out of him.

"Because she wants it to exist. She just doesn't want it to exist in her territory. If we leave it here, something bad will happen to it. Someone will eat it or break it or try to use it, and that's not what Night's Reach wants. She likes things as they are right now, and she's tasked me with keeping them that way."

Buoyed by Kiku's support, Marrow was still skeptical. "And you expect us to fight off the ogre and his yamabushi if things don't go according to plan?"

"I expect the hyozan oath to keep Hidetsugu in check. He can't attack us without endangering himself. As for the yamabushi . . . yes, I do expect you to fight if it comes to that. There may also be the odd oni to contend with, but I don't think—"

Marrow's fur stood up straight. "Oni?"

"One in particular. Hidetsugu sort of put his dog on my trail, so it's possible it'll come running as soon as I show up." He turned to Kiku. "That's your main job, by the way. If anything with four legs and horns shows up, I expect to see a bouquet of flowers in its eye sockets before it comes anywhere near me."

"But I still don't—"

"Hush, vermin." Kiku strode forward past Marrow, her eyes hard. "The more Toshi tells us about this job, the more I'm convinced he's not telling it all. The job is to grab the disk, get away, and break up the gang. If we have to fight along the way, we fight." She beckoned the ratman closer, and they stood shoulder-to-shoulder facing Toshi.

"Let's do it," Kiku said.

"Okay," Toshi said. "But there's one more detail I haven't mentioned yet . . . ."

* * * * *

Captain Nagao was even less pleased to see Toshi the second time around. He drew his short sword and stalked over to the new arrival with Silver-Foot close behind.

"See?" Toshi held up his hands in playful surrender. "Told you I'd be back."

It was broad daylight, so most of the survivors were awake to see Toshi arrive, but the windowless room was as gloomy and the mood as bleak as it had been in the dead of night.

Nagao glared at Toshi, clenching his blade tight. "Are you going to help this time, friend, or just talk?"

Toshi shrugged. "I can start helping right now." Behind him, his foot was still immersed in the shadowed corner of the room. With his hands up as they were, it was an easy task to reach out, grab Nagao by the shoulders, and haul the heavier man backward into the darkness.

Off-guard and overbalanced, Nagao grunted as he tumbled into the black expanses. Toshi held fast to Nagao's shoulders, concentrating on his chosen destination. It was far easier to travel alone, but it helped when he knew where he was going.

After a breathless lurch through the void, Toshi and Nagao erupted from the base of a stout cedar tree. Toshi recovered first, but Nagao was breathless as he clutched the dirt, trying to locate his sword by touch. He winced with each breath and clutched at his chest. Toshi saw blood seeping through a ragged bandage under the officer's chest plate. He realized Nagao wasn't just disoriented by the trip and the sudden change of scenery; he was also recovering from a serious wound.

They were in a lush, healthy forest of evergreens, the smell of moss and damp wood thick in the air. The sky was clear and sunlit, but the thick canopy of boughs and needles allowed only thin river of light to reach the ground.

"This is Jukai," Nagao said. He had found his sword and now struggled to his feet. "This is where the kitsune led by Lady Silk-Eyes came after the goblins attacked their village. Where we were before we went to Minamo."

"And it's probably just the way you left it," Toshi said. "The kitsune villagers are still living wild and loving it. You'll recognize more than a few familiar faces."

Nagao had completely recovered by now and he had regained most of his bluster. "Take me back to the academy," he said. "I'm the last one to be rescued, not the first."

"You're the leader," Toshi said. "I had to take you first so you can convince the others. You'll have to do it fast, though, because I don't know how much time we'll have."

Nagao hesitated. "Who is in charge here?"

"Hm? Oh, I don't know. There's a trio of old foxes everyone seems to listen to. And Princess Michiko is here, along with her kitsune minders. Oh, and that big dog is here, too."

The captain considered this. "And all are safe?"

"So far. They've been here for weeks with no troubles. I don't think even the kami have bothered them."

Nagao sheathed his sword. "Take me back at once," he said. "And then start bringing the others here as quickly as you can."

Toshi cocked his head, his voice cutting. "I need you to tell me that. Listen, soldier, that was always the plan," he said. "If you're done making conditions, how about we go to work?"

* * * * *

Ferrying the survivors from Minamo to the forest took longer than Toshi had hoped, but at least it went smoothly. Once Nagao convinced Silver-Foot that Toshi could do what he'd promised, the rest of the survivors were only too willing to trust the stranger.

Toshi could only take three people with him at once when he started, but soon he was bringing seven or eight at a time. It was strenuous work, but it was like running long distances—once he'd established a pace and a rhythm, it was just as easy to keep going as it was to stop and rest.

He said a silent prayer of thanks to his myojin for keeping Hidetsugu and the oni off his back while he worked. Between the ogre's nose and Toshi's connection to the oni dog, he had expected them to pounce within moments of showing up. He guessed that they hadn't because he never stayed in Minamo for long. Once the captains had the survivors lined up and ready to go, all Toshi had to do was show up and collect them.

Kiku stood quietly behind Toshi, never addressing or acknowledging the survivors, even when they tried to thank her for rescuing them. She was focused on the room's only door and the hallway outside it. If a challenge came, it would come from there.

Toshi had left Marrow-Gnawer on the roof of the academy to make sure the moth was not discovered. The nezumi had never flown before and he was as giddy as a schoolgirl when the great insect carried them up into the clouds. Toshi couldn't bring the Taken One into the realm of shadow, but he could cause it to fade as he did. Once they were both immaterial, all Toshi had to do was guide the stone disk up to the roof, where he could lash it to the moth. From there, he could take it anywhere in Kamigawa.

After half an hour of steady, nerve-wracking work there were only a dozen civilians and a handful of soldiers left to rescue. Toshi signaled for the next party of eight to approach him, but Nagao and Silver-Foot interrupted him.

"Captain Silver-Foot will stay with the others in Jukai," Nagao said. "But my men and I need to get back to Eiganjo."

Toshi shook his head. "This isn't a *ricksha* service, Captain. And if it is, no one's tipped the driver yet. I agreed to get you to safety, and I will. Where you go after that is your problem."

Nagao reddened. "I am a captain in the daimyo's army," he flared. "My country is at war and I have been here, helpless and besieged. Do you understand duty, friend? Obligation?"

Toshi inhaled to answer, but Kiku spoke first. "It's coming," she said. She casually sniffed the camellia on her shoulder and drew her fuetsu throwing ax.

A low, panicked murmur rose from the far end of the room. Three sets of black jaws had already appeared, snapping at empty air as they floated purposefully toward the remaining survivors.

Silver-Foot and Nagao quickly charged across the room and positioned themselves between the retreating survivors and the growing flock of hungry mouths. There were over a score of them now, with more appearing every second. The officers gestured to the other soldiers and these brave fighting men formed a line that stretched all the way across the center of the room.

One of the soldiers cried out as a savage set of teeth clamped onto his sword arm. With inhuman precision, Silver-Foot sliced the set of jaws in half from the rear, bringing the edge of his sword within a hair's breadth of the stricken soldier's skin. Separate, the upper and lower rows of teeth stubbornly clung to their morsel before they evaporated into smoke. In response, the other mouths oriented on the bleeding man and drifted toward him.

Under Silver-Foot and Nagao's careful command, the soldiers

carefully deflected and avoided the floating jaws away from the occupied side of the room. It was a good idea not to antagonize the All-Consuming Oni of Chaos any further, but Toshi feared it was an idea that had come too late. The demonic spirit had been struck, and now the smell of blood seemed to tell it there was prey to be had. The far corner of the room soon filled with hungry mouths that seethed and buzzed like a swarm of angry bees.

A survivor in academy robes moved up and clutched Toshi's arm. "Come on, man, what are you waiting for? Take us away from here."

Toshi shrugged the man off. "Wait," he said. "Try to keep still. It hasn't done any real damage yet, and it won't if we all just keep quiet."

The academician moved back, his eyes still wide and fearful. Kiku sidled up next to Toshi.

"How do you know that?" she whispered.

"I don't," he whispered back. "But I think the only reason they lasted this long was because that thing is in here with them." He pointed to the Taken One. "I think Hidetsugu's oni is afraid of it."

Kiku and Toshi watched together for a moment as the cloud of mouths rose up to the ceiling. Some of them turned and pointed themselves directly at the Taken One. Slowly, menacingly, they began to float towards the stone disk.

"Not anymore," Kiku said.

Silver-Foot appeared in front of Toshi, startling the ochimusha once more. He'd have to learn how the foxfolk did that trick without the blessings of a major myojin.

"Take as many as you can and go," the fox captain said. "We'll cover your retreat."

Toshi looked Silver-Foot in the eye. "No good," he said. "Anyone who doesn't make this trip will be dead by the time I get back."

"We are willing to make that sacrifice."

"But I'm not. If this place is overrun by the oni, I'll never get that thing out of here." Even as they spoke, the oni's ravenous jaws were encircling the stone disk, testing and biting the air around it.

Toshi had spent more time with the kitsune lately than he ever had before, so he was accustomed to reading their blank, inscrutable expressions. Silver-Foot's short muzzle crinkled and his eyes flashed. He was furious.

"Thief," he growled. "Is your treasure worth your own life? For I will cut you down where you stand unless you take these people to safety right now."

"Then we all die."

"So be it. I will not let you choose an inanimate thing over the lives of my charges."

Kiku stepped forward, sniffing her flower again. "That's not a decision you get to make, kitsune."

Simultaneously touched and disturbed by Kiku's sudden protective streak, Toshi considered his options. Silver-Foot's sword was out and Toshi glanced down at its glowing edge. He looked back at Kiku, then up at the kitsune, and then he smiled.

"What if I offered you a third option?"

"I would listen. Do it quickly."

"My treasure and your people are threatened by the same thing. Stand aside and I'll take care of both our problems."

"How can you do this?"

Toshi twirled his jitte. "Just pull all your people back . . . over there, away from the disk and the oni. I'll take it from there."

Silver-Foot paused. "We can help you."

"I don't need you to help. I need you to watch."

Visibly unconvinced, Silver-Foot made an angry clicking sound in his throat. But he turned and quickly went back to the line of soldiers. In a matter of moments, Silver-Foot and Nagao had herded their men and the remaining survivors into the safest corner of the room.

Kiku sheathed her axe. "Good luck, Toshi."

"Thanks."

"No, I mean it. If you die, I've got no way out."

"Oh. Well, I suppose that's all right, too. I suppose a kiss is out of the question?"

Kiku glowered as she withdrew to the far wall.

The oni's mouths had filled the far end of the room from floor to ceiling and they were still expanding, still increasing in number. A smaller cloud now encircled the Taken One, though so far none had been bold enough to test their teeth against it.

Toshi took a deep breath. He cleared his thoughts, picturing the vast expanse of darkness and void that housed his myojin. He pictured the Myojin of Night's Reach as he had always known her: a bone-white mask of a woman's face framed on a field of luxurious black fabric. The curtain of black was held by a pair of disembodied arms and was attended by pale, ghostly hands that followed her like servants.

Night's Reach was one of the oldest and most powerful spirits known. In fact, some of Kamigawa's religions believed that Night and Chaos were the first spirits, from which all other spirits drew their substance. Toshi knew for a fact this wasn't true, but he was heartened by the comparison. If he were going to pit his patron spirit against Hidetsugu's, at least they were of the same high pedigree.

O Night's Reach. Toshi's thoughts were as focused and urgent as a desperate whisper. *Grant a humble acolyte your blessings once more. In your name, I act. For your glory, I call for your aid.*

There was no reply, not in his mind or in the vast ocean of darkness he saw in his mind's eye. But a familiar sense of something huge began building inside him, like wave about to break or a bubble about to pop. He felt as if he had held his breath for an hour, and his lungs were screaming to exhale, like his sinuses were packed with ragweed and the upcoming sneeze would blow his head to pieces.

You honor me, acolyte. Go forth with my blessing.

Toshi opened his eyes. He grunted in savage triumph, intoxicated by the power suffusing him. It was all he could do not to throw back his head and laugh.

Nearby, the first set of needle-like teeth touched the surface of the Taken One. Pure white light flashed from the points of contact.

The oni's mouths went mad, chattering wildly and swarming toward the stone disk. If the oni hadn't recognized the power of the daimyo's prize before, it did now. The storm of jaws surged forward.

Too late, Toshi thought. For once, someone else is too late.

He raised his arms and felt the power of his myojin surge through him. Circles of black light bubbled around his hands, and then Toshi did laugh, raucous, mocking laughter in the face of this terrible foe.

The black lights coalesced into a cloud around his wrists as the oni's hungry mouths streaked toward him. When the first was only a few yards away, the cloud of light let out a terrible flash and a stream of pallid, cadaverous hands.

The river of palms and fingers blasted into the cloud of snapping jaws. Toshi directed the stream back and forth across the Oni of Chaos so that the demon's jaws were fully opposed by the grip of Night's Reach. The hands emerged identically: flat, straight, and with all the fingers pressed together, but they moved like living things once they touched the enemy.

Each pale-skinned hand clamped onto a pair of oni jaws and squeezed tight. When positioned correctly, they completely neutralized the voracious little beasts. If they missed the mark, they lost fingers to the insatiable appetite of the oni. Even these maimed hands continued to fight, however, pushing the invaders back to the doorway they'd come through.

Still laughing, still spraying the cloud of mouths with his myojin's attendant aspects, Toshi slowly advanced across the room. The oni's jaws could easily shred anything that came within range of their teeth, but the myojin's innumerable hands continued to clamp them shut and move them back.

As one, the oni's jaws opened and let out an enraged, ear-splitting shriek of anger and frustration. Untouched in the center of the swirling mass of hands, mouths, teeth, and fingers, Toshi raised his arms high and brought his palms together.

The impact boomed like a black-powder bomb. The concussion cleared a wide space around the ochimusha, which then quickly filled with disembodied hands. Safe behind a wall of the myojin's power, Toshi pressed forward, driving the oni mouths up against the far wall and the closed door. He gathered his strength, cried out in ecstatic spiritual frenzy, and then forced the last of the oni mouths from the room.

He stood for a moment in the gently swirling cyclone of hands, breathing heavily. Then Toshi pitched and fell to his knees, wincing as his arms, legs, and stomach cramped.

Kiku was there to help him up. "You did it," she said. The mahotsukai seemed impressed . . . but Toshi suspected that he was misreading her expression. Kiku was probably only surprised and perhaps a little put out that he had survived.

Toshi stood under his own power as soon as Kiku got him to his feet. "You bet I did it. I just sent Hidetsugu an engraved invitation to come slaughter us. That was his oni I just beat back. He's not going to be happy about it."

Kiku's eyes widened a bit. "What should we do?"

"Get them all ready to go. I'm taking everyone in one trip." He raised his voice. "And you, Nagao. You and your men will follow me to Jukai, now, without further discussion. Once we're all safe and alive, I'll consider taking you home."

Nagao glanced at Silver-Foot. The kitsune nodded and Nagao said, "Agreed."

Toshi stretched his arms, working the kinks from his muscles. "Line up, people. The last boat to Jukai leaves as soon as you're all on board." Kiku tapped him on the shoulder, and Toshi turned.

"And then?" she said.

"And then," Toshi answered, "we see if Hidetsugu will let us dissolve the hyozan reckoners without a fight."

Kiku nodded, her face calm. "That's not going to happen, is it?"

"No," Toshi said brightly. "But it's worth offering him the chance." He leaned in close and spoke into Kiku's ear. "I've got something in mind."

"I expect no less," the mahotsukai said. "Go on, Toshi. Get these sheep to safety. The sooner we're done here, the better."

The survivors all stood in a long line with their hands clenched. Toshi reached out to Nagao at the front of the line and offered his hand.

One by one, the survivors of Minamo crossed into the shadows, finally escaping the bloody slaughter of the hyozan's final reckoning.

CHAPTER 8

Hidetsugu sat glowering upon his throne of bones, thick black smoke rising from the corners of his eyes. He had felt the attack on his oni. He knew only one being audacious enough to attempt such an attack and powerful enough to accomplish it.

"Hunters," he barked. "Stand ready." Three yamabushi instantly bounded from the sides of the room to the throne. Once they'd landed, each dropped to one knee and planted a fist on the floor.

Hidetsugu was completely satisfied with his little raiding party. They fought well and obeyed without hesitation. Together they had bested Keiga the Tide Star, guardian spirit of the falls, and visited bloody vengeance on the academy students and staff. It had not been an easy campaign for them—only five of the original eight had survived. One had been slain as they stormed Minamo, one had been accidentally devoured by the All-Consuming, and one had simply dissolved his sky platform and allowed himself to fall five hundred feet onto the rocks below. Hidetsugu considered this last the only failure in the entire group.

The great o-bakemono stood, sending a fresh cascade of skulls and thigh bones rattling to the floor. Rib cages crunched under his feet as he made his way to the floor. Once there, he put two fingers in his mouth and whistled.

The oni dog appeared in a puff of charnel-house smoke. Even the yamabushi cringed as it stalked past them.

"Your playmate has returned," Hidetsugu told the dog. "Go find him and do as you were summoned to do. Indulge yourself. Make merry with his body and soul."

The dread creature snorted a jet of ashes from its armored muzzle. It reared up on its spindly hind legs, pivoted, and bounded from the chamber.

With machinelike precision, Hidetsugu attached a pair of armored plates to his shoulders and lashed a third across his chest. He stretched and flexed his powerful muscles, testing his range of movement. After readjusting the shoulder plates, Hidetsugu hoisted his spiked tetsubo club and swung it through the air like a willow switch.

He inspected the tip of the club, then fixed his eyes on one of the three yamabushi. "Come here," he said. The mountain warrior instantly sprang to his feet and approached his master.

"Stop there," Hidetsugu said. The priest halted with one foot still in the air.

"Good," said the ogre, and then he crushed the yamabushi to the floor with his tetsubo. The thin, solid weapon fairly ripped the yamabushi's body in half lengthwise and blood spattered over his fellows and Hidetsugu alike.

Moving quickly but confidently, Hidetsugu clamped his tetsubo between his teeth and scooped up the crushed yamabushi's remains. He spit coarse, painful-sounding syllables around the bloody club in his mouth. The victim's blood hissed and boiled where it touched the ogre's face. Hidetsugu spat out the club, swallowed some of the crimson drops that had collected in his mouth, and began to chant.

In the old language of the o-bakemono, he converted the blood of a trusted retainer into a barrier against those who might likewise betray and murder him. When the last of the victim's vital fluid had been squeezed from his corpse, Hidetsugu crammed meat and bone alike into his maw. In seconds, there was nothing left of the murdered yamabushi but a slick of red on the floor and similar droplets on the faces of the others.

Hidetsugu bent to retrieve his club. "Now," he said to the remaining hunters, "we . . . " The ogre's voice trailed off and his eyes locked on a spot somewhere beyond the south-facing exterior wall. His nostrils twitched, and then he tilted his head back and drew a long, deep breath through his nose.

"We have other guests," he said. "Follow."

Hidetsugu had days to explore the Academy while his oni feasted, so he led his hunters up one flight to take advantage of the huge windows there. The view here was even better than from the roof of the academy, which was almost perpetually wreathed in thick clouds. From here, one could see the falls, almost all of the lake, and out onto the plains of Towabara far to the south.

The ogre grumbled as he peered down toward Konda's territory. There was something moving down there, something coming toward the falls. Hidetsugu could scarcely credit what he was seeing, but he had lived in Kamigawa long enough to recognize an army on the march.

Konda's army, in fact. There were scores of battle-moths and thousands of men and horses all advancing on Minamo. They were moving quickly, too: When Hidetsugu had first seen them, he could barely discern them as men. Now he could see the daimyo's symbol on their battle standard and the awful, unearthly glow that surrounded the entire force.

Hidetsugu's eyes narrowed. So Toshi had been telling the truth, at least about this. Konda had raised a spirit army to reclaim the stone disk. And if Konda had traced it here, the great old serpent O-Kagachi could not be long in joining them.

The ogre's eyes crackled and he barked out, "Hah!" He turned to the pair of dead-eyed yamabushi and said, "Find the others. Go down and meet Konda before he reaches the shores of the lake. Harry him, harass him, do whatever it takes to halt their advance. The oni will be joining you shortly. Keep the fight away from here until I come for you."

The yamabushi bowed and bounded off. Hidetsugu nodded to himself. They were excellent minions, and he regretted the need to harvest one of them for the ritual.

The ogre drew his club and whipped it through the air again just to hear the sound it made. It would be worth the loss of one hunter, worth it to see the look on Toshi's face when whatever spell he had planned for Hidetsugu failed, rebounded, and consumed its caster instead.

Hidetsugu smacked his lips. He sank to his knees and began chanting in the old tongue once more, calling out to the oni in Oboro as well as to the All-Consuming busily gorging itself nearby.

Bloodshed and brutality beckoned. If Chaos held sway here, nothing could stop it from devouring all Kamigawa.

His message sent, the o-bakemono sat patiently until he felt his patron spirit's dire attention shift from its current meal to the approaching army. The All-Consuming started the long process of disengaging its horde of mouths from the academy library, while above, the lesser oni charged over the edge of the soratami capital and fell howling to the waters below, eager for slaughter and hungry for fresh human meat.

When all was in motion, Hidetsugu rose, sheathed his club across his back, and headed down to witness the end of Toshi Umezawa.

*   *   *   *   *

Toshi was in too much of a rush to worry about what effect touching the Taken One again would have on him. Once the last of the survivors was gone and Kiku had resumed her close watch on the only doorway, the ochimusha pressed his palms onto the surface of the stone disk and willed it to become insubstantial along with him.

He felt a similar jolt when he made contact, as if he'd grabbed an iron bar with one end in a furnace and the other in a block of ice. The feeling ended as quickly as it had started, and to Toshi's relief the disk proved as easy to manipulate and carry as it had before.

"Toshi," Kiku said, "if you're still here, get ready. Something's coming."

Toshi continued to maneuver his phantom burden toward the hall. He hated to leave Kiku alone, but he was almost home free now. All he had to do was reach the roof, and tie a few knots, and they'd all get away clean.

He heard something with claws moving quickly toward them but fought the urge to run. Nothing had been able to affect him in this phantom state; nothing had even been able to perceive him. He had strolled through the most formidable magical defenses as if they didn't exist, and he had stood unnoticed by some of the keenest kitsune trackers. The yamabushi, the oni, even the ogre himself would not be able to stop him if he just kept his head.

Kiku drew a throwing axe and conjured a purple bloom as she backed away from the door. A second later, the door exploded inward, dissolving into a hail of splinters and broken wood as the oni dog thundered into the room.

Throw the bloom, Toshi thought, unable to spare the energy it took to make himself heard. Forget the ax.

The four-legged brute lowered its armored head and growled at Kiku, its sharp tail scoring the stone wall behind it. The mahotsukai's face was grim but alert. She made no move to attack, but instead waited, her eyes locked on the oni's under its savage upturned horns.

The oni dog turned away from Kiku. It faced the spot where Toshi was struggling with the Taken One, roared like a bear, and then launched itself at the ochimusha.

At first, Toshi was too shocked to react. The dog was hurtling toward him with its terrible jaws open wide, and all Toshi could do was think, "But that's not possible."

Luckily, his instincts were stronger than his rational mind, and he threw himself away from the Taken One. As soon as his phantom hands left the disk's surface, the Taken One regained its weight and solidity. It thumped to the floor, rolled a quarter turn, and then fell so that the etched figure of a dragon was facing the floor.

Toshi backpedaled, his eyes darting for a shadow to dive into. The oni paid no attention to the Taken One's sudden reappearance. It growled and lowered its head almost to the floor. Pointing its muzzle directly at Toshi, the oni dog stalked forward.

It's tied to me, Toshi realized. Hidetsugu hadn't been exaggerating when he'd said the oni dog would find him anywhere. Somehow summoning the beast had linked him to it like master to hound . . . or in this case, like hunter to prey.

The oni lunged again. Toshi was able to dodge. He had to assume that if it could tell where he was in phantom form, it could also injure him. He didn't fancy getting caught by those jaws, so he kept moving, making himself as hard a target as possible.

Kiku, meanwhile, was still standing ready at the other side of the room. She had seen the Taken One reappear and she had watched the dog stalking the empty air, so she must know that Toshi was still here. He decided to gamble his speed against the dog's—if she struck as swiftly as she usually did, the dog would be dead before it had a chance to get him.

Willing himself solid, Toshi caught Kiku's eye just as the dog pounced.

"Plant the bloom!" Toshi said. Kiku reacted like the professional she was, casting her arm in a wide arc that sent the purple flower spinning toward the oni's broad rib cage.

Toshi commanded himself to fade once more, vanishing from sight just as the oni dog's teeth were about to tear into the flesh on his arm. The jagged fangs passed through Toshi without resistance, but blinding agony shot up his arm all the same. He cried out, more from the shock than the pain, but the pain lingered far longer.

Kiku's throw had missed. The camellia wriggled where it landed, thorny tendrils grasping for somewhere to take root. Well clear of the danger, the oni dog gathered its strength as it prepared for another leap.

Toshi's head began to spin and he fell to the floor. The bite seemed to be poison. He became solid just before he landed so that a resounding thump echoed across the room. Groggily, he looked across at his nemesis, their eyes exactly level.

He tried to summon the cold, but his mind was already too far removed from his body. He willed himself to fade again, but he had neither the strength nor the focus.

The oni snarled. It opened its mouth wide. Toshi could see multiple rows of slashing teeth, could smell the stink of blood and slaughter on its breath.

Kiku's throwing axe shot across the room into the dog's open mouth. It slammed into the brute's upper palate, sending a jet of blackish-crimson blood across the scroll case nearby. The axe handle wedged behind the oni's innermost row of teeth so that its killing jaw was propped open. The oni coughed and sputtered as it furiously tried to dislodge the weapon.

Without thinking, Toshi lunged to his feet and staggered toward the stricken dog. He heard Kiku's voice calling to him, yelling something urgent, but she was so far away he couldn't understand her words.

Toshi slammed into the scroll rack, knocking several ancient parchments to the floor. Clinging to the shelf for support, he drew his jitte and dragged the tip through a smear of the oni dog's blood.

A sharp wooden crack came from behind him. Toshi threw himself back, swinging from the scroll rack, until his back thumped into the wall. The oni dog had succeeded in bringing its jaws together, snapping Kiku's axe in half. The sharp head was still embedded in the roof of its mouth, and blood-flecked foam drooled from the corners of its lips, but it was far from mortally wounded. The oni shook its armored head, inhaled, and let out a huge, ragged roar.

Toshi held the jitte out in front of him. "Come on, then," he said. "I'm not going to be the only one who dies today."

The dog sniffed, growled again, and then turned toward Kiku. The mahotsukai already had another purple flower in hand, but she froze as the monster fixed its terrible gaze on her.

Toshi's vision went gray. He had to save himself, and do it quickly. Kiku might defeat the dog, but she couldn't stop the poison. He clumsily pulled a scroll from the rack and popped the seal with his jitte. He hastily scrawled a kanji on the back of the scroll (which seemed to contain a spell for sculpting crystals from sea water), clamped the parchment between his teeth, and then shoved off from the wall with all the strength he had left.

Incorrectly choosing Kiku as the more serious threat, the dog pounced at the mahotsukai before Toshi reached it. Kiku drew back to throw her flower, but the oni's powerful legs had ensured that it would land on her no matter what she hit it with on the way. Even if her flower killed the dog quickly, it would still have a chance to tear the mahotsukai's throat out.

Toshi fumbled for a handhold on the dog's spiky back as it went past him. Instead, he latched on to the demon's tail, and though his fingers were growing number by the second, Toshi clamped tight and held on.

The ochimusha's weight spoiled the dog's aim and momentum, dragging it to the floor well shy of Kiku. Toshi's tackle also pulled the dog clear of Kiku's bloom, which spun all the way across the room and bounced off of the far wall.

The oni's lower jaw smacked painfully into the floor. Enraged, it bent its powerful body at the waist and lunged for Toshi's face.

Toshi slapped the parchment with the paralysis kanji onto the base of the oni dog's spine. In an instant, with its savage teeth mere inches from Toshi's eyes, the brute went as rigid as a statue. Three malevolent eyes continued to dart in their sockets, and ghastly, choking breath still wheezed from its throat, but the oni was frozen fast.

"Wait," Toshi said. Kiku lowered her arm, which held another camellia, and looked at Toshi questioningly.

Toshi's legs worked, so he pulled himself up on the oni's body, using its spiked carapace for handholds. Without explaining, Toshi wiped the dog's blood off of his jitte and then slid the hooked truncheon across the oni's dripping teeth. With the same venom that was killing him, Toshi cut a healing kanji over the festering bite mark on his arm.

Kiku watched him silently. When he pushed back from the paralyzed oni and the color began to return to his face, she said, "Now?"

Toshi nodded. "Now."

Kiku tossed the delicate-seeming blossom onto the top of the dog's bony skull. Unable to move a muscle, the brute snarled, slavered, and growled as the lush purple flower punched thorny roots through the top of its skull. The oni dog shuddered and its three eyes rolled back in its head while the camellia grew larger, more vivid, and more fragrant. By the time the oni's skull was empty, the camellia's petals had completely covered its head and shoulders.

Toshi coughed up something nasty and spat it alongside the dead oni. "Feeling better now," he said, rising to his feet. "My thanks, oath-sister. I don't think we'll have any more problems."

Kiku sneered and started to speak, but an arrow suddenly sprouted from her collarbone. Kiku winced but did not cry out as she staggered and fell to her knees.

Toshi turned just as a yamabushi tackled him to the ground. It was the female sentry who had stopped Toshi at the gates, and he was still too weak to resist her as she quickly relieved him of his jitte and swords. Nearby, Toshi saw her male counterpart kicking the axe from Kiku's hand and twisting the mahotsukai's arms behind her, not even bothering to remove the arrow first.

In the hallway outside, Toshi saw Hidetsugu kneeling to peer through the door. The ogre was too large to easily enter the room, but he was already taking hold of the doorway to widen it for his use.

"Greetings, fellow reckoners," he said. With an ear-splitting crack, Hidetsugu tore a double handful of wall away. "Oath-sister . . . Toshi. Congratulations, you've bested a formidable foe."

The ogre shuffled through the hole he'd made. The room's ceiling was high enough for him to stand, and he did so. "But now," he said, "it's time to separate the loyal reckoners from the soon-to-be-stains on the bottom of my feet."

Toshi tested the yamabushi's grip, but her strength was still too much for him. He looked up into Hidetsugu's mad, glowing eyes, as awed and helpless as he'd been years before when One-Eye had sent him out as bait.

"You talk too much," Kiku called through her pain. "We aren't afraid, oath-brother. You cannot harm us while the hyozan is still intact."

Hidetsugu paused. He nodded at Kiku then turned to Toshi. "She doesn't know?"

Toshi gritted his teeth. He was about to lose the only ally he had, and there was nothing he could do about it.

"What?" Kiku flared. "What don't I know?"

Hidetsugu smiled patronizingly. "You're quite right, my dear.

You are completely safe from me, as are all who bear the true hyozan mark.

"But Toshi here," he waved his arm in a grandiose arc, "quit our little brotherhood some time ago. He is no longer oath-bound to me, or you, or the nezumi. He serves the Myojin of Night's Reach . . . and himself, of course . . . but he has no more connection to the hyozan than you did before he tricked you into joining."

Kiku forgot her wound and stared at Toshi in open shock. "You utterly contemptible bastard."

Toshi merely stared back at Kiku, holding her eyes as if he had nothing to hide, nothing to regret.

"Turn her loose," Hidetsugu said. "We will discuss things, she and I. And the hyozan will decide this traitor's fate together."

The yamabushi holding Kiku let go. He placed a hand on her collarbone, circling his thumb and forefinger around the arrow, and it popped out in a flash of orange light and a few droplets of blood.

Kiku inspected the site of the wound, but her skin had already healed and scarred over beneath the torn purple satin. With her angry eyes fixed on Toshi, Kiku very deliberately crossed the room and stood beside Hidetsugu.

"Kiku," Toshi husked, "don't listen to him. He's going to kill us all."

The beautiful mahotsukai glared at Toshi with pitiless eyes. She snapped her fan open and covered her face, fanning herself as she turned her back. The ogre began to laugh. Toshi endured the sound easily, but only because he could not have felt more desolate and bitter.

He had failed. He had been one short step away from achieving his goal without sacrificing Kiku or Marrow, but now everything had fallen apart. As if to confirm his bleak position, the second yamabushi also took hold of Toshi as Hidetsugu and Kiku advanced. Being held fast was bad enough, but the combination of gleeful grins and hateful stares on the faces of his former oathmates did not speak well for his immediate future. Still, there was time for one quick prayer, one last observance to his patron spirit.

O Night, he thought, *help me just one more time.*

Toshi licked his lips and struggled against the yamabushi's grip while he waited for an answer.

CHAPTER 9

Marrow-Gnawer enjoyed ascending to the academy's roof, but staying put once he got there was another matter.

The top of Minamo was like a small city of worthless buildings to the nezumi clan leader. There were patches of open space, like the one Toshi had tethered the moth to, but mostly there were peaked alcoves, scaffolding, and arcane equipment stations. It was cold and damp, and the roar from the falls made his ears throb. To further foul his mood, a thick mist filled the air from the nose up so he had to crouch if he wanted to see or smell clearly.

It didn't help that the moth was completely docile and required almost no attention. Toshi had told him to keep the moth from being discovered or getting loose until he or Kiku returned, but Marrow could tell the moth wasn't going anywhere, and no one would come up here exploring any time soon.

Worst of all, there was an entire building full of belongings left behind by important wizards and the scions of wealthy families. In his boredom, Marrow imagined an increasingly dazzling and powerful hoard of treasure that was just waiting for an enterprising nezumi to come along. As the hours wore on he convinced himself all he needed to fund his sudden early retirement was ten minutes alone in the teacher's dormitory and a heavy sack. No more burglary for the bosses, no more backbiting clan politics, and no more reckoners. They couldn't force him to avenge anything if they couldn't find him.

Once he'd made up his mind, it didn't take Marrow long to sniff out a way to the academy. A little muscle, a little tooth-work, and soon he had a hole big enough to squeeze through. He poked his face into the hole, saw that it led to some sort of attic storage space, and then pulled back onto the roof in a shower of masonry dust.

Something was happening. He couldn't see anything above or beyond the academy roof, but the nezumi tilted his head and listened carefully. He could hear snarls, roars, and terrible cries, but they all sounded far away, fading as if they were falling from the sky to the lake below.

Marrow shrugged. It was probably just another kami manifestation. Certainly nothing that should distract him from his retirement fund.

As he pondered his wealthy future, Marrow's hand exploded into a fiery ball of agony. It felt as if his bones were being crushed by a millstone and burned in a furnace. He hissed and cradled his hand against his chest. When he glanced down, the hyozan symbol scratched into his flesh was glowing white-hot.

The ratman struggled to his feet and skittered back to Toshi's moth. He checked the tether and made sure the food bricks were in easy reach. He stood and watched the great insect gently move its wings while burbling happily. If they needed to flee in a hurry, the moth was ready and waiting. Meanwhile, the pain in Marrow's hand was proving to be a summons he could not ignore. Hyozan business was happening somewhere nearby, and the oath was demanding he get involved.

Wincing from the pain, Marrow loped back to the hole he had made and disappeared inside.

* * * * *

Daimyo Konda was amazed by the resistance he encountered in the approach to Minamo but he did not let it sway his path. He did not understand how the fabled yamabushi kami-killers had come to fight alongside oni demons, but neither did he care. Whoever and whatever stood between him and his prize would be cut down like rice before the sickle.

Astride his perfect white steed, Konda galloped along the battlefront. He urged his ghost army forward where the oni were thickest and focused the moth riders on the high-leaping yamabushi as he himself led the charge for the academy. Konda had always been a fighting general, unwilling to send his soldiers into a battle without him, and he felt blessed to be fighting alongside his retainers once more.

The spirit army was the finest he had ever commanded, responding to his commands almost before he gave them. They were fearless, fast, and strong. They moved as a single coherent entity, overwhelming the enemy and always advancing like an irresistible tide.

Konda noted that the misshapen spectral warriors moved faster, struck harder, and glowed more brightly when he was beside them. To confirm that this was no trick of the brain or delusion of ego, the daimyo watched his warriors as he rode the ranks. The daimyo beamed as he galloped. It was true—with their leader to personally rally them, his ghost warriors were even more formidable.

Konda's grin faded into a disgusted scowl. The demon filth opposing his army was unworthy of their swords. Oni were mere monsters, twisted and vile brutes who wallowed in bloodlust and gluttony. This was not a war fit for his army. This was but extermination of a dangerous pest.

The oni were savage and numerous, but they were unable to stop Konda's advance. His army's phantom swords cut more keenly than steel and their arms never tired. Though the demons' claws could tear their bodies, the wounds never bled and healed almost as quickly as they were made. Against such invincible and well-disciplined troops, these mere oni were outnumbered and woefully overmatched.

The yamabushi were another matter. Trained to battle kami and other spirits, the mountain priests were striking down Konda's ghost army with alarming efficiency. They moved almost unimpeded through the crush of battle, felling spectral horses and phantom infantry alike with sword and staff and magic bolt. Though Konda's ranks never seemed to dwindle . . . those that fell to the kami-killers soon reappeared to continue the fight. He would have to intervene personally if the yamabushi could not be brought to heel.

Overhead, scores of gleaming battle-moths soared ever closer to the academy. Konda had kept them in reserve in case the yamabushi became a serious threat to his own progress, but so far the warrior priests had only been able to sting at his flanks with their powerful hit and run tactics.

With a thought and a wave, Konda directed most of the battle-moths to move on toward Minamo. The rest he called to him.

When they were circling overhead, Konda scanned the battlefield to note the positions of each yamabushi. He raised his face and clapped his hands, and the moths split into pairs, one pair for each mountain priest.

Surprised, the first yamabushi cried out as the moth-riders attacked. They converged on his position, each rider clasping his hands overhead. Moth and rider alike were enveloped by a cold, yellow glow, and then two braided streams of glowing eyes spiraled from each attacking moth to the yamabushi below. His face was wide and vacant, and he howled incoherently as the beam attack crushed him to the ground like a gnat beneath a stone.

Konda roared his triumphant battle cry. This was how it was meant to end, on the field of battle where he could conquer his enemies and win back his prize in the same master stroke. The Taken One was ahead, his eyes still fixed on it within the academy building. He would clear the field and ascend to Minamo on the backs of his beloved battle-moths. And if they could not carry him, he would climb to the heights of Kamitaki Falls with his own hands.

The daimyo stood in his saddle, thrust his sword forward, and cried for his army to follow him. His army roared their loyalty. Konda looked upon Minamo, knowing that his treasure was within, and he roared again.

High overhead, an ominous stream of black emerged from the academy. At first Konda thought it was a thundercloud or magical storm conjured by the yamabushi. It swelled to enormous size in seconds, billowing larger than the building it came from. Then the black mass began to descend toward the battlefield.

Three eyes opened in the top of the buzzing black cloud, and two sweeping horns extended up through the clouds. Konda felt two rushes, one of disgust at the vile creature before him and one of anticipation, for today he would utterly destroy it.

"Men of Eiganjo," he bellowed, "behold! The gluttonous Beast of Chaos! Once we have destroyed him, victory will be ours!"

The ghost army roared again. The moth-riders banked away from the school and streaked toward their new target, a cold, yellow sheen already glimmering on the moth's powdered wings.

Konda paused once, for the briefest moment, to appreciate the noise, the splendor, and the sheer scale of what he was about to accomplish. Then the daimyo spurred his horse and charged forward to meet the enemy.

* * * * *

"Did you really think I didn't know?"

Toshi noticed Hidetsugu's joy was rapidly becoming more manic and dangerous. Kiku still regarded Toshi with eyes of hate, but she had also taken a few steps back and away from the ogre.

As he often did when speaking to Toshi, Hidetsugu had sat himself cross-legged so he and the ochimusha were at eye-level. The ogre rocked back and forth slightly as he spoke.

"I knew the very moment you slithered out from under your mark, kanji mage." He yanked the metal plate off of his shoulder, revealing the hyozan triangle branded deep into his flesh. Hidetsugu then reached forward and hauled Toshi out of the yamabushi's grip, holding the ochimusha by his left hand. Toshi's sleeve immediately slid back, revealing the false hyozan mark. Hidetsugu spit on the forgery and smeared it with his thumb.

"Ours was a blood oath, Toshi. Do you remember? I told you

vengeance is based on blood and demands blood as payment. The oath would not have worked without our blood to power the ritual. My blood became steam under the branding iron, but I gave it willingly according to our deal. I offered you the brand and a sharp knife, but you chose the tattoo." The ogre snorted derisively. "You took the coward's way out, Toshi, but you still bled. With every tap of the needle, with every new drop of ink, you gave a drop of blood in return.

"Blood bound us, Toshi: your blood, my blood. Our oath. We are the true pillars of the hyozan. These others," he waved at Kiku, "they didn't bleed for their oaths. You cut into their flesh and you recited your silly spells, but they are subordinate, mere reflections of the oath we two maintain." Hidetsugu rocked forward so he was face-to-face with Toshi. "And now you have abandoned it. And you are mine." He released Toshi's arm and dropped him into the waiting clutches of the yamabushi.

Hidetsugu rocked back and leaned on his hands behind him. "Hurt him, my hunters. By now Toshi has regained enough of his faculties to become a nuisance. Shorten his breath."

Toshi gasped as something hard thudded into his stomach. It felt like the end of a staff, but it could have just been the yamabushi's fist.

From the other direction, the rock-hard edge of the other yamabushi's hand slammed into Toshi's windpipe. The ochimu-sha gagged and thrashed as the yamabushi kept his hands pinned behind him.

"Good. Now bring him here."

They dragged him forward, dazed and choking, and then forced him to stand straight before the o-bakemono.

Hidetsugu leaned forward, lifting Toshi's head up with a single thick finger. "I'm curious, Toshi. How long have you been working on a way to kill me in spite of our oath?"

Toshi's eyes flickered. "Not long," he grunted. "Since you sicced your oni dog on me over Oboro."

The ogre's face widened in honest surprise. "That is very disappointing," he said. "I've known how to kill you without breaking the oath since before it was cast."

Toshi's retort died in his throat.

"Didn't you know that? Didn't it ever strike you that I might have outsmarted you from the very beginning?"

"Lying," Toshi croaked. "No way out."

Hidetsugu smiled wide, displaying his terrible teeth. "Here," he said. "I'll demonstrate."

The ogre stopped his hand as it was about to close around Toshi's head. "Hang on. You quit the gang, didn't you? I could pop your head like a fat tick and the curse would never be invoked."

Toshi guessed what was coming, but he couldn't summon the breath fast enough to warn Kiku. In a blur of motion, Hidetsugu lashed out with his other hand and pinned Kiku within his massive fist. She struggled and squirmed, but he lifted her like a child's toy without even glancing at her. Held as she was, she could neither reach her throwing axes nor raise her hands to create a flower.

"Ours is a blood oath," Hidetsugu said again. "And so requires blood. You've always interpreted the spell as cursing us if we harmed or tried to harm one another. But I crafted it specifically to work only if one of us spilled the other's blood. Cut my throat, crush me under tons of rock, or run me through and the curse will claim you. But if we managed to kill one another without actually shedding any blood . . ."

Toshi watched the muscles in Hidetsugu's arm ripple as he

slowly clenched his hand around Kiku. Incrementally, bit by tortuous bit, he was crushing the life from her.

"Her bones won't break," the ogre said. "Her heart won't burst. But if I squeeze her just so." He shut one eye and made a show of concentrating. "I can prevent her from breathing in. Once I get the grip just right, all I have to do is hold it until her face turns blue."

Kiku moaned and her breathing became ever more shallow. Soon she was gasping soundlessly, her mouth wide open and her eyes bulging.

Hidetsugu cocked his head. "Surely you've noticed how often I've picked you up and squeezed you during our long partnership? That was me testing my theory . . . as well as my grip. I soon figured out exactly how hard I had to squeeze. After that . . . it was just fun."

The ogre suddenly loosened his fist. Kiku sucked in huge gasps of air as Toshi forced himself to breathe.

A thunderous explosion shook the building. Toshi thought he could hear the sounds of battle, of men shouting as magical energy sizzled in the air.

Hidetsugu sighed. "Our time grows short. So sad." The ogre lashed out, snatching Toshi from the yamabushi with his free hand. With Toshi in one fist and Kiku in the other, the o-bakemono rose smoothly to his feet and held them out to each side at arm's length.

"Goodbye, Toshi Umezawa. You were an amusing oath-brother. I will send you to the spirit world with your paramour. Let us see which one of you departs first."

Hidetsugu's powerful hands constricted around Toshi's chest, and Toshi's breathing simply stopped. He heaved and strained as best he could, but his lungs could not expand past his ribs, and his ribs were compressed to the point of breaking. Toshi's face began to tingle and his chest began to burn.

This is how Kobo died, he thought. If Hidetsugu allowed him any air, he might have pointed this irony out to the o-bakemono. Instead, Toshi sent his eyes darting around the room, searching for an out. All he saw was Kiku's panicked face and the ogre's dreadful leer.

Behind Hidetsugu, the door to the chamber cracked open. To Toshi it seemed like the door was very far away, at the end of a glittering tunnel. But glittering tunnels don't have rats, do they?

Toshi's mind came back to him and he recognized Marrow-Gnawer. What was the little vermin doing here? He was supposed to be on the roof. Not only had he abandoned his post, he was going to get himself killed.

Despite his lack of air and his impending death, Toshi tried to shout a warning. Hidetsugu was too enraptured with constricting the life out of his former oath-mates. The yamabushi were keeping a close eye on Toshi and Kiku. The nezumi had not been spotted, but if he struck Hidetsugu . . .

Oblivious to the danger, Marrow slid his black, rusty blade between his teeth. This can't happen, Toshi thought. It won't happen. Marrow was fraction of Hidetsugu's size and the ogre's skin was far too tough for a rusted nezumi blade, even if it was wielded by one of the most competent rats in all the world.

But Marrow was even more competent, brave, and resourceful than Toshi could credit. The nezumi carefully weighed the situation, plotted his attack by scanning the walls and ceiling, and then literally sprang into action.

The tough, powerful muscles in his legs carried him halfway

up the chamber wall to the left of Hidetsugu. His claws dug into the fabric covering the stone wall, giving Marrow enough purchase to launch himself all the way up to the ceiling. Were he larger or less strong, he never could have climbed so high so fast. Rats were made for climbing and jumping, and Marrow was a most exceptional rat.

As he rebounded off the ceiling, Marrow was spotted by the yamabushi. The female shouted, and the male raised his staff, but neither of them were quicker than a striking nezumi.

Marrow screeched from a few feet over Hidetsugu's head. The o-bakemono instinctively looked up at the sound just as Marrow struck with all his might, driving his dirty, jagged sword deep into the ogre's eye.

CHAPTER 10

Konda had never felt so alive.

The greater oni descended on the battlefield like a storm cloud, large and savage enough to engage all of the Daimyo's ghost army. His retainers threw themselves against the enemy's snapping jaws while the battle-moths hurled bolts of righteous fire at its eyes.

Both sides seemed inexhaustible. The greater oni grew darker and thicker, its multiple mouths larger and sharper no matter how much damage Konda's army inflicted. Likewise, his soldiers reformed and rejoined the battle seconds after being rent by those terrible jaws. If not for the fact that he was slowly and surely pushing toward the academy, Konda would have considered this situation a stalemate.

Konda felt a renewed rush of pride for his army and the justness of their cause. The beast was fearsome in battle, but Konda's army was beyond fear. They were the demon's equal in ferocity, stamina, and determination, and with Konda leading them it was only a matter of time before the prize would be his once more.

The oni's buzzing hive-body rumbled like the beginnings of an avalanche. The ground shook and the moth-riders were buffeted as the air itself pounded them. The great demon's form expanded briefly, then contracted down to half its original size.

Before Konda could shout an order, the oni's body exploded, sending hard, sharp teeth and a crushing wave of concussive force radiating outward across the battlefield. The daimyo himself was able to remain upright only by tucking his head behind his horse's and tightly gripping the animal's saddle.

Konda's spectral retainers were less fortunate. Those closest to the oni were torn to shreds by the shrapnel and the sheer power of the blast, which scoured a circular crater deep into the ground. Battle-moths were sundered from their grafted-on riders and hurled violently from the field, their broad wings useless in the gale. The oni's eyes and horns remained constant, mute witnesses to the bedlam and bloodshed below.

Konda glared at the oni, impressed but undeterred. It was an excellent blow, well struck, but it would not be enough to stop him.

The field was now covered in a thin layer of smoke and dust. It had grown deathly quiet. Then, as Konda's soldiers regained their feet and resumed their charge, their war cries sounded again, mingling with the feral snarls of the lesser oni. Yes, Konda thought, this battle is far from over.

He kicked to prod his steed forward but pulled back on the reins when something in the southern sky caught his attention. As he wheeled the horse around, Konda's eyes remained fixed on the academy, but the daimyo could still see the awesome and terribly familiar sight that was forming on the horizon.

Six new suns had flared to life, burning away the heavy banks of afternoon clouds. These fiery orbs moved in pairs, scanning the ground below as they increased in both size and brilliance. They drew closer to Konda, and he saw three reptilian faces forming around each pair of eyes. The serpent heads became sharper, more defined, and more terrible with each passing moment, perched atop huge, writhing necks covered in dazzling golden scales.

This was O-Kagachi, the ultimate guardian of the spirit world, the physical world, and the boundary between. Its rage had spurred the lesser kami to action when Konda brazenly raided their realm, and its ire launched twenty years of conflict. The multiheaded serpent had personally battered Eiganjo's walls to pieces and crushed the Daimyo's army in its rush to recover the Taken One. Konda took some small satisfaction from the fact that while he no longer possessed the prize, neither did the Great Old Serpent.

As a rival for the Taken One, O-Kagachi was Konda's mortal enemy. As the embodiment of the barrier preventing direct contact between kakuriyo and utsushiyo, O-Kagachi was his nemesis. The great serpent's arrival was a threat, but it was also an opportunity, for an abstract concept made flesh can be dangerous, but it can also be overcome.

Konda quickly weighed his choices. He could continue to battle the oni—the more timely his victory, the more likely he'd get to the prize first. Or he could turn and try to engage O-Kagachi, which would give his army the chance to avenge their own deaths but would also expose them to the oni's treachery from behind.

Neither of these options appealed to Konda, so he chose a third course. He concentrated, calling his best horsemen and five battle-moths to him. Together they would form a phalanx that would punch through the oni and enter Minamo while the main force continued to fight the demonic horde. O-Kagachi moved slowly while it fully manifested, so the daimyo was confident his retainers could win the day while he acquired the prize, all long before the old serpent joined the battle.

Konda waved his sword in a wide arc, drawing cheers from his personal phalanx. The daimyo spurred his horse, and the noble beast charged. By the time it reached the edge of the oni's crater, it had built up enough momentum to leap clear over the smoking hole created by the oni's blast.

Airborne, between the moths overhead and his soldiers on the ground, Konda felt the force of his true destiny pulling him forward. The prize, victory over the oni, revenge on O-Kagachi . . . eternal life, and ultimate power to wield for the glory of Eiganjo. Before this day was done, Daimyo Konda would have them all.

* * * * *

Hidetsugu raged and roared after Marrow's blade struck. He immediately dropped Toshi and Kiku as he fell back.

For several moments after tumbling to the floor, Toshi thought he had been crushed to death. His cruelly compressed lungs at first refused to reinflate, so he had to coax in a sip of air at a time. Marrow was there beside him before Toshi could rise or even clear his vision.

"Let's go, oath-brother," the nezumi hissed excitedly. "I hurt him but I don't think I stopped him."

Toshi shook his head. He grabbed Marrow by the shoulders and pulled him close so he could look in the nezumi's eyes.

"Find my sword," Toshi said. "The long one."

Marrow-Gnawer cocked his head. "What? What'd I do? My hand burned, I saw him hurting you, so I figured the oath was already broken. Like you said." Marrow quickly glanced down at the slightly smoking triangle scratched into his palm. "The oath is gone, right? I saved you. I did good." The nezumi's pleading eyes searched Toshi's face. "Didn't I?"

As the last syllable left his mouth, Marrow went rigid. He stood trembling and twitching as his face flushed. Toshi could see smoke rising from Marrow's fur and feel heat radiating from the nezumi's body.

He sadly shook his head. "No, Marrow. The oath is intact. You spilled Hidetsugu's blood, and now the reckoning is upon you."

Toshi couldn't tell if Marrow could hear through the throes of his seizure. Several feet away, Kiku lay on her side, coughing and struggling to roll away from the ogre. Something brittle crackled under her hip as she moved.

Hidetsugu had stopped roaring and knocking chunks of wood and stone from the walls. Blood and his ruined eye still oozed down his face as he gingerly tested Marrow's sword to see how firmly it was planted. The yamabushi stood nearby, unsure if they should assist their master or exact vengeance on the one who struck him.

Toshi spotted his sword belt. For Marrow, for Kiku, and for himself, he dived for his weapons and rolled, drawing his long sword in one hand and his jitte in the other.

He charged toward Marrow, his mind working feverishly. There was a chance they could still pull this off and stay alive. He could fix this and still capture the Taken One for his myojin. All he had to do was survive the next few minutes.

Toshi reached Marrow and sheathed his jitte. Keeping his eye on the yamabushi, Toshi brusquely pulled Marrow's arm out straight. He turned the rat's hand over to make sure the hyozan mark was still there, and then Toshi raised his sword.

"Sorry, oath-brother," he said. He swung the blade down at Marrow's wrist. As the edge touched the first hair on the nezumi's arm, a bolt of white light struck Toshi's sword in the center, shattering it into three equal pieces. Marrow's arm was barely even scratched.

"Don't do that, Toshi." Hidetsugu had regained control of himself and stood smiling, Marrow's sword still jutting from his eye socket. Next to him the female yamabushi held her stringless bow ready, a new bolt of magical force drawn and ready to fire.

"I've heard that the hyozan curse has only been invoked twice," the ogre leered. "And I didn't get to see the other one."

"I wouldn't worry," Toshi said. "You'll only see half of this one even if I do let you watch."

The o-bakemono chuckled. He seemed remarkably placid for someone who'd just been maimed. As Toshi watched and waited, Hidetsugu scrunched up the wounded side of his face and plucked the blade from his eye like a loose lash.

"Much better." He tossed the stained and rusty sword aside. "Now then. I was just about to kill you—"

A thick column of dusty black slammed into Hidetsugu's chest like a battering ram, cutting him off in mid-threat and hurling him back through the stone wall behind him. The entire room, the entire floor of the building shook, raining dust and bits of plaster down on the stunned yamabushi. Toshi was as shocked as they were by this surprising turn of events, and he followed their wide-eyed awe across the room to its source.

Kiku was in the same place Hidetsugu had dropped her, floating three feet off the floor and surrounded by a nimbus of shadow. Pieces of a brown ceramic disk lay broken at her feet. Toshi's stomach went cold as he recognized the kanji he'd crafted back in the swamp to contain the mahotsukai masters' curse.

"Kiku?" he called. She did not reply. From the shadows crawling over her perfect cheekbones to the dull black void in her eyes, Toshi guessed that she couldn't . . . and that the masters' spell had reclaimed its original vessel.

More thick columns of shadow sprouted from Kiku's body and bent down to the floor, lifting her up like a spider's legs. Suspended from this network of shadow limbs, Kiku's entranced body skittered over the yamabushi and through the hole in the wall after Hidetsugu.

Toshi turned his attention back to Marrow. One crisis at a time, he told himself. In swift, practiced motions, Toshi stretched out Marrow's arm and crisply lopped of the nezumi's hand at the wrist. It popped off of the rat's arm and landed with the hyozan mark facing the ceiling.

Marrow was too far gone to cry out, but Toshi felt the heat coming off him dwindle. Marrow's convulsions also eased. The ochimusha wrapped Marrow's bleeding stump in a strip of the rat's own shirt.

"I don't know if that will work," Toshi told Marrow's rigid body. "But I think one less hand is better than slow, agonizing death." He tilted Marrow's head so he could look into his eyes. There was no sign of conscious thought.

"I'll ask you again when you're able to answer," Toshi said. "If you disagree, I can always kill you then to make it up to you."

The yamabushi had recovered while Toshi had tended to Marrow, and the female was taking aim with her bow. For the first time since the oni dog had bitten him, Toshi had the strength and the focus to call upon the power of his myojin. "Hoy, skullcaps," he called. "You've done enough for now. Rest."

Toshi spread his fingers wide and then slowly clenched them back into a fist. Across the room, the yamabushi staggered as the air around them grew cold, then frigid, then arctic. A thin patina of powdered ice formed on their hair and eyebrows as the color drained from their faces.

The female shuddered and then sat right where she'd been standing. The bow clattered from her numb fingers, and her chin slowly drifted down to her chest. Her partner managed to stagger a few extra steps before he also dropped his weapon and crumpled to the floor.

Beside him, Marrow toppled onto his side. The rat and the yamabushi were out of the picture for now. That only left Kiku and Hidetsugu.

Toshi drew his jitte and sprinted through the hole in the wall. To his surprise, the next wall had a similar hole, and the wall beyond that. Whatever Kiku had hit the ogre with had not been a lover's tap.

In the room past the third hole, Toshi found his former oath-mates. Kiku was still entranced, black-eyed and unresponsive, but her shadow limbs had Hidetsugu pinned against the floor. With a separate column of shadow restraining each arm and leg, the ogre was slowly crushing the floor beneath him into powder and he heaved and strained against the ponderous black force.

Though it seemed Kiku had the upper hand, Toshi knew it could not last. Ten years of uneasy partnership had not helped him develop a kanji spell to defeat Hidetsugu, and he'd worked very hard to do so. The ogre was too strong, too tough, and too magically adept for Toshi's best efforts, even if he had the element of surprise. There was no reliable way to kill Hidetsugu or render him helpless with a single stroke, and the ogre's return blow was almost guaranteed to be lethal. Frankly, he was amazed Kiku had lasted this long.

Toshi racked his brain to come up with some way to help or call her off before Hidetsugu gathered his wits. Too late, he thought, as fire sparked in Hidetsugu's eye and he opened his mouth wide in a voracious grin.

"Magnificent," he cried, just before a plume of white-hot flame blasted into Kiku at the center of her shadow-cloud. Toshi registered that Hidetsugu was referring to Kiku's attack and not his own fire spell—it must have been decades since someone had knocked the o-bakemono off his feet.

The blast forced Kiku and her shadow limbs up through the ceiling, but the recoil also drove Hidetsugu the rest of the way through the floor. Masonry and planks rained down around Toshi, and he wondered how much more abuse this wing of the academy could take. Cracks had already formed along the exterior walls, and as Toshi watched, one huge slab of stone slid out of alignment, threatening to fall and crush anyone beneath it.

Four spidery shadow legs folded themselves around the hole in the ceiling and then dragged Kiku back into the chamber. Her blank eyes had narrowed and her mouth was closed, as if the ogre's attack had reminded her of the need for caution and considered action.

Before Kiku could pull the rest of her shadow limbs in behind her, Hidetsugu's muscular form rocketed up from the crater in the floor. The ogre slammed into the mahotsukai and wrapped his powerful arms around her waist. She was protected within her field of shadow, but Hidetsugu was far too strong to simply be ignored. Kiku's real and conjured limbs flailed as the ogre compressed her midsection, but she was unable to grab him or toss him clear.

Hidetsugu cinched his grip and locked his hands behind Kiku. He forced his head back, opened his mouth, and chomped down on the shadowy substance surrounding her. Kiku opened her jaws in a silent scream of agony as Hidetsugu tore a jagged hunk of darkness free and spit it back over his shoulder.

The nimbus reacted like a living thing, shuddering in what appeared to be pain. Hidetsugu bit again, ripping another piece of the material free, and it instinctively crawled away from his mouth. This left a patch over Kiku's torso thinner than the rest of the envelope, and Hidetsugu's next bite sank into the weakened spot.

Inside the cloud of shadow, Kiku suddenly blinked. The black glow that had occluded her eyes faded. She seemed shocked to discover herself in close combat with an ogre, but she remained Kiku of the mahotsukai: tough, smart, and capable.

She cupped her left hand, still pinned to her side by the ogre's hug. When she turned her hand palm up, it held a delicate purple bloom.

As he had with Marrow, Toshi opened his mouth to warn Kiku that the oath still applied to her but stopped himself. She was in the fight of her life and she needed every tool at her disposal. Hidetsugu was likely to kill her anyway, so why not let her do all that she could to get him first?

He beat back the inner voice that whispered of the other reasons he did not speak when he had the chance. Wasn't this what he'd brought Kiku and Marrow for? Whether they killed Hidetsugu, or he killed them, the end result was the same: easy access to the Taken One.

As he debated with himself, Toshi saw Kiku flick her wrist, tossing the flower clear of the shadow nimbus. The camellia spun as it arced up over Hidetsugu, gracefully drifting down toward the ogre's head.

"No," Toshi said. The purple kanji on his forehead flashed again, and the supple petals of Kiku's flower went brittle. Instead of writhing and digging in when it touched Hidetsugu, the frozen camellia shattered like a wafer of spun sugar.

Kiku's face snapped toward Toshi, murder in her eyes. Hidetsugu laughed.

"Thank you, ochimusha." With a brutal jerk, Hidetsugu twisted his body at the waist and tore Kiku loose from the legs that anchored her to the ceiling. He turned a somersault in the air and, as he completed the rotation, he straightened out his body and hurled Kiku violently against the exterior wall.

The impact blew a great gap in the stone, revealing the orange evening sky beyond. Kiku had the presence of mind to use her long shadow limbs to grip the edges of the hole, which saved her from plowing clear through the wall and falling five hundred feet to the lake below.

Hidetsugu landed heavily on the floor. The wall directly above Kiku collapsed, burying her in a pile of jagged stone. The tremors from the rockfall were still reverberating across the floor when Kiku forced herself up through the rubble.

But Hidetsugu was relentless. A volley of fireballs rained down on Kiku like hailstones, and the instant the last of these slammed home Hidetsugu himself crashed down upon her with both feet. The ogre rained kicks and punches on the shadow envelope, and though Kiku was protected by her masters' shadow curse Toshi could see the painful effects each blow had on her. The punishment continued, but Kiku did not respond. She was exhausted, and she was dazed. The last of the Numai jushi was beaten.

Standing on a blister of solid shadow, Hidetsugu roared with delight. He plunged his hand through the thick dark mass and clamped thumb and forefinger around Kiku's throat. The ogre tensed, planted his feet, and yanked Kiku free of the shadow nimbus like a pearl from an oyster.

"You are magnificent, mahotsukai." Hidetsugu settled to the floor as the shadow nimbus faded beneath his feet.

He held Kiku high over his head and turned toward Toshi. "Isn't she?"

Light from the windows above cast Kiku's shadow across Hidetsugu's ruined eye. He peered around the chamber, searching for Toshi.

"She is, old friend." Toshi's voice came from Kiku's shadow on Hidetsugu's cheek. "And she's the last magnificent sight you'll ever see."

Hidetsugu dropped the mahotsukai and leaped back, but it was too late. Toshi's short sword plunged through the surface of Kiku's shadow and up into Hidetsugu's remaining eye.

The ogre seemed to explode in pain and fury. Amid the dust, the shattering stones, and the thunderous peals of rage, Toshi backpedaled away from Hidetsugu as quickly as he could.

He took a moment to reorient himself, and then Toshi squeezed through a shadow made by a pile of rocks beside Kiku. The mahotsukai was unconscious but alive. For now. Her best chance of staying that way was for Toshi to concentrate on Hidetsugu.

Toshi stood, careful not to make any noise that would alert the ogre to his location. The o-bakemono may have been blind but he was far from defeated.

But Toshi had a plan for that as well. He silently drew his jitte, dragged the sharp tip across his forearm, and collected a few drops of his own blood.

Hidetsugu's roar ended as if his throat had been cut. Just as Toshi realized the folly of drawing his own blood in the same room as a keen-nosed o-bakemono, Hidetsugu lashed out with his foot. The rock he kicked broke in half—most of it disintegrated into a cloud of dust and sharp pebbles. The rest shot across the room and hit Toshi full in the chest, pinning him against the far wall and crushing a spray of red blood from his lungs.

The jitte tumbled from his fingers as Toshi sank painfully to the floor a short distance from Kiku. No help there; the mahotsukai was still unconscious.

Hidetsugu sniffed again, grinned savagely, and started toward the fallen ochimusha with careful, unhurried steps. He didn't taunt or threaten but simply strode with a definite purpose and a terrible, undeniable gravity.

CHAPTER 11

Toshi struggled to breathe, to roll away, to move at all. He failed.

Hidetsugu drew ever closer, unhurried, precise, and deliberate. Unable even to wipe the blood from his lips, Toshi scanned the chamber for some alternative to violent death. Kiku was out cold; Marrow was probably dead or would be shortly. And Toshi himself was no longer protected by the hyozan curse.

O Night, he prayed, *your acolyte needs your blessings.*

The voice that replied was cold, and distant, but not uncaring.

Nonsense, Toshi Umezawa. You already have all the power you need.

Desperate, Toshi thought, *Please, great myojin. I do not have my full wits about me. What must I do?*

What you did at the beginning. What you did when you first accepted my gifts.

Hidetsugu was almost close enough to reach down and grab Toshi. The ochimusha searched his memory . . . what had he done at first with Night's blessings? Called for silence? That wouldn't stop Hidetsugu's nose from locating him. Fade into nothingness? He didn't have the strength.

Toshi looked out through the massive hole in the exterior wall. Far below, he saw armies of twisted spirits and demonic oni. He saw the All-Consuming Oni of Chaos, looming as large as a small mountain. And across the southern sky, he saw the Great Old Serpent, O-Kagachi. Three of the most powerful entities in all Kamigawa, the rulers of humankind, oni, and spirit alike were all assembled to fight for the prize that lay all but forgotten just a few rooms away.

He had been beset by powerful forces the first time he'd called on Night's Reach. Then, he'd used her power to subdue the powerful patron of Jukai Forest, the Myojin of Life's Web. He'd struck at the great spirit through its worshippers, robbing her of strength by silencing her followers in mid-chant. Perhaps he could do the same thing in reverse now, attacking Hidetsugu through the oni he worshiped?

The idea crystallized quickly in Toshi's head. He scanned the field below to confirm. Yes . . . while Konda and O-Kagachi were fixed and oriented on the towers of Minamo, the All-Consuming was facing south, its eyes pinned to the great serpent's approach. The ochimusha spared one last look at Hidetsugu, who was sightlessly searching for him with wide sweeps of his massive arms.

Do you understand?

At last, Toshi realized he did. The three-way struggle developing on the shores of the lake provided information that Hidetsugu didn't have, information that would wound the ogre more viciously than any spell or blade.

Thank you, O Night.

Fare well, my acolyte.

Toshi ignored the pain in his chest and rolled onto his knees. The ogre's probing hands were only inches away.

"Hidetsugu," Toshi said, "listen."

At the sound of the ochimusha's voice, Hidetsugu lashed out and snared the front of Toshi's shirt. He lifted Toshi up and said, "No, my friend. Every time I listen to you, I lose. It would be more fitting . . . more dignified if you simply accepted your death in silence. Nothing you say will save you."

Swaying in the ogre's grip, Toshi said, "All right, don't listen. Smell. Point your ugly face south and tell me what you find."

Hidetsugu shook his head, but in doing so turned his face to the open air. The scent of battle reached him, familiar odors that could not help but fire his ogre blood.

"The All-Consuming," he said. "And an army of souls who fight even though they don't have proper bodies." Forgetting himself, Hidetsugu tilted his head back and drank deeply of the evening air.

"And an elemental force of amazing power. That has to be the fabled O-Kagachi." Hidetsugu sniffed again, momentarily forgetting his rage. "There are hundreds of powerful scents out there in the world, Toshi, but this one smells like all of them. It is the world itself."

Hidetsugu lowered his head. "And now I have listened, old friend. Good-bye." The ogre raised his powerful fist, preparing to crush Toshi against his own open palm.

"Before you kill me," Toshi said, "let me tell you the one scent you missed."

"Oh? Tell, ochimusha, tell."

"Fear," Toshi said evenly. "Fear of O-Kagachi. Whatever that thing is, it's more powerful than Konda, and it's more powerful than the All-Consuming. If it arrives here . . ."

"Nothing is more powerful than my oni," Hidetsugu said.

"Chaos is the fate of all things, living, spiritual, and in between. All that lives will someday die, all that is ordered will someday unravel. And when they do, Chaos reigns."

"Oh?" Toshi said, and he could see how his mocking tone annoyed Hidetsugu. "You seem certain. But is your oni?"

Hidetsugu huffed, but he did not strike. Instead, he turned once more to the opening in the wall and waited, drawing a steady stream of air into his nostrils.

* * * * *

A mere hundred feet from the shores of Lake Kamitaki, Konda's advance had ground to a halt. Even as his main forces threw themselves against the Oni of Chaos in endless waves, the demon held fast. In the sky and on the ground, even his personal strike force could not break through.

Konda was confident in his eventual success, but the approach of O-Kagachi threatened them all. The great spirit beast now filled the entire southern sky, five castle-sized heads thrashing and rolling down from the horizon. The battlefield and the entire world seemed to tilt toward the serpent's coils, as if the world were overbalanced by its presence.

The daimyo shouted for another charge, and his troops obeyed without hesitation. Doubt had crept into Konda's own mind as he weighed the risks of being trapped between two of the kakuriyo's most powerful spirits.

O-Kagachi roared then, adding its multiple voices to the cacophony of battle for the first time. The serpent's cries covered the entire range of pitch and timbre, from a high, shrieking wail to a low, ground-rumbling roar. Konda's army did not react to the terrible new sounds, but all of the oni did, from the lowliest foot soldier to their lord hovering and slavering overhead. The greater demon recoiled as if stung by a hot needle, and then its hissing, malevolent call stabbed through every ear and mind for a mile in all directions.

Konda's heart surged. Could it be? Was he actually hearing the sound he had heard in a hundred different battles from a hundred different enemies? Was the mighty Oni of Chaos sounding a retreat?

Like a squall on a sunny day, the greater demon suddenly soared up from the shore into the sky. It grew darker, heavier, and broader as it rose, its eyes aglow with crimson light. Thousands of sharptoothed black jaws coalesced around the oni's eyes and horns, giving it a distinct shape for the first time. Still rising, the Oni of Chaos boldly turned to face O-Kagachi. Its shape swelled, and then a river of snapping jaws erupted from below its eyes, streaming toward the five-headed serpent like a horizontal geyser.

Konda stopped, half-mesmerized by the enormity of the conflict in the sky. All around him, his soldiers and moth-riders slowed their advance, waiting for the daimyo to act. Even the lesser oni stopped fighting but stood dazed and almost frightened as their deity struck.

The stream of demonic jaws curled slightly as it streaked toward O-Kagachi. The closer its leading edge got to the serpent, the smaller and more comical it seemed. Konda let out a mocking laugh as the oni's attack made contact with O-Kagachi's closest face. The stream of vicious jaws splashed harmlessly off the old serpent's scales like gentle rain.

The stricken head then blasted forward at a speed greater than Konda could follow. He saw a flicker of movement and felt a rush of air and pressure as something huge rushed over him. It took but a split-second for him to jerk his head back to the oni. What he saw chilled him to his core.

O-Kagachi's return stroke had torn through the center of the Oni of Chaos, sundering the great demon in two. Two of its three eyes remained on one ragged half, opened wide with shock. On the other half, the third eye rolled back in its socket and lost its angry red glow just before the lid drifted closed. This smaller half of the oni's body jerked and twitched for a moment. Then it began to fall, leaving a trail of stunned and motionless jaws fluttering in its wake.

Before the disintegrating mass could splash into the waters of the lake, O-Kagachi's head turned and swallowed it whole in one single bite. As quickly as it struck, the great serpent's head withdrew, rejoining the other four heads and the huge crush of undulating coils.

Lesser oni on the battlefield screamed in impotent rage. Many disengaged from Konda's soldiers and disappeared into clouds of foul-smelling black smoke. As they cleared the field, the stunned greater oni still hovered overhead. Crippled, diminished, and chastened, it began to fade from sight.

The way to Minamo was now clear. Konda had secured his position as the greatest military leader in Kamigawa by seizing opportunities as soon as they arose. He raised his sword hand and his voice to rally his troops onward.

"Now, my retainers," he cried, "even our greatest enemy serves our cause today! Ride on! To Minamo! The prize shall be mine once again!"

* * * * *

Red tears dripped from Hidetsugu's empty sockets, but the ogre's face was a mask of rage.

"No," he said softly. "This cannot be."

Toshi took advantage of Hidetsugu's distraction to become immaterial. The ogre did not notice his intended victim's escape, did not even lower the arm that had held Toshi.

"It fled," he whispered bitterly. "It faced the great serpent and lost, and now it abandons its own kind. It abandons me, the truest acolyte it has ever known."

Toshi collected his jitte and went to check on Kiku. The mahotsukai was still unconscious, but her masters' curse had protected her from the worst of the ogre's attack. She lay next to a pile of rubble, her body painfully twisted but basically intact.

Kiku's skin was now a deep, perfect black like the heart of an onyx. She had been stained by the shadows, marked by the forces she manipulated. She was still strikingly beautiful, but her beauty was more dire and terrible than ever.

At the opening in the wall, Hidetsugu snarled and shattered one of the half-broken stones before him. He was cursing angrily in the old language of the o-bakemono.

Toshi limped back to the chamber where he'd left Marrow and the Taken One. The disk was intact where he had left it, so that was something. It didn't look good for the rat, however.

The nezumi was still rigid and radiating heat, but it would take several hours before he died. As Toshi feared, removing the hyozan mark slowed the curse but did not spare the nezumi from it. As intended, the spell would incapacitate the traitor and make him suffer until the rest of the reckoners came to put him out of his misery.

"Toshi," Hidetsugu called from the distant chamber. "Where are you, oath-brother?"

Toshi considered. He was not in immediate danger, but Hidetsugu had served him one surprise after another today. Since he was quickly regaining his strength and able to call on Night's Reach, Toshi felt safe enough to answer. He went through the holes Kiku had punched through the academy walls and stood on the verge of the chamber where the ogre and the mahotsukai were.

"Here, Hidetsugu. Though I think our time as oath-brothers has long since passed."

The ogre took a few steps toward Toshi's voice. The ochimusha was chilled by how steady and confident those steps were, how quickly he had adjusted to being blind. He was also leery of the raucous ogre's subdued tone.

"Nonsense," Hidetsugu said. "We are blood brothers . . . you, Kobo, and I. The hyozan oath may no longer bind us, but we have tasted each other's flesh. We are all still tied to one another."

"I never tasted anyone's flesh," Toshi said, annoyed. "That's your hobby."

"Of course you did. When we took Kobo into our brotherhood, you drank the water that cooled his brand. Kobo had already eaten of my flesh, and you in turn swallowed his."

Toshi considered this. To his growing unease, he realized Hidetsugu was right. "Does this mean you can still kill me somehow?"

A thin smile flickered across the ogre's features. "No, my brother. It means that we will never be free of each other until we are both dead."

"Oh. That's all right, then." He waited a moment for Hidetsugu to reply, then added, "So . . . what happens now?"

The ogre's brow furrowed over his bleeding eyes. "I have a favor to ask of you. For old time's sake."

"A favor?"

"Yes."

"What's in it for me?"

"Same old Toshi. Let me put it this way, ochimusha. I am blind. I am alone, having outlived my hunters and been deserted by my god.

"But I still hunger for vengeance. There are yet many who deserve my wrath. I wonder . . . when you travel on the power of your myojin, have you visited the spirit world?"

Toshi weighed his words carefully. "Not exactly. I have only seen visions of the kakuriyo."

"But have you gone to the *honden* of Night's Reach? Have you visited her place of power?"

"I have."

"Then help me. Send me to my oni's home. The honden of the All-Consuming."

"What? Why?"

Anger and menace slipped back into Hidetsugu's voice. "I did not devote my life to Chaos so that Chaos could turn its back on me. I summoned it here for a battle to the death as the world collapses around us. If Chaos will not fight that battle here, I must carry the battle it." The ogre's face was terrible to behold. "My god will live up to my expectations, or I will make it suffer."

Toshi waited for his heart to slow down before he spoke. "I don't even know if that's possible. And if it were, what can you do? Even an o-bakemono's power has limits."

Hidetsugu crossed his arms. "Perhaps you are right. Perhaps we should simply fight until one or both of us is dead. You are a wily trickster, Toshi Umezawa. You may yet find a way to destroy me before I bring this entire building down." For emphasis, Hidetsugu stomped one massive foot onto the floor, shaking more bricks loose from the broken walls.

"Agreed," Toshi said instantly. Behind the ogre, framed by the hole leading outside, Toshi saw several of Konda's twisted moth-riders circling ever closer. Beyond them, the sky was full of O-Kagachi. "But I must ask something of you in return."

The ogre bared his teeth, though Toshi could not tell if it were a smile or a threat. "I'm listening."

"Save Marrow from the hyozan curse. And help me carry the Taken One to the roof. Do this for me and I'll take you anywhere you want to go."

"The only way to avoid the curse is not to invoke it. I'm sorry, but my rat brother is doomed."

"Hmm. And this has nothing to do with the sword he stuck in your eye?"

"That had crossed my mind. But no, it is not a question of whether I will help him, but can I. I cannot."

"But you'll carry the disk for me? Time's running out, old friend, and I have to get it away from here or all this was for nothing."

"It always has been all for nothing," Hidetsugu said. "Nonetheless, yes, I will be your draught animal if you do as I have asked."

"Then we have another deal, blood-brother. Come toward the sound of my voice and I will show you the disk."

Toshi felt his sense of self-preservation screaming as he took the ogre's hand, but Hidetsugu did not lash out. Instead, he allowed Toshi to guide him through the rubble to the fallen stone disk.

"Here," Toshi said, but his unease did not subside. The Taken

One was lying faceup, with the profile of the fetal serpent clearly visible. Hadn't it landed facedown when the oni dog attacked? Hadn't it been facing right instead, whereas now it faced left?

Hidetsugu bent and fastened his thick fingers around the edges of the disk. He shuddered as his hands made contact, but he smoothly hoisted the prize onto his shoulder.

"This is indeed powerful," Hidetsugu said. "But well-camouflaged. Had I known, I would have inspected it far more closely while I had it to myself." With a grunt, the ogre turned toward the hallway.

"One moment," Toshi said.

"Why?" Hidetsugu replied. "Aren't we both in a hurry?"

"We are," Toshi said. "But I need to end the hyozan oath properly."

Moving quickly, Toshi made his way back to Kiku. The mahotsukai was still unconscious but breathing steadily. Toshi gently pulled her away from the rubble and covered her with a tapestry from the wall. He drew his jitte and deftly scratched a protective symbol on her jet-black forehead. The symbol glowed white for a moment, then faded. Kiku would be safe here until she woke up. Before he turned away, Toshi stole one last kiss from Kiku's sleeping lips.

"Farewell," he said, "last of the Numai jushi."

Kiku's eyes fluttered and her lips pulled back into a familiar sneer. "Kill you for that," she whispered weakly.

"Get in line." Toshi grinned.

The envelope of shadow began to churn around Kiku, bubbling like oil in a hot pan. In the center of the dark mass, Kiku opened her eyes and stared sleepily at Toshi. Slowly, she began to sink from sight, disappearing into the blackness that surrounded her.

"Remember who you are," Toshi called. "Remember who you hate. Cling to the things that mean the most to you, or the shadows will consume you in the end."

Kiku's eyes fluttered and she nodded. As the shadows rose up to her throat, a bright purple flower broke through the surface of the black mass. Kiku held the flower aloft for Toshi to see as the mahotsukai herself vanished from sight. Seconds later, the black bubble imploded in on itself, leaving the delicate bloom behind to adorn the cracked and shattered floor.

Without going anywhere near Kiku's parting gift, Toshi turned and went back to the main chamber.

Hidetsugu was waiting for him with the Taken One propped up on his shoulder. He showed no signs of strain, but he was grinning evilly.

"You have changed, ochimusha. A year ago you would have stolen her shoes while she slept and left an insulting note pinned to her clothing."

"We've all changed," Toshi said brusquely. "A year ago, I was much less weary." He produced the axe he had taken from Kiku's belt.

Hidetsugu must have smelled the freshly sharpened metal, or at least the residual blood that the axe had tasted. "You are going to do your duty by the nezumi?"

"I am. If he can't be saved, I can't just leave him to suffer."

"Careful, my friend," Hidetsugu said, his voice unkind. "You are dancing on the precipice of nobility."

Toshi did not reply.

"When you've done your duty," Hidetsugu said, "find my tetsubo and bring it along, will you?"

"Of course." Toshi turned to Marrow-Gnawer, still smoking and twitching as the curse held him fast.

"You were the best vermin thug I ever knew," Toshi said. "And a loyal reckoner. The hyozan salutes you, Marrow-Gnawer." The axe went up and came down with a terrible, terminal thump.

Hidetsugu waited until Toshi turned to face him once more.

"Are you ready, blood-brother?"

"I am." Toshi looked around at the wreckage he'd helped create. He shook his head and then shrugged. "To the roof."

* * * * *

The last of the oni had either fled or been cut down. The battle belonged to Konda and his ghost army, and O-Kagachi was still crawling across the horizon, slowly but inevitably headed for Minamo.

His moth-riders now circled the academy, concentrating on a large hole in the exterior south wall. Konda's eyes had fixed on the same spot, and he knew that total victory was within his grasp.

"Forward!" he shouted. "For Eiganjo! For Towabara! For the glory of all Kamigawa!"

"Konda!" his army replied. "Konda!"

Two moth-riders swept down on each side of the daimyo's horse. The grotesque hybrids of man and beast extended their glowing auras to surround Konda, and they now carried him and his steed into the air over Lake Kamitaki.

Though the lake and the shore alike were strewn with wreckage and fallen bodies, Konda had never seen such a beautiful view. Borne aloft on his retainer's wings, he felt more than a general, more than a daimyo. He felt like a conquering god. This was his true destiny, and that of the world—to be victorious and triumphant over all enemies.

The moths guided him to the south wall and tacked back and forth outside the hole in the wall. Though he was only a short leap from the building's interior, Konda sensed something was wrong. His eyes were no longer glued to this level of the school. The Taken One had been moved.

Anger and panic bubbled up through his euphoria. His wandering eyes darted across and around his face like maddened hornets in a jar. Disoriented, Konda could only sit and fume until he located his prize.

Overhead, thunder rolled down from the academy roof and a great flash of black lightning snaked across the cloudy evening sky. Even from this great distance, Konda caught the scent of sulfur and saw a ghostly vision of a vortex filled with sharp teeth and slavering jaws. A huge, vaguely man-shaped figure was falling into the vortex, howling in rage and waving a heavy spiked club. Then the vortex closed, swallowing the brutish figure and vanishing from sight.

Konda's eyes found their target. There, he thought. He craned his head up and saw a single living battle-moth ascending from Minamo into the clouds above. The Taken One, the great stone disk that Konda had risked so much and fought so hard for, was lashed securely to the colorful creature's back.

Without a word or a gesture, his moth-riders turned and gave chase. The two escorting Konda were the first to move and the fastest in flight. Even with their burden, the ghostly moths rapidly closed the distance between the daimyo and his prize.

Konda saw a single man on the moth's back, and while the distance was still too great to identify him, the Daimyo's eyes would not be fooled. This was the thief Toshi Umezawa and he was once again stealing Konda's treasure. The daimyo urged his bearers forward, willing them to go ever faster.

The sky ahead of the thief was growing darker even though it was closer to the setting sun. The ochimusha steered his moth into the blacker mass of clouds and air ahead, and then he and the Taken One were gone. Not even Konda's eyes could find them, even after the daimyo himself had plunged into the wall of darkness. Seconds later, he emerged from the other side to find an empty sky stretching out before him.

This was intolerable. He had both thief and treasure within his grasp, but now they were both gone without a trace. Was Night itself the ochimusha's ally?

To the south, O-Kagachi let out an anguished roar. Its thrashing coils became quiescent and the giant serpent heads paused, fixing their star-eyes on the patch of sky where Konda raged. Then the dread guardian of the kakuriyo turned away and cast its eyes east, the direction the ochimusha had gone. Like a typhoon, the serpent ponderously changed course, ignoring the academy and the waterfall.

Daimyo Konda bellowed in frustration. Victory would not be his today.

With a thought, Konda summoned his army and directed them to follow. The Taken One had gone east. O-Kagachi would follow, but the serpent was not as quick as the daimyo's ghost army. Once he could lock his gaze upon his prize, Konda would ride down upon the ochimusha and crucify him. The prize would be back in Eiganjo before O-Kagachi ever came close.

The daimyo gripped his horse's reins and clenched his teeth. The next time he came this close to his goal, he would die before he let it slip though his fingers.

* * * * *

Toshi willed himself and his moth solid as soon as they were clear of the falls. He had chosen his steed well. The live moth had so far proved fast enough to keep him out of Konda's clutches, provided he maintained the lead his myojin had given him.

Night's Reach had been pleased with Toshi's success in keeping the Taken One from Konda and O-Kagachi, so she was extremely accommodating in the matter of escaping the daimyo's pursuit. In addition to hiding Toshi as he flew, she had also delayed Konda's progress. She had also been unexpectedly enthusiastic about sending Hidetsugu to confront the All-Consuming. Night's face was literally an unchanging mask, but Toshi thought he saw joy and excitement in his myojin's demeanor.

He tried not to dwell on the cost of pleasing his patron. Hidetsugu was gone, Marrow was dead, and if Kiku remained herself she would still be forever changed. He hoped the rough stone disk was worth it, but it would take someone else to convince him.

thank you

Toshi started at the sound of a voice in his head. The most powerful mages and spirits could speak mind-to-mind, but this voice was unfamiliar to him. That's all I need right now, he thought, another interested party.

saved me

Toshi shivered in the cold night air. I'm not hearing this, he insisted to himself. I'm not listening to any new voices.

release me

Slowly, Toshi turned in the saddle. Behind him, the Taken One was still securely bound to the moth's harness. The serpent's face peeked out between leather straps.

To his mounting terror, the etched image of the Taken One moved, stretching like a cat after a long nap. It turned to face Toshi directly, and, though its line-drawn mouth did not move, its voice came clearly to Toshi's ears even as the rushing wind filled them with its roar.

thank you
saved me
release me
NOW

Toshi struggled for words. He had thought his recent success had come from the Myojin of Night's Reach, but now he wasn't so sure. His mind was choked with questions. The stone disk was talking to him. Had it talked to Konda? What else could it do?

The image of the serpent strained. The tip of its nose broke through the surface of the disk, and Toshi stifled a yell.

Not here, he thought. Not now.

release me

"I will," he said, though he had no idea how. Whatever the Taken One had been in the spirit world, whatever it had become in this world, it was alive. And making demands.

The strain of breaking free from the disk proved too much for the etched serpent, and it settled back into two dimensions. It remained focused on Toshi, however, fixing him with its baleful eyes.

"I can't do it alone," Toshi said quickly. "And I need to rest and heal before I can even try. But I promise I will do whatever I can, as soon as I can." He swallowed nervously. "Trust me."

The serpent slowly settled back into its original pose, showing Toshi its profile.

waiting

Toshi nodded, awash with relief. "Thank you," he said. "You won't have to wait much longer."

He watched the motionless image for many long minutes before turning his back on it once more. There was nothing for it but to press on. Night's Reach wanted this thing kept from Konda and O-Kagachi, and Toshi meant to honor her wishes for the time being. His promise to the Taken One would have to wait. After all, he couldn't help it if they were both captured or killed, so his first priority was to avoid that.

As the great moth carried him east toward the Jukai Forest, Toshi lowered his head and tried to think who in the world would be ready, willing, and able to help him. He was still thinking hours later when the first rays of sunlight speared over the horizon.

PART TWO

DAUGHTERS OF FLESH
AND SPIRIT

The great Jukai Forest was almost as large as all the surrounding territories combined. A vast tangle of massive cedars and tall, grassy hills, Jukai was so large it could experience five different types of weather at once. The eastern edge of the woods had never been mapped, as no survey team had ever found it and returned.

This remote corner of Konda's domain was some of the wildest and most dangerous country in all Kamigawa. There were very few human tribes, and those that did dwell in the east were extremely religious and intensely private. The orochi-bito snakefolk held sway in these deepest recesses of the forest, and while over thirty tribes had been identified, no one was truly sure how many snakes there were.

It was upon this remote wooded expanse and against these fabled creatures that the soratami descended. Their warriors came down from the sky in huge cloud chariots, raining ice-blue magic and silver arrows upon any orochi they saw. As the crescent moon smiled sharply on the horizon, wave after wave of silver-white war machines stooped down to the treetops, unleashing a grim tide of armored soratami clad in shimmering mail armor.

To any observer it would have seemed as if the pale, slender warriors were lashing out at the forest itself, blasting thick stands of trees with their crystalline magic and piercing great hedgerows with volleys of spears and arrows. The moonfolk left little more than shattered trunks and broken boughs as the lifeless bodies of camouflaged orochi fell from their hiding spots.

Mochi, the Smiling Kami of the Crescent Moon grinned, and the actual moon turned so that its points were facing up. As was his custom when manifesting in the utsushiyo, he now took the unthreatening form of a small, chubby, blue-skinned cherub with bright eyes and a dazzling smile. As Mochi became solid, the moon overhead returned to its normal position.

So far, the campaign was going splendidly. There were hundreds of soratami warriors already in the forest, with thousands more arriving or on the way. Almost the entire Oboro garrison had been mustered and sent into the woods. They had not found the homes of the largest orochi tribes yet, but he was certain they would. When they did, the dominant snakes would fall as easily as the small pocket of resistance his army was devastating right now.

The soratami were spectacular in all-out warfare, a study in grace blended with power wrapped in a shroud of stealth. It was something everyone should be able to see and appreciate, even if it meant they had to be on the wrong end of the moonfolk's swords.

First came the *shinobi*, scouts and spies who could walk through walls and dance on dust motes without drawing attention. The orochi had to breed for generations before they could blend into the deep woods as effectively as Mochi's agents did with just a few weeks' preparation, and the soratami were not limited to the forest. They could disappear just as easily on the plains of Towabara or the marshes of Takenuma.

This invisible advance team had located all of the orochi dens and gathering places, even mapping the most likely shelters they would be driven to when attacked. When the fighting started, the soratami warriors knew exactly where to look for their prey.

The warriors themselves were a special point of pride for Mochi, as they wore his crescent moon standard, and their enchanted mail perfectly mimicked the shine of moonlight on pure silver. They were armed with traditional katana and they floated like ethereal dancers through the moss and cedar, blades flashing and spinning through the trees. Mochi could easily imagine there were no orochi at all and that his army was simply performing an intricate military exercise . . . if not for the vile hissing of the snakes and the stench of their watery green blood.

Overhead, scores of cloud chariots waited for the chance to deposit more warriors on the field. Mochi folded his chubby fingers over his bulging belly and sighed happily. Things were working out so well.

His agents in Eiganjo had told him of Konda's plan to raid the spirit world as soon as the daimyo consulted them about it. Instead of seeing this as an outrageous blasphemy like any decent kami, Mochi saw only opportunity. Like many spirits who have frequent interaction with the physical world, Mochi had been exposed to his worshippers' way of thinking. He had experienced enough of their worldview to understand and even share it.

Konda was intending to disrupt the natural order of things, the balance between physical and spiritual. Such an act would have dangerous, unpredictable repercussions, and so Mochi decided that he would not only allow it, but also facilitate it.

In the twenty years of strife since Konda made his raid, Mochi had time to reflect on the wisdom of his actions and their true motivations. His introspection revealed three important things:

One, he did not know what to expect as a result of Konda's crime, but he was sure he could capitalize on it for his own benefit; two, if Konda succeeded it meant the oldest and most sacred laws could be broken by someone with enough will and power, which he could capitalize on for his own benefit in the long term; and three, it was a waste of time second-guessing his own genius because he made good decisions even when he didn't have all the facts.

A trio of orochi turned on a pursuing soratami and enveloped him in their strong, flexible bodies. Too late to save the warrior, Mochi directed a nearby squad of soratami to avenge their fallen comrade. It pained him to lose his noble followers, but this war was for a great cause, and sacrifices had to be made.

When the kami attacks started, Mochi knew that Konda's reign would not survive. The daimyo had done a remarkable job uniting the different peoples behind him, but once he was gone they would undoubtedly fall back into petty skirmishing and tribal warfare. Mochi knew the soratami would be largely unaffected, safe in their cloud cities, but he also thought the soratami destiny was to be more than elite survivors. They were exalted beings who worshiped him, after all. If anyone was fit to rule Kamigawa, it was the moonfolk.

If he had conceived the plan on his own beforehand, Mochi might have tried to bring Konda down or perhaps even challenge him on the field of battle. The soratami had a far smaller army than the daimyo, but Mochi would put a single one of his warriors against a whole platoon of Konda's in any situation.

Once Konda had decided his course, however, it became unnecessary to take action in order to topple him—he had doomed himself by his rash act. It might take decades, even centuries, but eventually the spirit world would come to claim what the Daimyo had stolen. When it did, Mochi intended for the soratami to rise in Konda's place as the dominant culture in Kamigawa. The soratami armada had stayed primed and ready for years, and could wait another century if necessary.

Thus, when O-Kagachi manifested and attacked the tower at Eiganjo, Mochi knew his time had come. His moonfolk had been carefully building their base of power in the Takenuma underworld for years, but he had always intended to openly attack the orochi. Of all the tribes in the world, the snakes were the ones with the purest and closest connection to their patron kami. It galled Mochi, but he knew it was true because the snakes and other wild tribes of Jukai were mere beasts. They didn't have the capacity to examine their choices; they simply saw a powerful spirit that made the trees green and the grass grow and that was enough for them.

Further, the forest myojin was one of the most violently aggrieved by Konda's crime. Except for O-Kagachi himself, Life's Web was the spirit most closely tied to the natural order. Like all beasts she was aggressive, hostile, and fierce when it came to protecting her territory. She would have punished Konda for his actions and undone the damage before Mochi had a chance to make use of it. He had arranged for Life's Web to be diminished so that O-Kagachi would have time to manifest, and now Mochi was determined to wipe out her followers so that she would never rise to challenge him again.

A flicker of regret marred Mochi's celebratory mood. Dealing with Life's Web had been a tricky business and required his personal intervention, but it had been effective. The price he paid for removing the most dangerous obstacle to his plans was the introduction of an even more troubling player: Toshi Umezawa.

The ochimusha had snatched the Taken One from under

O-Kagachi's nose just as the great serpent was about to level Eiganjo with Konda inside. Worse, Toshi brought the prize to Oboro's doorstep and even had the temerity to attack Mochi himself. If he weren't protected by the Myojin of Night's Reach, Toshi would never have been able to cause so much trouble, but with such a powerful patron, he was a dangerous provocateur.

Night's Reach, now there was a spirit that had traffic with the physical world. Even the dumbest forest brute understands the power of darkness and either curses or blesses it, depending on its position in the predator-prey relationship. She was old and vast, more so even than Mochi himself, and she was a puzzle to him even now. She had supported Mochi against Life's Web, but now Night's acolyte actively worked directly against Crescent Moon.

The little blue kami smiled, bathing the surrounding forest in pure moonlight. Toshi had been a problem, but even with the support of his patron he had not been able to stop the soratami's ascension. There were thousands of dead orochi who could provide mute but unshakeable testimony to Mochi's success. There had been setbacks, of course, but Minamo, Oboro, and virtually all of Kamigawa was a small price to pay if he and his could rebuild the world to their liking and rule it as they saw fit.

Smiling, Mochi rose up into the sky. In the trees below, the advancing soratami were setting mystical fire to a large pile of brush and dead snakes. It had been a dry winter, and without magical help the fire would consume uncountable acres of living forest, along with every living thing therein.

The moon kami spun slowly, drinking in the full panoramic view of the slaughter. Every life lost, every snake cut down and every tree burned diminished his enemy and empowered him. When the snakes were all dead or routed, Mochi would construct a new capital in the clouds right above this very spot. It would commemorate this moment when he, the Smiling Kami of the Crescent Moon, had seen the shape of soratami victory. Let fire and carnage and the ultimate spirit beast raze the world down to the bare soil. The moon would go on shining, and the soratami would remain above it all.

Sparkling as he rotated, Mochi flashed another blinding smile and disappeared.

* * * * *

Mochi reappeared in the largest cloud vessel in the armada. The massive conveyance was as large as a warship and had not descended to the forest. This was the soratami headquarters and flagship, and it was buzzing with activity.

Two soratami women were waiting for him in the innermost chamber. The room was lavishly decorated with bolts of luxurious cloth and huge satin couch-pillows. The women did not speak as they lounged around a lacquered table. At the center of the table was a shallow bowl filled with vivid blue liquid. A single candle floated on top.

Both women had the soratami's exquisite white skin. They wore their hair in a tightly wound pile that was somehow unruly and severe at the same time. Their long ears were each wrapped tightly around their heads.

On the left sat Uyo, the silent prophet. Most soratami were androgynous, and Uyo was no exception, though her features were especially fine. She never physically spoke, but Uyo's voice carried more authority than any other single soratami in the entire world. She was the high priestess of a powerful cult who had honed the power of their minds. Uyo herself had the unique ability to see into the future, though her visions were difficult to interpret. Mochi and Uyo had been a great help to one another, he assisting her with interpreting her visions, and she providing him with advance information that only a prophet could know.

On the right sat Chiyo, one of Uyo's most talented students. She had also had especially elegant features, but lately she had taken to wearing a large, metallic mask of the crescent moon that completely hid half of her face. The upper point of the crescent hung high above her forehead while the lower jutted out below her chin. The edge of the curve descended across her face to cover one eye, her nose, and half her mouth. There was no opening for her to see or breathe through, but the surface of the moon-mask was covered in glittering, incandescent dust that wafted around her head like a halo.

The visible half of Chiyo's face still displayed her strong features, but the muscles were tight and her expression dour. She had barely survived the oni's initial assault on Oboro and would have been killed if not for the city's defenders. She never shared the details of what happened to her, but Mochi knew. Out of respect for her years of dedicated service, he had never openly questioned her account of being badly mauled by an oni. It was technically true, after all, but not entirely true. Still, whatever the cause, she now believed herself disfigured and had adopted the crescent mask to both soothe her pride and honor her kami.

Chiyo had always been one of the fiercest soratami, intimidating even the most seasoned warriors, but the mask made her even more daunting. Mochi intended to give her a city of her own to rule once the soratami nation was established, and he expected her to become as powerful as a queen before she was half Uyo's age.

Greetings, my children. Mochi always hailed Uyo and her followers mind-to-mind, as a sign of his personal favor and to keep their discussions private.

Greetings, Mochi-sama. Unlike her pale and stoic exterior, Uyo's inner voice was rich and throaty, alive with intellectual force and just a hint of carnal possibilities. *How goes the war?*

Splendidly, thank you. Though I see you have something even more relevant to share.

Uyo turned to her student. Chiyo's visible eye was a cold, cruel blue and her inner voice was seething and bitter.

He has come, Chiyo sent. *Toshi Umezawa.*

The ochimusha, here? I applaud his energy, if not his judgement. Has he . . . ?

He has. The Taken One is nearby.

Well, this is an interesting development. What do you propose to do?

Chiyo turned away angrily. Uyo's throaty voice smoothly broke in and she said, *Chiyo has some definite ideas on that. Suffice to say she wants to kill him with all available speed. She has already asked for a squad of shinobi and bushi to accompany her, but she is ready to go alone if you so wish it.*

I do not. Mochi's cheeks bunched up as he grinned. *This is a matter of some concern, but nothing that demands such drastic action. I have a better plan in mind for our friend.*

Uyo nodded. *You see, my student? Mochi-sama always has a better plan.*

Chiyo's eye narrowed. *Then I ask to be a part of that plan.*

The little blue kami folded his hands over his belly and rose into the air. His voice was playful. *You are, my dear. Intimately and necessarily, you already are.*

CHAPTER 13

Toshi slipped into the wilds of East Jukai unnoticed. He was intent on staying unseen and undisturbed until he had time to recover after his ordeal in Minamo and his flight from Konda. The journey from the waterfall to the woods took all night and most of the morning, but in the breaking dawn he was able to find a hidden glen that could conceal him and the moth.

After landing and tethering the moth, Toshi carved a series of protective kanji on the trees leading to his bivouac. His ribs burned with every breath and he had trouble raising his stiff arms, so the symbols were rough. They would alert him if anyone came too close, however, and that was all he really needed right now.

When he felt safe, Toshi dined on borrowed soldier's rations and sat with his back against a century cedar. Fatigue forced his eyelids down, but he struggled to stay alert. He found it difficult to take his eyes off the stone disk for fear of missing it move again. Part of him wanted to hear more of what the Taken One had to say, and the rest of him was just plain scared of it. It had finally stopped glowing and steaming after it called out to him, but that did nothing to boost his spirits. For all he knew, that just meant it was saving its strength to break free. No wonder the daimyo went mad after spending twenty years with it.

He imagined Konda sitting in his tower alone with the stone disk, endlessly staring as he waited for it to speak or move again. How long, Toshi thought, before my eyes start drifting out of my head like the daimyo's? There were times when it seemed about to come to life, but they only came when the Taken One was in the corner of Toshi's eye. If he looked at it directly, it remained inanimate, a lifeless chunk of shaped stone.

Gingerly, Toshi tested his ribs. His kanji magic was extremely limited when it came to healing, but he carried enough medicinal herbs and magical charms to speed his recovery. He couldn't cure himself in a single stroke as he had with the oni dog's venom, but he could encourage the bones to knit more quickly.

His eyelids fluttered and his head fell back. Though he hit hard enough to crack the bark, he barely noticed the blow. The major downside of his healing treatment was that it demanded long, uninterrupted hours of sleep to be effective. As his face lolled forward and consciousness faded, Toshi still fought to stay alert. He had too many enemies and too important a burden to let his guard down.

I will stay awake, Toshi thought, even as his eyelids closed and he proved himself a liar.

* * * * *

Toshi awoke on a barren field of gray stone. A strong, gritty wind kept his eyes nearly shut. He shielded his face and looked around, still groggy from the healing medicine.

He was no longer in Jukai. There was nothing on the plain of rock except him—no moth, no Taken One, no forest glen. Toshi turned a full circle and saw only an endless stretch of dull granite.

"Hey," he called. The world vanished into the cold dry air, barely even echoing off the flat stony ground.

There was no reply except a stinging gust of wind-driven rock particles. He had seen a great many bizarre and terrible things, so now his mind ran wild with potential explanations for what had happened to him.

Night's Reach might have brought him here for one of their rare face-to-face conversations, or to give him a new task now that he had possession of the Taken One. But that wasn't likely, because Night's honden was a gleaming platform of white against an endless black void. This place didn't look or feel familiar.

Konda or O-Kagachi might have imprisoned him by some spell or artifice so that Toshi couldn't keep running with the Taken One. Both of them would like nothing more than for the stone disk to stay in one place long enough for them to claim it. But Konda's army did not usually rely on spells in battle, and O-Kagachi seemed far too vast and alien to bother with anything less than broad strokes. It was more likely to flatten the entire forest into toothpicks than to pin down one ochimusha at the center of it.

Or, the Taken One itself might have switched places with him, so that it was loose in Kamigawa and he was trapped in the stone disk. No immediate counterargument presented itself. In fact, if he put himself in the stolen kami's place, he could easily see how it might leap at the first chance it had to escape. Assuming its earlier warm words were only a ruse, being swapped was looking like the most likely explanation. Even if it did think it owed him for taking it away from Konda, being kidnapped and held immobile for twenty years would make any entity irrational.

"Uh," he said, "Taken One? Spirit in the stone disk? Have you brought me here?" Toshi spun around, trying to see in all directions. "Where is here, anyway?"

The wind rose. Over the rustling howl in his ears, Toshi heard a cold, callow voice say, "You are where you should be. You have died, Toshi Umezawa, and all that remains is to determine which hell claims your soul."

Toshi blinked. "I don't feel dead. But then again, I wouldn't know."

The voice seemed thrown, but it soon spoke again with the same eerie authority. "This place asks the same question of all who pass through it. Your answer will determine your status in the next world. Are you ready?"

"No," Toshi said. "Absolutely not."

"Nonetheless, I must ask." The disembodied voice paused, then said, "What have you done to deserve your reward?"

Toshi kept shuffling his feet, turning in tight circles as he scanned the horizon. "How long can I think about it?"

"Do not toy with this place. Your answer, now."

"But I don't understand the question."

After a pause, Toshi guessed the voice would not be drawn into further debate. He sighed and said, "Okay. I have tried to lead a virtuous life. I paid my debts on time. I honored the promises I made, each to the letter. I avoided material pleasures . . . well, I didn't take more than my share of material pleasures. Actually, let's move on from material pleasures. In general," he said with a flourish, "I meant well."

"And you have nothing to recant? Nothing to regret or set to rights?"

"Nope," Toshi said. "I mean, obviously, mistakes were made. But in all, I'm quite satisfied with me."

"You are a liar," the voice said calmly. "You are a thief and a thug. You have committed violence for monetary gain and for its own sake. You have blasphemed the spirits and broken the laws of man. I name you villain, outlaw, oath-breaker, and murderer."

Toshi pursed his lips. "Is that you, mom? I wondered where you ended up."

"Silence. Look upon the victims of your crimes and laugh, if you can."

The wind swirled and became visible, white streams of force curling and breaking like a wave. A blinding glare filled Toshi's view of the barren world, and when it faded, a long line of people stood before him.

Boss Uramon was the first, with her sallow eyes and motionless face. "You swore to serve me," she said. "Instead, you betrayed me. You broke your oath to my reckoners. You abandoned your comrades in arms and cowardly refused to fight. You stole the power of the Shadow Gate from me. And when you were done, you killed me and scores of my loyal servants."

"I didn't kill you," Toshi said. "Kiku did."

A sneer flickered across Uramon's lip as the boss walked past Toshi and vanished in the wind.

Godo was next. Though Toshi had never met the *sanzoku* bandit king, it was no challenge to recognize him. Godo was huge and brawny, almost seven feet tall and powerfully built. He carried a massive spiked log on a chain.

"You cursed me with the yuki-onna," Godo said. Sweat steamed from his bald head. Though he spoke angrily, his face was solemn. "You offered her as a weapon against Konda, but you knew she would turn and consume my people as well. Hundreds have died in the cold, thanks to you."

"I underestimated her influence," Toshi admitted. "But it's my problem, too. I'm the one who took her power upon himself. Besides, I only gave the kanji to Hidetsugu. The o-bakemono convinced you to break it and let her out in your territory."

Godo spat on the cold dry rocks and stormed past Toshi.

A young man in Minamo robes came forward. He had spiked, snow-white hair, and his eyes burned with hatred as he glared at Toshi.

"You killed me," Choryu said. "You sent me to the ogre so that he would torture me. After weeks of indescribable agony, you returned and murdered me as an afterthought."

Toshi looked unflinchingly into Choryu's eyes. "And?"

The white-haired wizard continued to glare until Toshi waved him off with an impatient flutter of fingers. Choryu shuffled forward and disappeared.

The next figure was small, dark, and covered in coarse hair. For the first time Toshi felt his throat close and an uncomfortable feeling rise from his stomach.

Marrow-Gnawer extended his left arm, which ended in a ragged, bleeding stump. The nezumi shook his head sadly. "You used me," he said. "You led me into danger so that you wouldn't have to face it. You admitted me into your gang only to sacrifice me when it came time to fight the ogre. And when you had done that," he waved his bleeding stump again, "it still wasn't enough. You maimed me and murdered me so you wouldn't have to watch me suffer."

"This is a dream," Toshi said. The cold, numbing sensation in his stomach faded as he realized the truth. "None of you actually talked like this. I'm having a nightmare brought on by stress and too much healing magic. Either that, or someone's playing a game with me."

The glare rose again, eclipsing the field of stone and the line of accusers. The cold, disembodied voice said, "You will be back soon, ochimusha. When that time comes, you will be made to answer for your crimes."

"Do me a favor," Toshi shot back. "Stand on one foot while you're waiting."

Then he fell into a blinding storm of white light where the only sound was the rising wind in his ears.

* * * * *

Toshi awoke with a start. Cringing from the pain in his chest, he forced himself to relax and settle back against the tree. His ribs felt better, but they were still far from healed.

Three orochi snakefolk were kneeling around him in a semi-circle. Beyond them, more snakes explored his hidden campsite, their long tongues flicking in and out. It was hard to get an exact count from where he sat, but Toshi calculated there were at least eight.

Toshi held very still. His previous experience with the orochi had taught him that they were much faster than he was . . . physically, anyway. If he went for his jitte there were a dozen ways they could stop him before it ever cleared the sheath.

Up close, he could see his reflection in the orochi's gleaming red eyes. Unlike Hidetsugu's, which glowed like hot coals, the snakes' eyes were a dusty crimson, like drops of blood that hadn't fully congealed. They shined like glossy, polished stones.

"Who are you?" The snake closest to him leaned forward, tasting the air in front of Toshi's face. His voice was soft and sinister. "Why are you here?" He pointed back at the stone disk with his long, spearlike arm. "And what is that?"

"That," Toshi said, "is the curse of Eiganjo. A great and terrible spirit beast seeks it and will destroy anything that gets in its way. I was sent by the highest authority to take it to the edge of the world and throw it off." He sat forward, and the orochi tensed. "Who's in charge here?"

The orochi who had spoken said, "I am."

"No, not here," Toshi gestured around the glen. "I mean in this region of Jukai."

"This is Kashi-tribe orochi country," the leader said. "Sosuke is our chief."

"I have a message for him. All I want is to fly over his land with my terrible burden. I'm heading east into the unknown lands. All I require is safe passage. I make no demands," he added carefully, "but I must give you this warning: to delay me would mean disaster for us all."

The leader looked at the other two orochi flanking Toshi. The one to his left hissed, "What do you think?"

The leader glanced at Toshi. "I think he's not a soratami," he said. "But he could be one of their agents."

Toshi's temper flared, and for once he spoke with the passion and surety of truth. "I am not a soratami agent. They and their patron kami are my sworn enemies."

"If you say so. But you're coming with us to Sosuke. I would just kill you here and chop that thing up for food." He gestured over his shoulder at the battle moth. "But you're probably more valuable than you seem. I'll let the chief decide."

"Very wise," Toshi said. He fought the urge to fade away. He was recovered enough to do it, but he saw no advantage. "I only ask that you leave my steed and my burden alone. Once Sosuke hears me out, I'm sure he'll want it out of his forest as quickly as I can carry it."

"We owe you nothing, human."

"No, you don't. But if that goes missing in your territory," he pointed to the Taken One, "it becomes your problem. I'd make sure Sosuke understands the risks before you let that happen."

The orochi narrowed his shiny red eyes at Toshi. He craned his long neck back over his own shoulder and said, "You three. Stay here. Keep the big moth tied to that tree and don't let anyone near the disk." He turned back to Toshi. "If you're lying," he said, "we'll break that stone over your moth's back and roast you both over a hot fire."

"Fair enough," Toshi said. "Quickly now, to Sosuke. The longer we delay, the more danger your little patch of woods faces."

The orochi lifted Toshi to his feet with their long, powerful limbs and marched him into the denser woods.

CHAPTER 14

Toshi had been in parts of the eastern woods and he had seen vast stretches of Jukai from the saddle of a battle-moth. As the orochi led him through the thick growth and massive trees of their territory, he realized he hadn't the slightest inkling of how big, vast, and crowded the forest was. From above, the canopy concealed worlds.

It took them the better part of an hour to reach the Kashi-tribe orochi stronghold, though they only traveled a few hundred yards. Toshi tried to pay attention as they walked so that he could find his way back if he had to run, but the trees were too similar and the hills too numerous to keep them all straight. Also, the orochi led him through underground tunnels and through titanic deadfalls that so turned and twisted his sense of direction he was no longer sure which way they were going.

He didn't know he was among the local snakes until they broke cover—their natural camouflage was perfect so long as they didn't move. A native of the swamps, Toshi had an innate distrust of creatures who lived in the clean green. The orochi's suspicious behavior and slender, flexible bodies made him feel especially isolated and vulnerable. There were no forest monks this far east, and

Toshi reckoned he was the only human being in the entire region.

Still, his ribs were healing well despite the forced march. The soratami attacks had given the snakes a reason to capture and interrogate strangers instead of killing them on sight, as the orochi farther west were prone to do. If Sosuke was sharp, Toshi might even be able to get some good information from him regarding the soratami. In exchange, he could tell Sosuke a very interesting tale based on his own experience with the moonfolk.

Toshi began to spot more snakes hidden among the brush. It helped to have so many in plain sight where he could determine their usual sizes, shapes, and colors. He saw fierce snake maidens glaring over their weapons and tiny orochi children slithering silently among the cedar leaves and juniper bushes. Each had four long arms and spindly stork legs that made their movements unsettling and comical no matter whether they walked or slithered.

There didn't seem to be enough orochi to stand against the soratami armada, but the snakes were experts at concealing their true numbers. Could venom and wooden spears stand up against silver blades and soratami magic? Toshi didn't intend to linger long enough to find out for himself, but he still wondered.

To his mild surprise, the scout party led him through this heavy concentration of orochi and onward into the thick woods on the other side. Another hour's hard slog took them to the crest of a stony ridge that was covered in bright green moss. Toshi stepped up to the edge and peered over, gauging the fall to be about twenty feet. Not lethal, but also not a drop he'd take voluntarily.

"How much—" Toshi stopped when he realized all his escorts were gone. They had melted into the forest and left him alone on the ridge.

"So this is the hero who wants to save us all." The voice came from underneath the lip of the crest. Toshi looked closely at the mossy rock and started when a huge green head separated from the larger mass.

"If you are Sosuke and chief of this tribe, then I am the hero you mention. I have come to talk with you."

Sosuke rose like a long stream of smoke, sliding up the rock until he was standing upright beside Toshi. He was taller and broader than most of the other snakes, which meant he was only half as wide as Toshi. His body was lean and powerful, and his muscles rippled under his green-brown scales. He held weapons in three of his hands—a sword, a dagger, and a staff—while the fourth toyed with a carved green amulet around his neck. Sosuke wore a glittering headband that marked him as a tribal chief, but it was much simpler than the other ceremonial gear Toshi had seen important orochi wear.

"I am Sosuke, war-chief of the Kashi-tribe orochi." He pointed at Toshi with his free hand. "What are you doing in Jukai?"

"Passing through," Toshi said. Since he'd had trouble with orochi and their myojin in the past, he decided not to mention his name. "I am no friend to the soratami and I wish you well in your struggle against them. But I carry a terrible cursed totem that has poisoned my homeland and I do not want to see its bad luck take root here. All I ask is to be left alone to rest and feed my steed before I go on my way. One day is all I need."

Sosuke shook his head. "We are at war, stranger. I will not let random humans wander freely through our land."

"Not through," Toshi said. "Over. My steed is a moth, and we have flown all the way from Kamitaki Falls without ever touching the forest floor."

"Until now."

"Until now. And by your leave, once I get back in the saddle, we won't come down again until we're beyond the eastern border of the forest."

Sosuke laughed a cruel, hissing snort. "You say that with such certainty, but even I don't know where the forest ends."

"Nevertheless, I intend to find it. If you like, I will return some-day and tell you what I saw there."

"You presume too much. You won't leave this ridge alive, much less reach the eastern edge of the woods."

"That is your choice, war-chief. I am alone and woefully over-matched. But please believe me: I am the only one who can dispose of that terrible stone disk I carry."

"This curse," Sosuke said, "can it be directed?"

"Against the soratami? Perhaps. But it brings danger to anyone nearby. You could direct it, but not precisely enough to harm them without harming yourselves."

"Then you have nothing of interest to me." The orochi bared his fangs in a hard smile. "But you have my thanks for attempting to save us all from this terrible curse. Perhaps I will strap your body to the disk before I launch it at the soratami."

"Sosuke," Toshi said sternly, "I do not take my duty lightly. Kill me if you must, but do so with respect." He thought that might appeal to the pragmatic warrior without overtly fawning. Anything that turned the discussion away from Toshi's dead body was a good thing.

The war-chief measured Toshi with his hypnotic red eyes. Unmoved by Toshi's false righteous anger, he simply said, "Done." Sosuke turned his long neck and hissed over the edge of the crest. In response, a half-dozen orochi warriors crawled over the lip of rock and moved to surround Toshi.

The ochimusha smiled confidently. "Well done, war-chief. I would have been disappointed if your favor could be had for the asking."

Sosuke held up his free hand, stopping the orochi closing in on Toshi. "You have something else to offer?"

"I do. The soratami have invaded your territory by now, have they not? If you name the spot, I can help you destroy them in large numbers. Your warriors won't even have to fight."

"But we want to fight. I was born to lead my brothers into battle, and we all want to feel their pale skin pop under our fangs and taste their blood."

"Who doesn't? But you have not seen the full strength of the invading armada. I have. Unless you want soratami warriors on your doorstep for the next ten years, you need to do something drastic. Something that will wipe out a large portion of their army and discourage the rest from ever coming this far east again."

Sosuke thumped his staff into the mossy rock and spread all four of his arms wide. "You make sense, stranger. But if I have not seen the full might of the soratami, you have not seen the full might of the Kashi-tribe orochi. We have the power of Life's Web behind us, the most powerful myojin of all. Even now my sister gathers and focuses the power of the forest against the invaders."

Toshi could have mentioned that he himself had bested Life's Web with the help of his own myojin, so the forest spirit wasn't as powerful as Sosuke claimed. Instead, he decided it was time for him to leave. He cleared his mind and prepared to fade away, but a signal cry from the north caused him to pause.

More precisely, Sosuke's reaction to the signal cry caused Toshi to pause. The war-chief's color changed from mottled green to bold, almost angry emerald. His red eyes widened and his flickering tongue tripled its pace. "You will see now, stranger, one way or the other. The soratami have come." He stretched his neck as high as it would go and tasted the air to the north. "Bring him," he said to the snakes surrounding Toshi. "Let him see how we fight. If he tries to run or warn the enemy, kill him where he stands."

Strong, sinewy hands clamped around Toshi's arms and hands. They propelled him along the ridge past Sosuke. Toshi did not resist, but he twisted his neck and called, "Listen to me, war-chief of the Kashi-tribe orochi. In a matter of days, a new threat will come from the sky. If you want to cripple the moonfolk armada, launch the stone disk as you said you would. Drop it into the heart of the soratami command. Then run for your life and don't look back."

Sosuke did not reply, but he nodded grimly as Toshi was man-handled away. Apparently he had meant it when he agreed to treat Toshi with respect. Then the war-chief turned and slithered over the edge of the crest.

The orochi half-shoved, half-carried Toshi along the ridge, their twisting path confusing him and disorienting him once more. The ache in his chest was almost completely gone now, so he could fade away or travel by shadow whenever he took the notion. He let them carry him because they were going farther from the Taken One, and while he could return to the glen in a matter of seconds, they would have to spend an hour or more retracing their steps. He knew he needed time to subdue the sentries they had left behind before taking to the air again.

Without resistance or complaint, Toshi let the orochi lead him to another tall ridge overlooking a wide green valley. Bright sunlight shone through an opening in the canopy to illuminate the valley. Through this opening Toshi saw the first soratami cloud vessels. They descended with clear purpose, aiming right for the space and the valley below.

The orochi struck as the first cloud broke through the canopy. There must have been something solid beneath all that thick white mist, because half a dozen snakes sprang from the cedars and latched on. The cloud vessel tilted crazily as it came to the ground and landed with an ear-bruising crash.

Scores of orochi swarmed from their hiding places and covered the cloud chariot. The dozen or so soratami struggled to get their swords clear of their scabbards and grappled with the long-armed snakes, but the sheer weight of their numbers crushed them beneath a squirming mass of scaled bodies.

Two more cloud chariots burst through the canopy, widening the hole. The soratami in these vessels were ready for the snakes, and as the orochi once more attempted to board and upset the cloud in flight, blue-steel swords flashed in the dazzling sun. The orochi boarders fell in pieces to the forest floor. The second wave of soratami landed safely and streamed out across the valley.

It some ways, this battle was the opposite of the one Toshi had seen in Oboro. Here, the snakes outnumbered the soratami, but it was the moonfolk who quickly gained the upper hand. The two sides seemed evenly matched in terms of strength and fighting spirit, but the soratami were far more lethal with their exquisite weapons than the snakes were with fang and claw. For every soratami that fell to caustic venom or a crushing embrace, an orochi lost an arm, a leg, or even a head. In these close quarters, the soratami worked more effectively as a unit instead of a collection of individuals—Toshi counted over a dozen pairs of moonfolk fighting back-to-back, as they cut orochi to pieces with weapons in both hands. All the while, more soratami kept coming down into the valley to further tilt the odds in their favor.

If this was what Sosuke had dragged him to see, Toshi would have to reconsider his good opinion of the Kashi war-chief. His warriors fought bravely, but they were up against a foe that was as strong, determined, and fierce as they were, but much better trained and equipped for this sort of conflict.

Then Toshi saw Sosuke halfway up the trunk of a massive cedar tree. The war-chief was accompanied by a smaller female orochi who had the similar features and coloring. Was this the sister he'd mentioned?

The female orochi folded two of her arms in meditative prayer, clinging to the tree with the rest of her limbs. Other snakes perched in the trees echoed her rasping hiss, and a swirling tendril of green fog formed between them, linking the trees fifty feet up.

The bark on the tree occupied by Sosuke and his sister shifted and rolled, reforming into a smooth brown mask of a human face. Toshi recognized the Myojin of Life's Web before the powerful spirit completely manifested, and he faded away before she could in turn spot him. The last time he'd seen that wooden mask he had laughed merrily as he drove the myojin back to the spirit world. She was sure to remember something like that and still probably held a grudge.

The orochi guards hissed angrily as their charge slipped through their grasp. They shouted at each other, each demanding to know what the others had seen. Still standing in the same spot, Toshi watched unnoticed as they spread out and began searching the surrounding woods with their heads stretched low and their tongues flicking the ground.

There were plenty of shadows for Toshi to use on the ridge, but he stayed just to see the orochi's gambit play out. He expected a wall of brambles or poisonous thorns to erupt beneath the soratami's feet, or for Sosuke and other key warriors to acquire the strength of giants.

Instead, the line of green fog thickened and became solid. It glowed faintly as it twisted itself into a burly braid of thick, green, woodlike material. A ripple of energy traveled along the braid's surface and it tightened, drawing the giant cedars closer together. As the green, swirling band solidified, it took on the appearance of a huge, burly green dragon. The snakes all hissed the same name, "Jugan," and Toshi dimly recalled it as the name of Jukai's other powerful guardian spirit.

Sosuke lunged, plucking his sister from the tree trunk and folding her up in two powerful arms. He slithered headfirst down the tree, traveling far faster than if he'd simply jumped. When his tongue touched the soil he sprang off the tree and cut through the underbrush, away from the valley.

The dragon Jugan continued to swirl around the trees, encircling them in a green ring of energy and force. The linked cedars groaned again as the magical bond tightened. Trapped in the ring of trees, soratami and orochi both stopped fighting and cast worried eyes upward. On the largest and thickest trunk, the face of Life's Web mouthed a series of silent words. In response, Jugan roared and began to move faster. The massive ring of cedars shuddered, and Toshi heard a deafening crack.

Bending at the center as if jointed, the trees all seemed to bow toward the center of the ring. Together, they formed an organic enclosure, a huge drum-shaped cell with dirt floors, cedar-trunk walls, and a solid ceiling of leafy green boughs. Muted hissing and screams came from within the closed drum, but nothing else escaped from the unbroken wall of living lumber.

All the bark on the exterior of the drum shifted and reshaped itself, forming a gargantuan mask for Life's Web. The myojin's face did not move, but her hollow eyes and mouth were wide open as she stared through the canopy into the sunlit sky. Then, the great enclosure contracted, sending shock waves rippling across the valley floor and almost shaking Toshi's ridge to pieces. Safe in his phantom form, Toshi stepped back from the edge but still kept his eyes locked on the spectacle below.

With Jugan circling ever faster around it, the enclosure collapsed in on itself like some great clenching fist. The noise of breaking wood drowned out any sounds from within the drum, which Toshi took as something of a blessing. His dreams had been troubling enough without more dying wails to haunt them. When it was half its original size, the cedar cell started to sink into the hard-packed forest floor. The ground broke and tumbled into an ever-deepening pit forming beneath the cell. Trees on the edge of the valley toppled into the pit as well, their roots robbed of their foundations.

Toshi watched the incredible display until the top of the cell was only a few feet higher than the rim of the pit. He didn't know if anyone was still alive inside, or how far down they'd burrow, but it was safe to say that these soratami would not make war on Jukai again.

Toshi shook his head. He was no soldier and he had never gone to war, but even he knew you didn't defeat an army by killing half your own in the process. If the snakes could harness the power of Jukai and make the land itself fight for them, they had a chance. Otherwise, the soratami would surely scour them away in a matter of weeks.

Without looking back, Toshi stepped forward into the shadow of a cedar sapling as the green dragon roared and the valley continued to swallow itself.

CHAPTER 15

Toshi emerged from a dark patch beneath an overhanging rock. He arrived at the edge of the glen near the moth, who was still securely tethered and happily slurping its food bricks. There was no sign of the orochi sentries who had stayed behind. Toshi didn't wonder too deeply about their disappearance—it was enough for him that they were gone.

He circled the largest tree to where he had left the Taken One. The stone disk hadn't moved, but something about the scene made Toshi uneasy. The image on the disk was static, and he didn't feel the gathering pressure of an impending kami attack, but the air around the Taken One felt different. All of Toshi's exposed skin tingled.

The ochimusha crouched beside the tree and peered at the clearing around the stone disk. All looked normal, except for three piles of what appeared to be white sand. Maybe salt, Toshi thought.

Fine white dust swirled off each pile as a soft wind blew through the clearing. Toshi stood to his full height and paced around the stone disk. Three piles, three orochi sentries. The mounds of white grit were positioned fairly evenly around the Taken One. If three able-bodied warriors were attempting to lift something of this size, they could easily have taken these positions.

"Hey," Toshi said carefully to the disk. "They touched you, didn't they?"

The fetal serpent remained motionless and the only sound was of wind playing in the dust.

"Look," Toshi said. "I've got to move you, and I've got to do it quickly. With . . . " He paused, almost overwhelmed by the absurdity of what he was about to say. " . . . with your permission, I will carry you to the moth so he can carry us away."

Toshi felt even more foolish when the disk didn't respond in any meaningful way. Had he dreamed that, too?

He screwed up his courage and placed his hands on the Taken One. It felt just like ordinary stone. Pushing his questions aside, Toshi willed himself insubstantial and took the stone disk with him. Less than a minute later he had maneuvered it onto the moth's back. The great insect sagged as the stone disk regained its mass, but it held the burden long enough for Toshi to lash it into the harness.

They wouldn't have to go far. The orochi would have their plates full with invading soratami, so he only needed to leave the immediate area. Between the invaders, the myojin, and the guardian dragon, there were far more important things to do than hunt down a mysterious stranger.

Toshi figured he needed only a few more hours of rest before his ribs would be fully healed. He had slept more than enough the previous night. Right now he just wanted one medium-long period of not running for his life, if the spirits would allow such a thing. Then he'd be ready to look into the visions and voices he'd been experiencing.

The great moth beat its wings and carried Toshi into the midday sky. Jukai was indeed impressive, but there were far too many plants for his liking. Too much dirt and not enough taverns. His mind began to wander as the cedar canopy rolled by beneath him, and he wondered why he had come this far east in the first place. The chances of finding Mochi were slim, and luring O-Kagachi and Mochi to the same place was even more unlikely. The best he could hope for was to re-create the confusion at Minamo and hope that either O-Kagachi or the daimyo took their toll on the moonfolk raiders.

A surge of fatigue ran through him, and Toshi's shoulders sagged. Everything had changed when the Taken One spoke. Toting the inert disk around was one thing, but if it were going to make demands and desiccate orochi all willy-nilly he'd have to make a new plan. He didn't have what it took to deal with matters of this magnitude on a regular basis. The sooner he could consult someone with a better brain and a nobler heart than his, the better.

Suddenly morose and sullen, Toshi urged the moth lower and redoubled his efforts to find a suitable spot.

* * * * *

Once more, Toshi awoke on a barren field of gray stone.

"Muck and mire," he spat. He shielded his eyes against the glare and the wind-driven grit. "Haven't we been through this?" he called. His mind seemed sharper in this dream than it had last time. He didn't recall landing the moth or falling asleep. Wasn't it still the middle of the day?

Without preamble, a line of three burly figures appeared,

marching toward Toshi through the haze. They were indistinct phantoms in the glare, but they were all significantly larger than Toshi. Perhaps he'd be pilloried now by bigger-than-life versions of the instructors, tutors, and constables he'd offended as a boy.

Annoyed, he folded his arms and waited. This must be some sort of side effect of the healing magic he used, or his proximity to the Taken One, or a combination of both. He was quite used to being accused of horrible crimes while awake, but it was beyond the pale to endure it while he slept.

Toshi's pique withered as Kobo emerged from the glare. The huge bald youth was as scarred and gnarled as he'd been in life, his crooked nose almost smeared across his face.

"Oath-brother," he said, "you left me to die. You let me take all the risk, stood back and let me do all the fighting. While I was being murdered, you didn't even bother to wake up."

"I didn't—" Toshi stammered. "That . . . that isn't the way it happened."

Kobo bowed respectfully and strode past Toshi. Impulsively, the ochimusha reached out, but his hand passed through the ogre's apprentice.

"Well, my friend," said a familiar voice behind him. "Where to begin?"

Hidetsugu swelled to his full size as Toshi turned to face him. He towered over Toshi and smiled, his eyes empty, hissing holes.

"I'm sorry," Toshi said, cutting the ogre off before his first word. "But you were always too big, too powerful, and too smart. You scared me. I knew that if I wasn't one step ahead of you, you'd find some way to punish me."

"And you were right." The o-bakemono smiled. "In the end, you could never have beaten me. But you're here, and I'm gone.

How did that happen?" Without waiting for a reply, Hidetsugu snorted derisively and trod past Toshi. The stone plain shook beneath his heavy feet.

"I'm sorry," Toshi called again, but the words felt slimy and bitter in his mouth. Was Toshi truly hearing his own voice? Was it him saying these words?

Sick and dizzy, Toshi stumbled and fell to his knees. Something was wrong, terribly wrong. He should not be feeling like this.

The final figure came into focus through the glare. It was Godo the bandit king once more. This time he was pale, drawn, and shivering, but his chestnut eyes still burned with fury.

Toshi's throat hitched. "I'm sorry," he said again. He felt like he was watching a terrible actor perform his innermost thoughts and getting most of the words wrong.

Godo nodded and leaned down to whisper in Toshi's ear.

"It's not too late," he said. "You can undo what you did."

The bandit king pulled back. Toshi's eyelids fluttered and he swayed on his knees.

"What?" he managed. "Undo?"

"I'm not dead yet," the figure of Godo said. "But I am very close to crossing over. You can help me. You can make it right. You don't have to come back here, Toshi. You don't have to listen to us forever."

"How?" Toshi said. "What can I do?"

Godo dropped to his knees and seized Toshi by the shoulders. "Return to the mountains," the bandit king said. "Capture what you have unleashed. Cage the beast and you will be one step farther away from this." Godo raised his eyes and spread his hands. Then he stood, placed a palm on Toshi's shoulder, and walked into oblivion.

A sharp, cold spasm creased through Toshi's guts. He doubled over in pain. As he sat and waited for his muscles to unknot, two tears splattered on the gray stone.

"Enough," he said. He inhaled slowly, gently expanding his chest. "Enough."

* * * * *

Toshi awoke on the forest floor, grappling with a pile of cedar needles. His face was wet and his stomach ached.

He staggered to his feet, confused to the point of panic. The sky was dark. He was in a wide gully between two hills. The moth sat nearby, its tether trailing in the evening breeze and the Taken One still lashed to its back. However and whenever he had gotten here, Toshi had made no attempt to conceal himself or his cargo.

Wooden and unfocused, Toshi stumbled forward. He drew his jitte and started scratching symbols in the dirt. His hand shook and his eyesight was blurry, so he didn't even know if the symbols he drew were the symbols he intended.

Angrily, he scratched out the abortive kanji with his jitte and struggled back to a standing position. His wild eyes darted around the gully until he found a low-hanging branch with a fat shadow beneath it.

Without hesitation, Toshi went toward the branch and slipped into the shadows like he was diving into a bottomless black pool.

* * * * *

Aboard the soratami flagship, Mochi held another audience with Uyo and Chiyo.

The war ebbs and flows, he said. *The orochi are doomed. It will take time, but we have plenty of time. But now, I wish to hear better news, stories of more measurable progress.*

Uyo smiled enigmatically. *I am delighted to accommodate you, Mochi-sama. We have been making the most splendid progress in that other matter you mentioned.*

Mochi beamed and rose into the air. As he began to rotate, he said, *Tell me all.*

Though untrained, his mind protects itself remarkably well. If not for this so-called hyozan reckoner gang, we might never have found purchase.

Go on.

The charge of "oath-breaker" stung him the most. The images of his oath-brothers shook even his composure. Once we found this chink in his armor, he was ours.

Outstanding. Your abilities continue to amaze even me. Mochi interrupted his rotation and spun to face Uyo directly. *Where is he now?*

On the wings of Night's Reach, bound for the Sokenzan hinterlands.

And the prize?

Abandoned. Left behind. He was not in possession of all his faculties when he left on this latest journey.

Excellent. You see, Chiyo? Even a most despised foe can prove useful. Toshi has done us an immeasurable favor. All we need do now is herd the orochi into the general area of the Taken One. Anywhere nearby is fine . . . O-Kagachi will pulverize huge tracts of the forest when it comes for its offspring. We simply have to prepare to disengage and withdraw quickly so that the serpent doesn't also pulverize us.

The soratami in the crescent mask turned angrily away from her mentors.

Ahh, I've offended you, my dear. Forgive me. Was it my playful tone? Or were you appalled by the inappropriate parental metaphor?

Master, Chiyo said, *Umezawa still lives. We have not punished him, only banished him. Do not leave his death to chance. Godo will not recognize Toshi as his enemy. And Toshi has escaped the yuki-onna before. We cannot rely on them alone.*

Mochi began to spin slowly once more, his eyes merry. *My dear,* he said, *whatever made you think we would?*

* * * * *

Toshi stood on a crest of rock at the foothills of the Sokenzan Mountains. It was cold in this barren, dreary place, but the chill of winter that cut through his clothes had as much to do with magic as it did with the season.

Icy wind whipped his sleeves against his wrists. The cold stung, but it did nothing to beat back the numb, haunted feeling that oppressed him.

The jagged rocks below him were littered with bodies. He had seen far too many corpses lately, from the carmine remains of the Numai jushi to the bleached bones at Minamo.

This killing ground was thick with the frozen bodies of Eiganjo soldiers and Sokenzan bandits. Each was fully dressed in cold-weather gear, but each was frozen solid, their faces twisted into masks of terror. Some were literally encased in sheaths of hard, transparent ice. One such display featured two of Konda's soldiers locked in a desperate embrace to stave off death.

The wind carried Toshi's breath from his chapped lips in wisps of snowy white. This was his doing, his and the snow-woman's. Toshi had hijacked her lethal cold and turned it to his own ends. He had also trapped her essence within a clay tablet that came down from her home in the Tendo Peaks and brought it here, to the northern border of bandit territory. As far as Toshi knew, Godo himself had broken the tablet, and soon afterward the curse of the yuki-onna had taken root, making this stretch of frozen rock her new hunting grounds.

How many had she killed since then? How many lives ended in bitter cold and crippling terror? Two score? A hundred? Two hundred? All victims of Toshi's careless pursuit of power.

The ochimusha continued to stare at the frozen corpses. He cupped his hands and blew on them, the momentary blast of warmth bringing sensation back to his fingers.

"You'll need more than a puff of hot air to survive this night."

Toshi recognized the voice from his dreams. Trembling, he slowly turned and saw Godo the bandit king in the flesh for the first time.

Godo was drawn and weary, as he had been in the second dream. He was still large enough to crush Toshi just by sitting down, and he led a massive mountain yak easily with one hand. The yak bore Godo's gigantic spiked club strapped to its side.

Godo wore heavy wool wraps over his bandit armor. His skin was pallid, gray and unhealthy, but his eyes were strong and alert. He stretched out his arm and offered a woven blanket to Toshi.

"Take this," the bandit said. "I can see you're not one of Konda's, so I hope you survive the night. You've picked a strange place to visit, my friend, and a terrible time. If you've got the strength, you should move on. Sleep somewhere else tonight, as far away as you can get."

Toshi mechanically took the blanket and tossed it over one shoulder. "Thank you," he muttered. "Much better."

Godo turned, and Toshi blurted, "Why do you stay?"

The bandit chieftain stopped trying to maneuver the yak with its turn half-completed.

"I mean," Toshi said, "if it's so dangerous."

Godo glanced back at Toshi sideways. "You don't know where you are, do you? Or who I am?"

"Pretend I don't."

"I'm in charge here," Godo said. "And Daimyo Konda's got a full division just over that ridge." He pointed to the north. "If someone doesn't stay here to keep him out, Konda will roll into the Sokenzan like he rolled into every other place. We are free people, friend. I decided a long time ago I would rather die than live under Eiganjo's rule."

Toshi nodded, his eyes distant. "I suppose it would help if you didn't have this to deal with as well." Toshi gestured to the field of icy bodies below.

Godo's eyes sharpened. He looked Toshi over and said quietly, "What do you know about dealing with this? Do you know the o-bakemono? Hidetsugu?"

"No," Toshi shook his head. "But I've heard the stories. I didn't start my journey completely uninformed." He smiled thinly. "Just incredibly uninformed."

Godo returned the pale grin. "The ogre said a kanji mage had made this happen. He also said that mage would return to reverse what he'd done."

Toshi adjusted his blanket. "What would you say to that mage if you met him?"

"Do your job," Godo said instantly. "Clean up your mess so I can go back to protecting my people from the daimyo, not some curse that belongs up in the peaks."

Toshi nodded. He turned his face into the wind. Nearby, Godo shrugged and led his yak back down the path.

Toshi felt the weight bearing down on him again. He felt bloated and diffuse. The tears were lurking in his throat, just waiting for the chance to escape through his eyes.

"If I ever see him," he said, "I'll be sure to pass that along."

CHAPTER 16

The Heart of Frost stood among the dramatic Tendo Peaks, a day's hike from where Toshi met Godo. Like all the Sokenzan Range, the Tendo's most infamous mountain was a tall, narrow spire of rock that connected the drab soil with the clouds above. None of the locals would go more than a few hundred paces up the ragged trail, for the Heart of Frost was cursed by the yuki-onna. No people meant no victims, and in a few decades she became little more than a potent folk tale told on a snowy night.

That was before Toshi came. As he had several weeks before, the ochimusha ascended the base of the Heart of Frost, bound for the clearing the yuki-onna called home. It was there he had performed his ritual, bound the winter spirit, and taken her power for his own. It was there he intended to return, to restore the snow-woman and surrender what he stole.

The morning air was frigid and the trail narrow, but Toshi did not waver. He felt a hollowness in his stomach and a great weight on his back that had nothing to do with the cold or fatigue, but he took some pleasure in the monotony of the hike. Walking in a straight line was about as much as his dulled senses and distracted thoughts could handle.

He made steady progress until about a third of the way up the mountain. There, he found the first of a series of kanji he'd carved along the path several weeks ago. The character was meant to draw the yuki-onna in and keep her away from Toshi long enough for him to complete his preparations farther up the trail.

It had worked spectacularly well—somewhere, the spirits of dead kanji masters were toasting him. No one had ever managed to do what he had done. It was the equivalent of catching a lightning bolt and tying it into a bow. Even in his maudlin state of mind, Toshi took a small shred of pride from the novelty of his achievement. People would talk about it forever if they knew. They might not say nice things about him personally, but they would talk about the grand, terrible thing he'd done.

Pride evaporated when he came within reach of a trail marker carved into the bark of an evergreen. Toshi stared at the symbol for a moment. Then he pulled his jitte and set to excavating all the bark around the symbol, changing a series of lines and curves into a square blank patch of naked wood. When he was through, Toshi scooped up the shavings from the base of the tree and scattered them into the wind.

He repeated the process on the next kanji he found. This second one had been drawn on a smooth rock in his own blood, so Toshi poured some of his water on the rock and scrubbed it with the edge of his hand until the flesh was raw. With the kanji washed away, Toshi washed embedded bits of rock from his flesh and went on up the trail.

He had been very careful about making the marks so it was easy for him to remember where they were. He spent the better part of the day hiking, finding kanji, and obliterating them. Each time he erased a trail marker, he felt some the fog in his brain lift and the heaviness of his limbs ease. He didn't feel right . . . none of this felt right . . . but he did feel better.

It occurred to him that he could have skipped the hiking and just gone directly from kanji to kanji by travelling through shadow. He barely considered the idea before continuing on foot. Something about the effort of walking soothed him almost as much as removing the symbols.

Overhead, the sun had set, and darkness colored the sky. Last time, it had taken him days to reach his destination. Today, he had covered almost all the ground he needed to in a few hours. This was another unexpected benefit of his fuzzy-mindedness: he had no sensation of time passing, no other weariness than what he'd started with. The entire day had blurred into one long, slow moment, from meeting Godo to scratching out the kanji in front of him now.

Toshi shivered under the blanket Godo had given him. It got much colder on the Heart of Frost at night, even without the yuki-onna prowling for victims. Cold enough to kill anyone who didn't take shelter.

Toshi went on to the next kanji. He didn't want to die, but he didn't want to settle in for the night, either. The idea of falling asleep filled him with dread. Better to press on and finish the job while he still had the wits to focus.

Toshi wiped clean another kanji, and then another. The moon rose, peaked, and started to set before he stumbled and fell heavily to the cold, hard ground. Something cracked on his face, and at first he thought he had ice in his hair. A touch-inspection of his face revealed that it was the skin on his forehead that had dried and split. Blood trickled from the split flesh on his face, staining his fingers.

The sight of his own blood brought Toshi closer to consciousness. He hated to see it go to waste. The stuff was even more precious to kanji mages than it was to everyone else, for characters drawn in blood were always the most powerful.

Though his fingers were thick and clumsy, Toshi dragged them across his forehead again until they were smeared with crimson. He forced himself to stand and lumbered toward a rocky overhang that would blunt the cutting wind. For a moment he stood swaying in the quiet alcove. Then, he leaned forward and drew a ragged pair of symbols on the rock face.

The alcove quickly warmed as if he had lit a fire. The sensation returned to his face and hands, stinging as his nerves registered the damage done by the cold. Barely able to stand upright, Toshi wrapped the heavy blanket around him and leaned against the rock. He was asleep before his body finished sliding to the ground.

* * * * *

He dreamed not of the gray granite plain, but of the Heart of Frost. He found himself trudging up the same mountain trail as the same scathing wind tore at him. Now there was definitely ice in his hair, and his eyebrows, and crusted across his lashes.

He had lost track of how many symbols he had eradicated and how many yet remained, but he recognized the section of trail he was on. Over the next rise was the clearing where he had trapped the snow-woman. Almost done, he thought.

Toshi cinched the blanket around his neck and shoulders and proceeded over the rise. The large circular clearing was bounded by a series of sheer cliffs with a narrow opening on the north side that led to the peak of the mountain. Frequent snowfall had covered the floor of the clearing in a light dusting of white, but Toshi knew that the snow concealed a ring of kanji carved into the rock. He ought to know: he had spend hours making it.

He trudged through the ankle-deep snow and wondered why this dream was so different from the others yet so similar to the waking time he had spent on the mountain. He caught his foot on a hidden rock and fell onto his hands and knees. Was this his afterlife, then? An endless trek to erase the things he had done, with nothing to look forward to but an ever-increasing numbness of body and brain?

Toshi dug his hands into the ground and clenched two fistfuls of dirt and snow. No. This would not be his fate. This would end here. He straightened his arms and his back and continued toward the hidden ring of symbols on all fours. It took almost an hour, but as the purple-black sky lightened to cobalt blue on the horizon, he finally reached his goal.

He carefully crawled around the edge of the circle, wiping dusty snow off the kanji until he had exposed the entire ring. Taken together, the symbols laid out a long, clumsily worded sentence that described their purpose and effect. Destroying one of the symbols would break the spell, but he would have to remove them all to completely restore what he had altered.

Something white fluttered in the corner of his eye. Toshi rocked back onto his knees and shielded his eyes from the wind. At the center of the circle stood a tall, female figure in a flowing white robe. Her head was tilted forward so that her long black hair hung down and obscured her features. She stood motionless for a second as the wind whipped her garments, and then she took a single step forward.

Toshi recognized the yuki-onna but he was beyond fear. He didn't feel anything save a wave of resignation, unable even to summon the energy for some clever last words.

The woman in white took another step toward Toshi. He simply sat and stared, his jitte held tight but almost forgotten in his hand. Then, the cold figure straightened and lifted her head, tossing back her silky black mane and revealing her elegant, sharp-boned face.

The yuki-onna's skin was jet-black except for her lips, which were painted a vibrant purple. She scanned Toshi with her glittering black eyes and shook her head in disgust.

"What are you doing, oath-brother? What could you possibly be doing?"

Toshi blinked, sending flakes of ice fluttering down his cheeks. "Kiku?" It was definitely the mahotsukai's face beneath that veil of hair. Confusion pricked the back of Toshi's mind. The yuki-onna often took the form of someone familiar, someone beloved. Did Kiku qualify?

Had the snow-woman ever spoken before? And weren't her eyes supposed to be bottomless black holes without pupils?

Kiku made a dismissive wave. "I am disappointed in you, ochimusha. With all the games you play, I expected you to recognize this for what it is."

"A dream," Toshi croaked. "This is all a dream brought on—"

This is no dream, my acolyte.

Toshi's eyes opened wide. Kiku was gone, and in her place stood a thick black curtain with a bone-white mask at its center.

Look around you, Night's Reach said. *You are not sleeping in a rocky cubbyhole. You are here, on the Heart of Frost, in the very clearing you seek. You have been manipulated here by powerful magic.*

The sight of his myojin and her voice helped Toshi concentrate. "Manipulated," he muttered.

Since you arrived in the forest. Perhaps even before. You are no longer in control of your own mind.

Toshi shuddered. His voice became sharper. "Who is?"

You know, but have forgotten. Or rather, you know, but they will not let you remember.

He tried to stand, but his legs would not hold him. "Help me, then," he said.

I could erase their influence with a thought. But I do not choose to reveal myself to them directly. Not yet.

Irritation seeped into Toshi's tone. "What are you waiting for?"

The right time. Now be still. Gather your thoughts. When you call for my assistance again, I will give it gladly.

The myojin began to fade from view. Toshi raised his hand to stop her, but caught himself before he spoke. His eyes fixed on the jitte still clutched in his fist. Realization hit him and he said, "Those pale-skinned aristo bastards."

Angrily, the ochimusha stood. His limbs were still leaden and unresponsive, but pure, clear hatred had punched through the fog in his mind. He steadied himself and looked down at the exposed kanji at his feet. Then Toshi snarled and fell to his knees once more, hacking at the carved character with his jitte.

Toshi. Night's voice was still strong, though her physical body was gone. *What are you doing now?*

"What I came to do." He barely interrupted his attack on the symbol. Chips of stone flew past his face.

That is what they want you to do, not what you came to do.

Toshi chipped away the last of the symbol so that there was nothing but a shallow indentation in the ground. "It is now."

* * * * *

Back at the Sokenzan border, Godo faced alone the nightmare that was consuming his army one man at a time.

The bandit numbers had dwindled so much that Godo himself was reduced to standing watch on the border. He had been safe for two nights running, but this night his luck ran out. He had sensed this was his last night long before he saw the woman in flowing white robes and the long, concealing veil of hair.

When she came, she came slowly, walking up the ridge toward Godo on his yak like a long-lost friend. The bandit chief fought the urge to run—he was too weary and too stubborn to abandon his post. Visions of Konda's army riding unchallenged across the border were even more hateful to him than his own meaningless death. When he died, they would say he died resisting Konda to the end.

The snow-woman crept closer, now mere yards from Godo. He flexed his cold muscles and took the heavy, spiked log from the yak's back.

"Come on, then." He tried to sound strong and sure, but he had used up the last of his reserves long ago. It was a challenge just to swing the heavy log, especially because he knew it would do no good. You couldn't beat back the cold with weapons of wood and metal.

Just out of arm's reach, the yuki-onna raised her head and tossed back her hair. Godo gasped when he saw the endless black pools of her eyes. He felt a flicker of disappointment in not recognizing the snow-woman's features. Perhaps she was so gorged on his men that she didn't feel the need to appear as someone he loved. Perhaps she had taken on the face of someone dear to him, someone from his distant past that his addled brain couldn't consciously recall.

"Hail to you, curse of the mountain. I am Godo, chief of the Sanzoku bandits. Take me if you can, but promise me this: once I am gone, continue to haunt this place. Claim as many of Eiganjo's men as you can. Make this border a bane to all so that none will try to cross through here ever again."

His speech energized Godo, and he swung the spiked log with the last bit of strength in his powerful frame. The thick weapon plowed into the yuki-onna's side, and for a moment it seemed as if she would be swept aside by it. But the log sailed past her and she still occupied the same space.

The snow-woman stepped within arm's reach of Godo and extended her hand. Summoning all his courage, Godo stared directly into the face of the killing force and waited.

The yuki-onna seemed to wince as if stung. She withdrew her hand and slowly tilted her head back toward the Heart of Frost. Godo fought off a surge of relief as those terrible eyes turned from him.

The dread spirit folded her hands into her sleeves and tilted her head forward. Her face disappeared behind the veil of hair, and as Godo watched, the yuki-onna's entire body slowly disintegrated into a stream of icy crystals borne up by the wind.

The cold, oppressive atmosphere on the ridge immediately warmed and lightened. Godo exhaled and sank to his knees. He giddily noticed that his breath no longer appeared as a thick cloud of white fog.

Exhausted but alive, Godo pulled himself back up by gripping the yak's leather harness. For the first time in weeks he felt a faint stirring of hope. Many of his warriors had died or fled. Konda's army was still waiting just beyond the border. The Kami War still raged across the nation. But the border was secure, and Konda would not come to enslave them this day. However it happened, the yuki-onna had gone just as mysteriously as she had come. And because of that, the Sanzoku bandits would live to fight another day.

Godo swung himself into the saddle and headed down to rally whomever he could find. As he rode off the ridge, the bandit chief leaned low and snared his spiked log, dragging it to him by its long metal chain.

Konda's army could not possibly know how their situation had changed, and Godo was eager to exploit this to his advantage.

CHAPTER 17

Dawn had not quite broken on the Heart of Frost, but the sky was growing lighter by the moment. Hidden in the shadows of the clearing's high walls, Toshi continued to work. He had erased a select set of kanji from the circle, wiping out almost half of the total before the yuki-onna appeared.

The real thing was a far more formidable presence than the illusion Night's Reach employed. The actual snow-woman carried the cold around her like a voluminous robe. Toshi could feel her drawing heat to her from the entire clearing.

"Greetings," Toshi called. He was still on his knees, hacking at the symbols with the tip of his jitte. "I don't know if you have the sort of mind that recognizes people or holds grudges, but we've met before. And I think you have a good reason to hate me."

The yuki-onna stood silently just outside the half-circle of symbols. Slowly, she lifted her head so that the wind carried her long black hair away from her face. There were the features Toshi had seen before, familiar but unknown to him. The bottomless black eyes, the sharp, square chin, the porcelain cheekbones were all as they had been when he had first performed his ritual. Like Godo, he was slightly put off by not recognizing a loved one, but he was especially aggrieved and somewhat relieved that he wasn't again face-to-face with Kiku.

The snow-woman gave no sign of recognition, but she took a menacing step toward Toshi nonetheless. He mouth hung open, but instead of words only the cold, rising wail of the wind passed her lips.

Seemingly unconcerned, Toshi moved on to the next symbol. "I borrowed your power," he said. "But now I'd like to give it back. Not that you missed it. You managed to stay quite busy even without what I took. I think on some level you ought to be grateful. I'll bet you haven't hunted that well in almost a century."

The yuki-onna showed no more signs of gratitude than she had anger. She simply continued to stalk toward Toshi with her arm outstretched, though she had not yet reached the line of kanji.

Toshi paused. "No," he said. "I didn't expect you'd agree." He went back to his labor. "You don't owe me and you don't hate me. You're not much like us at all, are you? All you care about is your role, your job on this mountain. I must say, you do it very well."

He finished breaking one final kanji and sighed. "All done," he said. "You can come get me any time now."

The snow-woman had stopped just shy of the remaining kanji on the ground.

"If you were the kind of creature that recognized faces and held grudges," Toshi said, "you'd be right to be cautious. That's strong magic there. Even with half the words erased, the sentence is powerful enough to affect you."

The woman in white lowered her arm. She took a step back and her wind-wail changed pitch.

"Bother," Toshi said. Well, he thought. There's no value in half-measures.

He stood as quickly as he could and lunged toward the yuki-onna. He imagined that very few of her victims charged her, at least not after she had shown them her true face. Whether through shock or simply because she didn't fear Toshi, the snow-woman made no effort to avoid him.

His hand crossed the line of kanji and clamped onto hers. She felt solid to him, and he hauled her toward him as hard as he could. Pale purple light flashed where their hands met and they both threw their heads back, their mouths open in twin silent screams. The same light glowed from Toshi's forehead, inscribing the character that had given him access to the snow-woman's power. At their feet, the broken line of kanji also shone brightly in the quickening dawn.

Toshi's voice caught up to his mouth and his screams echoed off the clearing walls. With a wrench, he jerked his hand free of the yuki-onna and staggered backward, falling on his seat in the dusty snow.

His arm burned from the intense cold. He cradled it against his chest and massaged it with his free hand. Nearby, the yuki-onna stood with her hand outstretched and one foot planted firmly on a glowing purple kanji in the rock below. She was motionless, her head still tossed back and her mouth open wide.

Toshi glanced up at the rising sun. He didn't have much time. He scrambled to his feet and went as far as he could go from the snow-woman without leaving the kanji circle. Then he settled onto the ground with his legs crossed, placed his tingling hands on his knees, and closed his eyes.

Despite his pounding heart and the danger, Toshi felt relaxed

and comfortable as he allowed himself to drift off. After fighting
sleep for so long, it came quickly when he called it, like an old and
faithful dog.

* * * * *

Toshi tried to feel nothing, to think nothing as he appeared on
the hazy plain of rock. He also ignored the jitte strapped to his hip,
which had not been there the last few times he'd visited this place.
He was an expert at setting traps and drawing the quarry in, so he
knew the most important thing a presumptive victim could do was
let them think they had you.

"I did as you asked," he called. "Why am I here again?"

After a pause, the voice that greeted him when he first came
here spoke. *Liar*, it said. Toshi hadn't noticed before how rich and
throaty the voice sounded. *You have sent the snow-woman back
to her mountain, but you have not relinquished her power. Is this
how you set things right?*

"Yes," Toshi said. "About that. I have a few questions about the
arrangement we've come to. I want a guarantee."

*You are shockingly bold, ochimusha. Your fate in the next
world hangs in the balance, and you still quibble over terms?*

"I just like to make sure I'm getting a fair deal. I mean, if I'm
going to go around making amends, I need to know someone's
keeping score. I'd hate to redeem ninety-nine sins and still be
damned for the hundredth."

*There is no bargain you can strike with destiny, Toshi
Umezawa. Fight it or accept it, but do not seek to modify it.*

"Right there," Toshi said. "That's where we disagree. I'm sure
you know a great deal about life's rewards and punishments, far

more than I do. But I, in turn, know something you do not."

The voice stayed silent, refusing to be drawn any farther into this mad debate.

"I know who you are," Toshi continued. "And I know whom you serve. Look," he said. "See the power of my patron spirit.

"O Night," Toshi intoned. "If you please?"

The pale haze covering the rocky plain darkened from glaring white to dirty gray to thundercloud-black. When Night's voice echoed from the nothingness around him, her voice was strong, almost playful.

I am here, acolyte. What troubles you?

"I'm here on the doorstep of the cold gray hell," Toshi said.

No. You are not.

"Sorry. My mistake. I'm here in my own mind, dreaming a dream that someone else inserted against my will."

Go on.

"As your acolyte, I believe my mind, body, and soul belong to you. It's very presumptuous for someone else to intrude here, isn't it?"

I would take such an action as a direct insult, if not a direct attack.

"As do I. And I've got every right, because it's my mind. But back to my point: dreams fall within your purview as well, don't they?"

They do. Night is the time for dreams, and thus all dreams and dreamers are partially mine. In this, I contain multitudes.

"Then this transgressor cannot go unpunished. Her mind is still connected to mine?"

I have ensured that she cannot leave until we are done with our discussion.

"Excellent. Would you . . . bring her here, please?"

The black fog separated in front of Toshi. It left a small, humanoid-shaped hole. The empty space went translucent and slowly cohered into the body of a small, elegant soratami.

Toshi cocked his head. "You're not the one I expected. I didn't mess up your face on the hallowed streets of Oboro. If you were her, this would at least make some sense. Who are you and why are you here?"

The regal soratami did not answer. Her eyes were angry, but her face and demeanor were chillingly calm.

Toshi shrugged. "No matter. My myojin and I have something for you."

The soratami seemed to be struggling, but the fog thickened around her and held her fast.

Don't do this, ochimusha. The soratami's lips did not move, but it was the same throaty voice that had hectored him before.

"Why?" Toshi sneered. "Is it a sin?" He drew his jitte and slashed it angrily through the fog. When he was through, the same symbol that adorned his waking forehead hung solidly in the air before him, the symbol of the yuki-onna and her lethal cold.

The soratami grimaced, clearly straining to escape. She was in Night's grasp and Toshi's mind, however, and they were not about to let her go.

The kanji floated forward, gathering speed as it approached the soratami.

"Tell Mochi he's next," Toshi called. The kanji punched through the layer of fog and disappeared into the soratami's chest. She shivered and heaved but still could not move. The only sound that escaped her pale blue lips was a gentle wheeze, like the whisper that fails to awaken a sleeping child. Then the moonfolk matron's body withdrew into itself, disappearing into the kanji inside her like water circling out from an unplugged basin. To her credit, she didn't scream once, not even with her mind.

When the soratami was completely gone, Night released the constraining fog and said, *Hurry now. You must finish what you began on the Heart of Frost and return to Jukai. The soratami armada and the orochi rangers are about to receive a vast and terrible guest.*

Toshi paused, watching the stony landscape fade and disperse. If he waited long enough, the ground beneath his feet would soon crumble.

He sheathed his jitte and sat once more with his legs crossed. There was no need to wait and every reason to hurry. Toshi closed his eyes and let himself fall back toward his body.

* * * * *

Toshi awoke with a start. The sun was now fully visible overhead. The yuki-onna still stood transfixed where Toshi had left her. As he rose, Toshi felt the mark on his forehead fade. The glow emitting from the kanji ring also diminished. Slowly, menacingly, the yuki-onna's head tilted forward until her terrible eyes were once more locked on Toshi.

"Thanks," he said. "But we're done now." He got to his feet and dashed to each remaining kanji in turn, brutally marring and cracking the symbols with his jitte. With each lost character, the glow on those remaining receded more. With each lost character, the yuki-onna regained focus and vigor. She crossed the line of symbols and strode purposefully toward Toshi.

Toshi tried to ignore her and went to work on the last kanji.

Sweat ran into his eyes and fell from his brow, melting the snow where it landed. He scraped his knuckles on the rough ground. The tip of his jitte was chipped and cracking. He hacked harder and faster, the snow-woman's shadow almost upon him.

Toshi cried, "Ha!" as the last recognizable bit of the last kanji disappeared in a spray of sharp pebbles and grit. She would never reach him now. Toshi turned his face toward the yuki-onna and grinned.

The dread spirit kept coming. Toshi awkwardly threw himself back and skittered away from the yuki-onna on his hands and feet, still facing her. He quickly bumped up against the wall of the clearing and pressed himself against it as tightly as he could.

"It's over," he told the advancing figure. "The sun's up, the kanji are gone. Why are you still here?"

If she heard him, she did not react. Standing over Toshi, she reached out with her pale fingers to caress his face.

Reflexively, Toshi made himself insubstantial. The yuki-onna's hand passed through his forehead, and the pain seared him like ten year's worth of frigid, skin-chapping wind. Toshi screamed in agony, struggling to press deeper into the rock behind him.

She held her hand in place for several seconds, and then withdrew. The yuki-onna turned away from Toshi and folded her arms into her sleeves. She took several steps toward the path that led to the Heart of Frost's summit, fading as she walked. Before she cleared the ruined ring of kanji, the yuki-onna vanished into the cold, clear sunlight.

Toshi remained a phantom until his heart stopped pounding. He was alive. As he materialized, he felt melting snow seep into his clothing.

"Thank you, O Night."

You have earned my blessings, acolyte. Now rise, and earn them once more.

"Right. Back to Jukai." Toshi pushed himself up against the rock wall, slapped the snow from his legs, and slid into the shadow of the overhanging cliffs.

* * * * *

Mochi appeared in Uyo's chambers on the soratami flagship. He had received an urgent thought-summons from Chiyo, and while her thoughts were jumbled and confused, he didn't need her to inform him something had gone horribly wrong.

He found the moon-masked maiden pacing angrily around the room. Uyo sat half-sunk into the broad couch pillows in a meditative posture. The silent prophet's eyes were open, but her mind was obviously far away.

Mochi floated up to Uyo and stared into her eyes. Then he turned to Chiyo and said, *Has Toshi . . .*

"Night's Reach," Chiyo seethed. In her fury, she was incapable of achieving the clarity of thought required for mind-to-mind contact. "We had him. He was in the yuki-onna's hands. And he slipped through, as I warned you he would."

Mochi's cherubic face darkened and he floated toward Uyo's student. *Have a care, Chiyo. I am not your enemy.*

The masked soratami bowed her head. She took two deep breaths and said, *Forgive me, Mochi-sama. I have been trying to break through to my master, but her mind is closed to me. I cannot determine what was done to her, or the lasting effects. Will you help?*

Of course. Mochi drifted back to Uyo until he was at eye level.

He concentrated, reaching out to her with his thoughts.

Instead of responding, Uyo's eyes flickered as if she were trying to focus them on something minute. She drew a long breath in through her nose. She parted her lips and sighed. The exhalation was white, frigid, and full of ice particles.

A coating of frost crept across Uyo's open eyes. A single tear slid down her cheek, but it hardened and cracked on her blue-white skin. Then Uyo pitched forward, rigid as a statue, into Mochi's arms.

The little blue kami caught Uyo's body, but the sudden stop was too much for her. With a sickening crack, her head rolled off her brittle neck onto the low table in the center of the chamber. There was no blood, as the silent prophet's body was frozen solid. The rest of her crumbled in Mochi's arms as the head rolled to the floor and shattered like a fine glass globe.

Chiyo sobbed in fury. Seemingly stunned, Mochi carefully placed the pieces of Uyo he had caught back on the luxurious pillows. He folded his fingers over his belly and rose into the air, rotating to face Chiyo.

Toshi Umezawa is now your responsibility, he said. *Do what you will. Take whatever and whomever you need to finish him once and for all. Report back to me when he is dead.*

I need no one. Chiyo clenched an angry fist. *It will be done.*

Of that I have no doubt. Go now, Chiyo. We both have much to do. You have a reckoning to see to. Mochi smiled coldly. *And I have a war to win.*

CHAPTER 18

Konda's moth-riders soared over the wilds of Jukai in perfect formation. The Daimyo himself rode at the front of the wedge suspended between two beams of magical force. He had left his horse on the ground long ago, unwilling to abandon the noble beast in the thickest and most dangerous part of the forest.

The daimyo's vision had led him unerringly east, though sometimes it seemed as if his prize had simply ceased to exist. His eyes would shudder and spin, unable to fix on a single position. When this happened he would call for a halt, land the moth-riders, and wait. It was agonizing, but even with the extra days it took to regain the trail he was heartened by their progress. When his army did move, it moved quickly.

The landscape below fascinated Konda. Neither he nor his armies had ever pressed this far east before. After he reclaimed the Taken One and restored the tower at Eiganjo, he would consider sending a proper expedition to finally map eastern Jukai and beyond. If there were nations at the far side of the woods, they must also come under Konda's protection. Someday, he expected, even the orochi will be brought under his banner.

The rolling sea of green stretched on as he flew, the hours

blending into each other. Lost in memories of his prize, Konda didn't notice the changes in Jukai until he crossed over a great smoking hole in the canopy. The daimyo waved his hand, and the moth formation slowed, gently beating their wings just enough to keep themselves stationary over the rising warm air from the fire.

Though his pupils remained fixed on a location even farther east, Konda looked down at the obscene bloodbath directly below. The vivid greens and rich browns of the forest were charred black by fire and splattered with gore. Hundreds of dead orochi had been heaped in the center of the killing ground, and more were pinned to their beloved trees.

The Daimyo felt a monarch's rage swell up in his breast. The orochi were prone to intertribal conflict, but they would never desecrate enemy dead in such a barbaric fashion. Neither would they use fire as a weapon—Jukai was damp all year round, but its trees still burned.

Konda signaled the moths to descend. No, the orochi fought wars in small groups, sometimes even settling disputes by single combat between champions. Some other tribe must have done this. Some foreign power must be conducting large-scale military actions on Konda's own doorstep.

His moths circled the site, and Konda grimly impressed the details on his mind. This must not stand, would not stand. As soon as he recovered the Taken One, he would turn his ghost army east and root out the invaders. He would slaughter them to a man for their brinkmanship, and in the process he would build a bridge between Eiganjo and the orochi for the first time ever. He had often admired their fighting skill and wondered about the wild mysteries they were said to explore in their isolated green home. Uniting against a common foe could not help but foster closer ties.

Konda waved again and his moths rose back into the sky. He reoriented on the Taken One and pressed on, but as he went Konda kept a close watch on the landscape below. If he saw any armed conflict of any size, he intended to investigate and identify the aggressors.

First he would reclaim his prize. Then he would punish these bold invaders. These were the first steps he would take to rebuild his kingdom.

* * * * *

Toshi was relieved but not surprised to find both the moth and the Taken One exactly as he had left them. The great insect was the most docile and accommodating creature he'd ever encountered, and he expected even a mortal wound wouldn't interrupt its happy burbling. As for the stone disk, it seemed quite capable of protecting itself.

Two more piles of salty dust greeted him from beside the Taken One. Toshi wondered if they were more orochi or simply wild beasts that had wandered too close, but he decided not to ask. He was tired of talking to the stone disk and feeling the fool for it.

Toshi paused as something like a good idea crossed his mind. He stepped back from the Taken One and sat with his legs folded. He cleared his mind and then called out to his myojin. She had far more knowledge than Toshi did. Perhaps she could tell him if the prize was alive and, if so, what to do about it.

He sat waiting patiently until his legs began to stiffen. Shortly after that, he opened his eyes and swore.

Inscrutable as always, Night was either unwilling or unavailable to talk to him. He shouldn't complain—she had just personally saved him from the soratami's mind tricks, and she must have millions of other acolytes to look after. Still, she had saved him to do what he was now doing, so she should at least acknowledge his request for an audience.

release me

Toshi started and jerked his head toward the Taken One. The etched dragon was moving again, readjusting its position with the rough sound of stone on stone.

"Absolutely," Toshi said. "That's where we're going next, I promise."

now

"I can't now," he said. "Not by myself. We have to go get some expert advice." Toshi hoped the people he had in mind counted as experts, and that they would have advice. He didn't know where else to go.

To his horror, the disk began to tremble violently. It vibrated against the cedar sapling Toshi had propped it against, making an angry tapping sound. The image of the serpent was pressed up against the surface of the disk as if it were a window. Her tail thrashed angrily.

father

Toshi instinctively looked up, expecting to see multiple giant heads bearing down on him. The sky was empty but for a few trails of black smoke drifting in from the west.

father is coming

"I know," Toshi said. "But we'll be long gone. He's a little slow to get going, as I see it."

The Taken One rattled loud enough to crack the sapling and then shot into the air. The stone disk hovered and turned with its face to Toshi, but the image of the serpent stayed fixed at its center.

coming now

"He isn't," Toshi insisted. "There's no sign of him." He waved to the sky, wondering how much it could see beyond its stone prison. Then the disk began to glow and smoke as it had in Konda's tower, only the smoke hissed angrily now and the glow withered the plants nearby.

"What can I do?" Toshi shouted in frustration. "What do you want?"

The disk snapped to a halt and let out a withering blast of smoke and ash. The glow scintillated across its surface, and tiny arcs of energy leaped to the nearby trees and scorched their bark.

freedom

In spite of himself, Toshi grinned crookedly. "Who doesn't?" he said.

The stone disk did not respond, but slowly turned like the wheels on a cart. The etched serpent stared solemnly at Toshi, but all he could do was shrug.

Then the Taken One flashed like lightning, sending a brilliant column of white rocketing into the sky above her. Toshi was carried back by the force and he smelled his own hair burning.

Dazed, he rubbed his eyes with one hand while he patted out his hair with the other. When his eyes cleared, there was a gleaming column of white stretching from the Taken One all the way up to the clouds. Even in the bright afternoon sun, the gleaming tower burned brightly enough to make Toshi's eyes water.

. . . father protect me from father protect me from father protect me from . . .

"Oh, good," Toshi said, his ears ringing from the fury of the plea. "Just perfect."

* * * * *

Konda had seen amazing things during his long, fabled life. He had seen the tower at Eiganjo rising from the Towabara plains long before the first shovel had broken dirt. He had seen the mysteries of the spirit world laid bare before him. He had gazed upon the splendor of his prize and seen the answers to eternity therein. These things all amazed or enlightened him, but the sight of the soratami armada razing Jukai outraged him like nothing he had seen before.

They came in huge numbers, a massive force of the noblest beings in Kamigawa. He had considered the soratami his closest allies. He had permitted them to keep their distance from the rest of the world and seclude themselves in their cloud city. He had done so out of respect and to allow them to explore their mystical and cultural pursuits . . . not to raise and train a standing army. Had he even dreamed the moonfolk had a military, he would have kept them under much tighter control. They were of course entitled to defend themselves, but this . . . this was an army of demigods large enough to meet him on the open field.

This day in Jukai, against the orochi, the soratami armada was an unstoppable force. They drove the snakes east from the ground and above, shattering the orochi's beloved trees and burning their territorial homeland. Soratami warriors used blades and spells to maim and kill, their perfect rows hardly noticing the steady stream of reptilian bodies. From above, the soratami seemed like a silver-white plow blade, separating the soil as it ripped through the forest. Only this soil was made from living beings Konda hoped to have as allies, and the plow driven by intimates who had already betrayed him.

"Unacceptable," he growled from his place at the head of the moth-riders. "Completely unacceptable." Konda turned back to the east, where the bulk of his ghost army was charging to catch up to him with all possible speed. They would arrive here at this cursed site in a matter of minutes. Would it be soon enough to stop the slaughter?

A plaintive cry ripped through his ears and Konda grimaced. The sound was simultaneously foreign and familiar, like a stranger singing new words to a melody he knew by heart. Before the pain had faded, Konda recognized the Taken One.

His eyes had never wavered from the right spot, but now Konda turned his face, his body, and his entire being toward his goal. There, in the distance, where the column of light touched the sky. It was there, well within range of his moth-riders. It was so close he could feel it, so close he could leap to the ground and run to it.

The moth-riders responded to their lord's unspoken command and soared up over the canopy, gathering speed as they bore down on the tower of light.

Faster, Konda thought. Faster.

The moths would carry him to his prize. His army would follow behind, engaging the renegade soratami on the way. Once Konda had recovered the Taken One, he would carry it triumphantly back and rejoin his ground forces. Together they would punish the presumptive soratami and decimate their army.

The closer he came to the brilliant white beam, the more anxious he became and the faster his moth-riders flew. Konda put his hand upon his sword, every muscle in his body tensed and ready. I'm coming, he thought. You will be mine once more.

Below him, Jukai became nothing more than a blur as he closed in on his goal.

CHAPTER 19

Toshi saw the moths bearing down on them and cursed the double burden of his duty and his stubborn insistence on avoiding that duty. It would be so easy to run now if Night's Reach hadn't just gone out of her way to save his life. Would it make such a difference if he were to escape into the nearest shadow and let Konda have his prize? The daimyo could contend with O-Kagachi; let those two determine how important it was that the Taken One was showing signs of life and self-interest. All Toshi would have to do would be to keep his head down for a year or so and these truly important entities could all kill each other off without his help.

Toshi scrambled to his feet and rushed to the stone disk. Abandoning the disk was not an option he could pursue . . . at least not yet. Better to load it up on the moth and take to the sky. He had outrun Konda and his ghost-moths before, and with Night's help he was sure he could do it again. In fact, he was eager to do it again, just to imagine the look on Konda's face.

The Taken One still floated just above his head, so Toshi placed his hands on the lowest edge and pushed. Whatever was keeping the disk afloat also allowed Toshi to move it easily without turning it insubstantial. In fact, it was faster and easier to move it this way, as he could really dig his heels into the turf and use his body weight to hurry things along.

He reached the moth in short order and guided the disk into the harness. This would be a narrow escape, but it would still be an escape.

father

Toshi paused as the Taken One's voice echoed in his head. When the lingering sound faded, so did the shining white tower. Toshi continued to squint, dazzle-blinded. The half of his body closest to the Taken One's beacon felt seared and tender.

His eyesight returned to normal just as he completed tightening the last strap. He started to swing his leg up over the moth's back, but something heavy seemed to be pressing in on all sides. He glanced up to check on Konda's approach and noticed the ominous purple sky glowering from the east. Had it grown much darker all of a sudden? Or was the storm casting a shadow over all of Jukai?

Twelve flaming suns suddenly ignited around the spot where the tower of light pierced the sky. Toshi stood frozen and agape as O-Kagachi materialized behind the six sets of sun-eyes, appearing whole and solid in one fell swoop. Six square, horned heads roared from massive, swaying necks. Its coils formed an impossibly large and complicated tangle of muscle wreathed in jagged scales, and their bulk filled fully half the sky from here to the horizon.

Toshi still stood motionless, awestruck by the titanic beast hovering so close. O-Kagachi opened all six of his mouths and roared. Back to the east, Konda's moths had begun their descent, silent but no less threatening than the old serpent.

Toshi's eyes darted back and forth across the sky. Konda

himself was streaking toward them and he was surrounded by an unsettling glow. O-Kagachi opened one set of jaws wide and likewise drove down at Toshi and the stone disk. There were only seconds in which to decide. One way or the other, the chase for the Taken One was going to end here.

Or, Toshi thought suddenly, I can do things my way. He took hold of the moth's tether and made himself insubstantial. The leather strap separated from the tree and fell to the forest floor. Then Toshi became solid, unbuckled the harness, and slipped it off the moth so that the leather straps were still fastened to the stone disk. He slapped one hand onto the surface of the Taken One and pulled, guiding the prize over to the closest tree.

"You're free," Toshi told the moth. "You lucky bastard." He slapped the moth lightly on the rump. It burbled one last time and rose into the air.

Toshi locked all ten fingers around the Taken One's harness and swung himself like a child on a rope swing. His weight pulled the Taken One down so that when he slipped into the shadow at the base of the tree, the stone disk was pulled along with him. The last things he saw were Konda's furious face and a wide-open mouth that could have swallowed a mountain.

Then he and his cargo/passenger floated safe and alone through an endless black ocean of silent darkness.

* * * * *

Konda's roar of frustration was almost as loud as O-Kagachi's as they both watched their prize follow Toshi into the shadows and vanish. Fortunately for the daimyo, his moth-riders were far more agile than O-Kagachi's crashing coils, and they veered off as soon as it became clear that their target was gone. The old serpent was not as maneuverable and he plowed into the forest.

The ground exploded in a white-hot blast of destructive energy. The back of the moth formation was blown across the sky like leaves in a typhoon while the front was merely buffeted. Konda's escorts tilted him perpendicular to the ground before regaining control.

The daimyo's eyes had lost sight of their quarry and they darted maniacally across his face. He commanded his moths to turn about so he could confront O-Kagachi—he would at least avenge the attack on Eiganjo. In the time it took to return to formation and complete the about-face, the great serpent had already begun to fade away. As the terrible serpent went, the bright light of early afternoon reclaimed the sky.

Konda swore viciously. How many times would this thief vanish from under the daimyo's nose? How often did he have to track down and corner the prize before he could reclaim it once and for all? He had traveled to the farthest reaches of his kingdom for nothing, and now he must go on for what would almost certainly be more of the same. He needed to find a way to pin this man down, to force him into a situation where he could not run. But how?

The daimyo's eyes suddenly snapped to the northwest and stayed there. Konda's rage cooled as he felt the presence of his prize. He was and would remain connected to it, no matter where the ochimusha took it.

Perhaps this was how he could finally catch Toshi. So far, it was the visible approach of his army that gave the thief time to prepare his escapes. If Konda led a much smaller, less obvious party that relied on stealth and Konda's unerring sense of direction, he could easily surprise the ochimusha and cut him down.

His full army would ride openly and in triumph once he took back what was his.

Pleased with his new plan, Konda called out to his infantry with the intent of summoning them to follow at a distance. In the crazed rush to seize the Taken One, he had forgotten that they were already engaged. A cruel smile crossed Konda's lips.

Here was the place for a demonstration of his full might, in the forests of Jukai. The soratami had come expecting a slaughter, and Konda would see that they got it. Responding instantly to their lord's thoughts, the moth-riders banked and headed back to the site of the armada's latest battleground.

The war-torn clearing had grown far larger as the soratami battered and burned their way east. Moonfolk samurai still poured from their cloud chariots, sometimes leaping off the vessels high above the forest floor and floating safely down with their feet wreathed in fluffy white fog. A significant force of new orochi had joined the faltering defenders and slithered out to face the invaders head on. Brutal close combat raged across untold acres of forest with devastating effects on both sides.

The orochi had mustered themselves into ranks instead of individually concealing themselves and waiting to ambush. They seemed to be organized around a single individual who sent them against the invaders in carefully timed waves. The forward edge of his attack was a line of brightly colored orochi who only attacked with their long, sharp fangs. They snapped and bit the leading soratami, not seeking fatal wounds but seizing whatever body part they could latch onto. Once they had struck, they forced their flexible limbs and bodies deeper into the soratami formation and bit again. In this manner they envenomed dozens of soratami without giving the moonfolk time to strike back. Their toxin seemed especially virulent, blackening the flesh and stiffening the lungs of every soratami it touched. Dozens of samurai faltered and fell, disrupting their graceful formation and throwing their charge into confusion. This left the invaders vulnerable to the next wave of orochi, who were among the biggest and best-equipped snakes the daimyo had ever seen. Most had metal weapons harvested from the soratami themselves in all four hands, and while they were not expert they were able to inflict serious damage on the moonfolk. The rest of this second wave fought with bare hands, but those hands were so numerous and powerful that the soratami found themselves stymied and unable to press forward.

Konda approved of this change in tactics. It was better to keep them off balance and use their numbers against them. It was what he would have done. Whoever the orochi leader was knew his business. Konda looked forward to meeting him when the fighting was done.

A larger cloud chariot came down from the canopy, shrouded in a decidedly blue-tinged mist. Konda wondered what made this vessel different, and as he ordered his escorts in for a closer look, the reason became clear.

A single soratami female levitated from the center of the blue chariot in shimmering blue robes and a ceremonial headdress. She stretched her pale, thin arms over her head, pressed her palms together, and then jerked them apart. A small blue ring of smoke formed between her hands and began to spin.

Quickly, Konda had his moth-riders soar up above the canopy. He maintained his view of the blue cloud chariot long enough to see the soratami wizard hurl the ring of smoke down to the forest floor. It fell like a stone.

The ring burst the moment it touched the loamy soil. The blue smoke vanished, and a bitter wind rose, churning the leaves and other debris into a huge funnel cloud. The whirlwind gathered speed and strength, thickening as it rolled east. The orochi in its path held their ranks until the leader hissed, and then they broke and scattered, melting into the brush.

The blue cyclone tore trees from the ground as it approached, and then gouged the ground itself as it passed. The terrible funnel-cloud plowed on, scattering the forest defenders and flattening a wide alley in the tangle of ancient cedars.

Overhead, Konda paused to respect the tacticians on the soratami side of the battle. This was both how they were moving so quickly through the thick woods and driving the orochi back. Their powerful wind magic served both purposes at once, with the added benefit of breaking up the orochi into smaller groups that were far easier to defeat. In fact, as soon as they were out of sight and earshot of their field general, the orochi fell back to their more comfortable but far less effective strategy of attacking the soratami individually.

Konda drew his sword. Fortunately for the orochi, he was able to inspire his army no matter where they fought, or against whom. By the stirring in his heart and the sound of hollow-voiced war cries coming closer, Konda knew he was at last in position to chastise the arrogant soratami.

The first of Konda's spectral retainers broke through the brush into the scorched battlefield. They did not need to assess the situation or formulate a strategy, for Konda had already done so. Without hesitation, the ghost army of Eiganjo tore into the soratami's flank, creating a gruesome cloud of pale limbs and thin, sticky blood.

Konda guided his escorts down, both to give him a better view and to allow the moth-riders to support the infantry. Now the soratami would face an army that was in every way its superior: Konda's troops were better trained, better armed, and more aggressive than the moonfolk. They also had the element of surprise and, since their resurrection, were as strong and fast as the soratami were . . . perhaps faster and stronger.

The sudden arrival of a new enemy shattered the soratami's precise formation and made their battle plan useless. They had come to fight wild snakes in the woods, not unkillable crack troops with decades of experience in large-scale engagements. The soratami warriors lived up to their reputation, fighting bravely and fiercely against the new arrivals, but the outcome of the battle was never in doubt. The ghost army's warped and twisted retainers cut them down like stalks of wheat.

Konda himself took his moth-riders back across the burned-out clearing and circled over the blue cloud chariot. He could see the small crew of moonfolk and the blue-robed wizard inside. They were scrambling to steer their vessel away from the circling array of ghostly moths.

Konda pointed his sword. "You too, must be punished," he said.

Clouds of glittering yellow force formed around the moths' antennae, similar to the force that held Konda suspended between his escorts. The force continued to collect and gather until each glowing cloud touched its neighbor. Then, a dozen streams lanced from the moths down to the cloud chariot, rivers of sparkling gold that swam with naked, glaring eyeballs. The orbs rolled and jostled against each other at first, but as they bore down on the blue chariot they locked onto the moonfolk inside.

The eye-beams struck, and the chariot exploded. Glittering

gold snow fluttered down to the killing floor, and a mournful wail rose from the beleaguered soratami.

Higher up among the clouds themselves, Konda saw many more of the soratami chariots. They would be dealt with in similar fashion, harshly, and soon. Below him on the ground, his army had completely surrounded the soratami samurai and were in the process of grinding them to bits. There was no sign of any orochi whatsoever, but Konda considered this to be tactical prudence instead of cowardice: if the ghost army won the day here, there was still plenty of Jukai left to defend.

Konda had his escorts and one other moth veer off to the west. The others he sent up to dismantle the soratami armada and demonstrate once and for all who ruled Kamigawa.

On the ground, a small force of about twenty split off from the fighting and raced after Konda's trio of moth-riders. While the bulk of his ghost army would continue to drive the soratami out of Jukai, these retainers would be his honor guard, the smaller, less obvious force that he would take to surprise the thief Toshi.

The daimyo soared on, eager enough to open a wide lead between the aerial elements of his honor guard and the ground forces. He refused to wait one second longer than he had to. Konda swore the next time he laid eyes on the Taken One it would not leave his sight until he reclaimed it, preferably over the dead body of that cursed lowlife.

* * * * *

The voice of Night's Reach boomed through Toshi's head scant seconds after he entered the realm of shadow.

TOSHI, she thundered, *YOU HAVE DISOBEYED ME.*

"I had no other choice, O Night. I had to weigh your wishes against each other. You did not want the Taken One retaken, yet you also didn't want it in your domain. I could not accomplish both, so I picked this."

The myojin's voice grew softer, but she was no less sharp. *You have chosen unwisely, my soon-to-be ex-acolyte. Rectify this situation immediately. Begone, and never return.*

The void around them boiled and churned. Toshi felt a rush of motion and a painful jolt before he tumbled painfully to the cold, hard ground. Behind him, he heard the Taken One make a similar rough landing.

Toshi quickly got to his feet. They were still in the forest, surrounded by cedars and ferns, but the landscape was different from eastern Jukai. This was more like the western edge of the forest, closer to the civilized regions of Eiganjo and the kitsune nation.

Before Toshi could fully get his bearings, Night's Reach sprang up before him on a curtain of black.

"You'll never see it here again," Toshi said quickly. "On my honor, I swear it was unavoidable."

Be silent. I have seen what your honor entails. My blessings count for nothing, my patronage counts for nothing unless it suits you.

"You wound me, O Night. I tried to ask for your guidance and you did not reply."

And that justifies doing precisely what I instructed you not to do? Have I not made you powerful? Have I not intervened and saved you when you were at the mercy of your enemies? And this is how you repay me.

Toshi shrugged. "I was desperate. Mistakes were made. Forgive me, O Night, but I don't see the harm."

And that is why you have failed me so completely, Toshi. The myojin's expression was static and unchanged, but rage and frustration both seeped from its porcelain surface. *My interests hinge on not drawing O-Kagachi's attention. Bringing that to my domain is like lighting a candle that he will always see. In seconds, days, or years, he will come. It might take centuries, but he will remember that I was the one who concealed his missing progeny. If he comes here, if he even fixes his gaze upon this place, I will suffer. And it will take far longer than your life span for me to recover.*

Toshi tried to think of a graceful way to excuse his actions or deflect Night's anger, but before he spoke another disembodied voice joined the discussion.

release me

Real panic crept into the myojin's voice. *What was that?*

The ochimusha paused. "Actually, that's what I wanted to ask you about. It's alive," Toshi shouted. "What do I do with it?"

What have you done? It is connected to O-Kagachi; it has tasted the old serpent's power. If it has awakened, we are all in terrible danger.

Toshi looked into the face of the stone disk. The image of the serpent was facing outward, both its etched eyes fixed on the Myojin of Night's Reach. Its tail waved in angry slashes.

His vision doubled and for a moment Toshi saw two stone disks and two angry serpents. Something heavy pushed against his entire body as a small white spark flashed on the surface of the Taken One.

A sharp, sleek needle of force shot out from the stone disk. It lanced directly into the myojin's face and punctured the mask, sending a spiderweb of cracks radiating outward from the center.

Night's Reach wailed, but the sound faded as quickly as the

pieces of the shattered mask. Toshi continued to stare at the space where his myojin had been until a flicker of motion drew his eye back to the Taken One.

On the surface of the stone disk, the fetal serpent drew its long, forked tongue back into its mouth. It disappeared into the etched mouth with a curious popping sound, and then the serpent resumed her profile position.

release me now

"I'm working on it," Toshi said. He paused, scanning the area for familiar signs. There was only one course left to him now, only one group he could turn to. And if they didn't kill him on sight, they might actually listen to him and try to help.

CHAPTER 20

Lady Pearl-Ear of the kitsune had been at Princess Michiko's side since the very moment the princess was born. At first the fox-woman served because of her great love for Yoshino, Michiko's mother, who died shortly after the birth, but as the child grew Pearl-Ear saw what a remarkable person the princess could become and swore to be the mentor and friend Lady Yoshino never had the chance to be.

Pearl-Ear did not think of herself as a second mother—she would not wish to dishonor Yoshino's memory, and also their species were too fundamentally different. Pearl-Ear did consider herself as family, but as a caring and perhaps overly concerned aunt rather than a parent. She would teach Michiko what she could about the world, but the princess herself would have to make her way in it.

Here in a village of kitsune made refugees by the Kami War, Pearl-Ear realized her guardianship of Michiko was nearly complete. Despite the horrors of the Kami War and the knowledge that her father's crimes had caused them, Michiko-hime was blooming in her self-imposed exile on the western edge of Jukai. Pearl-Ear had never seen the princess Michiko so confident and determined, or so focused. She attended every meeting of the kitsune council and made frequent (and sometimes heated) contributions to the discussion. Pearl-Ear took secret pride in the way Michiko presented her concerns, for it was the kitsune who taught her to reason, to argue, and to address an august assembly. As a representative of the people of Eiganjo, Michiko was a passionate and welcome voice at the table.

Pearl-Ear's eyes crinkled in amusement. Some of the council members had openly mentioned Michiko's only shortcoming as a diplomat: her all-too-human impatience for action. During one discussion, Elder Silk-Eyes explained that the kitsune were always more inclined to observe the situation and meditate on a solution. For all creatures, especially humans, the world revealed itself only to those who took the time to consider it.

Michiko had bowed politely, but her words had been sharp. "Venerable elder," she said, "the kitsune live for hundreds of years. You can afford to meditate. Humans have to act more quickly, else we'd never accomplish anything."

Silk-Eyes spoke kindly. "Well said, Michiko-hime. You have the floor. What would you have us do?"

So once more Michiko had reddened and fallen silent in frustration. There was no answer. The dire situation around them had not changed, and they were still unable to affect it. Simply surviving was a major victory.

Now Pearl-Ear watched the princess from a broad, flat cedar stump as Michiko trained. The princess had thrown herself back into her magical and martial studies, working harder than she ever had in Eiganjo. Pearl-Ear encouraged this to further Michiko's ability to protect herself, but also to give her frustration a constructive outlet. Life was almost idyllic for Michiko in

Jukai, surrounded by her closest friends and most revered elders, but Pearl-Ear knew her student was on the cusp of an explosive outburst. The isolation and guilt she bore on behalf of her father were weighing on her, and she was responding to a primal urge to simply *move*.

Below, Michiko galloped down a long lane the villagers had cleared on the far side of the encampment. War steeds were scarce among the refugees, but there were a few of Konda's cavalrymen eager to contribute to his daughter's training. She was tall and beautiful, though she looked considerably rougher and wilder in the woven linens of the kitsune than in her flowing palace robes. With smooth, practiced motions Michiko nocked and fired six times at six targets as she galloped along the lane. She scored three hits in the center, two in the inner ring, and one on the outer.

"Excellent," said Sharp-Ear, the princess's *yabusame* archery coach and Pearl-Ear's brother. He stood on top of a huge fallen log that marked the outer edge of the horse run. He was small, lithe, and quick even for a fox, and his short-muzzled face was always on the verge of a wink or a playful shrug. Like many of the kitsune, Sharp-Ear was crafty and prone to playing tricks and games on friend and foe alike. In Pearl-Ear's opinion, he was an irksome scamp who should have been named "Sharp-Tongue" for his cutting wit and his quick grasp of any situation . . . but he was a loyal friend and a valuable ally even if he was an exasperating brother.

Sharp-Ear was something of a journeyman, expert in a number of different disciplines. He could harness the magic of field and forest, he was formidable on the back of a horse, and he was devastatingly accurate with the bow. He worked the princess hard during her yabusame training and his combination of good cheer and frequent drills helped Michiko progress far more quickly than she ever had with Pearl-Ear. If Pearl-Ear was a stern but caring aunt to the princess, Pearl-Ear was her boyish, indulgent uncle.

The refugees had been abuzz lately from a series of sudden arrivals. First, Isamaru, Konda's dog and Michiko's companion, had inexplicably turned up. The great pale akita bounded into the village unannounced and unexpected, barking happily at anyone and everyone until Michiko came calling his name. Isamaru had been trained to hunt, but his age had begun to catch up with him. This meant he couldn't catch the rabbits of Jukai, but he was more than happy to join the chase. Some of the refugees were soldiers from Konda's army, and they regarded the dog as a combination lucky charm and good omen. As long as he was there, they allowed themselves to hope.

The second round of visitors was even more remarkable. The honor guard of Eiganjo cavalry and kitsune samurai that escorted Pearl-Ear and Michiko to the academy was thought to have been killed in the massacre. Days after the main party had escaped Minamo, the soldiers joined them, bringing tales of terrifying brutality and the curious, taciturn ochimusha who brought them to safety.

Pearl-Ear recognized the soldier's description of Toshi Umezawa, and she added his heroic actions to the growing list of inexplicable things he had done. In a matter of weeks he had kidnapped the princess, battled the orochi and a major myojin to a standstill on her behalf, murdered one of Michiko's closest peers, freed her from house arrest, and rescued her when ogre and oni came to Minamo. Now for some reason he had returned to the school, and Pearl-Ear had a strong idea what that reason was.

Except for Konda himself, Toshi was one of the only people in Kamigawa to lay hands on the Taken One, and he had left it behind when he rescued Michiko and Pearl-Ear from the school. He must have returned there to take it back, or to exploit its mysterious power for his own use.

Pearl-Ear could not bring herself to trust or respect the man, but Toshi had done them great service as well as great harm. He was a mercenary and an opportunist and he always seemed to be one step away from catastrophe . . . the kind that claimed him and everyone around him. Pearl-Ear looked for the best in everyone she encountered, but she feared Toshi's ambition and fecklessness would destroy him long before he matured enough to rise above them.

Sharp-Ear clapped his hands. "Again," he said. "One more pass and we'll call it a day." Michiko nodded and spurred her horse back up the lane as Riko and a young kitsune replaced the wooden targets.

Michiko reached the starting point, wheeled her horse into place, and waited for Sharp-Ear's signal. It never came.

Instead, a long-haired figure dressed in black emerged from the edge of the woods bordering the horse run. He had bright green eyes and one arm raised, waving to catch the princess' attention. His other arm was extended back into the cedar shadows behind him, but the kitsune's eyes were sharp enough to see what lay beyond. The man's hand was resting atop a large stone disk he had propped against a tree.

Pearl-Ear shot to her feet, but cries of alarm were already echoing through the trees. The soldiers who guarded Michiko closed ranks around her an instant after the visitor appeared. Sharp-Ear sprang from atop the fallen log and nocked an arrow into his bow as he somersaulted to the ground. He trained the bolt on the intruder as his feet dug into the turf.

"Wait," Pearl-Ear called, for she had recognized both the man and his burden. Her brother and the other warriors did not lower their weapons as they advanced, and Pearl-Ear wondered if that was because they didn't recognize Toshi and the Taken One or if it was because they did.

The ochimusha held both empty hands up to show he was unarmed. Pearl-Ear noted that he still had his jitte strapped to his hip but both swords were gone. She would have felt more confident if he'd had the blades and lost the tool he used to inscribe kanji—Toshi's symbol-magic was as dangerous and unpredictable as the fellow himself.

"Stand easy." Toshi quickly scanned the approaching warriors. Pearl-Ear saw a flicker of recognition when the kanji mage saw Sharp-Ear, but Toshi's face visibly brightened when he saw her atop her stump.

"Lady," he called, waving to Pearl-Ear, "I need your help."

Toshi lowered one arm and gestured at the Taken One, its edge barely peeking past the trunk of the tree. "And if you don't want to help me, help yourselves. Look. See what has become of Konda's prize."

Pearl-Ear focused her keen eyes on the stone disk. She watched it for a moment, then gasped when she saw part of the etched serpent move along the disk's edge.

release me

Toshi stayed in his awkward position, grandly presenting the Taken One with one hand and surrendering with the other. "See?" he said.

"Do as he says. Stand down." Michiko's voice rang out from the center of the phalanx of human soldiers and kitsune samurai.

The warriors parted, and Michiko cantered forward on her horse. "That man," she pointed to Toshi, "works for me. I sent for him. And that item," she nodded at the stone disk, "is my responsibility. Sensei." She turned toward Pearl-Ear. "May we present ourselves to the elders for an audience?"

Pearl-Ear nodded. "As you wish, Princess. Wait here and I will convene the council." Before she turned, Pearl-Ear made sure to make eye contact with her brother. Kitsune were subtle creatures and could read a person's body language as easily as a schoolboy's primer. She and Sharp-Ear had also been siblings for almost one hundred years and so could speak volumes with the slightest nod or facial tic.

Don't let Toshi out of your sight and don't let the warriors drop their guard, Pearl-Ear's knowing look said.

Sharp-Ear's scornful expression clearly and succinctly replied, *I need you to tell me that.*

Lady Pearl-Ear left Toshi surrounded by a half-dozen swords and at least as many arrows as she hurried to gather the elders.

* * * * *

Toshi somehow expected more from the wise council of kitsune shamans. Three wizened and scrawny old foxes just didn't justify the reverential treatment they received. Toshi knew next to nothing about the kitsune and he hated the woods, but even he knew that proper fox-elders had more than one tail. Maybe all the really important elders were engaged elsewhere.

The soldiers kept him under close watch but they left his hands free. The littlest kitsune male, Sharp-Ear, had made sure to relieve Toshi of his jitte.

Since offending Night's Reach, Toshi found he could no longer become immaterial or travel by shadows. The kanji that bestowed these powers were still visible on his arms but they no longer functioned. The kitsune still monitored him as if he could come and go at will, and he was determined to keep them misinformed for as long as possible. If they were guarding him as if he were a phantom, they might leave some other avenue of escape open to a more normal prisoner.

So Toshi sat on the stump-platform at the edge of Michiko-hime's riding lane, the Taken One nestled safely against a tree nearby. They had at least taken his advice and not tried to move it. The three elders, Pearl-Ear, and Michiko had all climbed atop the fallen log that bordered the training lane to listen. Pearl-Ear made introductions, Toshi bowed to the venerable foxes, and he told them (with several minor omissions) about his experiences over the past few days.

When he was done they simply stood and gave each other meaningful stares. Michiko looked grim and determined as she watched her teacher. Pearl-Ear in turn waited for the elders' reaction, and so Toshi stood watching his hosts watching each other.

"I don't think you understand the urgency here," Toshi said to Sharp-Ear. The little fox was always nearby. He seemed to have taken a personal interest in minding the prisoner. "A day, two at the most, and we're all in the same trouble I left in the east."

Sharp-Ear continued to stare at Toshi intently, but he answered quietly. "I daresay you're right. But they didn't get to be elders by being fools. Give them a chance to consider the options."

"What options?" Toshi hissed. "It keeps saying, 'release me.' Where's the mystery? It wants out, I say let it out."

"It's not that simple. There's your credibility to consider."

"It is that simple. That thing's alive; everyone can see it. If you were frozen solid, you'd want someone to crack you loose, right?"

"Sadly, I speak from bitter experience. Yes. I did want that when I was frozen and I would want it again."

"Sure you would. What else could they possibly be considering?" Toshi peered up at the silent elders. "*Are* they considering? It looks like they've forgotten why they're here."

"Be quiet," Sharp-Ear snapped. "Or show more respect. You came to us for help, remember?"

"That's because I thought you would know what to do. You don't know any better than I do."

"So what? Even if that's true, what do you propose? Shall we give it back to you and send you on your way?"

"That's a start. If you foxes want to sit and contemplate its true nature, be my guest. Just don't make me wait around to watch." He looked up into the sky.

"We have decided." The elder in the center of the trio spoke. Toshi remembered her name as Silk-Eyes.

"This," she pointed at the Taken One, "is a living thing. Everything else is mere speculation."

Toshi called out, "That living thing 'speculated' three orochi into piles of salt."

Silk-Eyes smiled patiently. "You left snakes and came back to salt. That does not mean the entity is responsible."

"Of course it does. I also think that because it keeps asking to be released that means it wants to be released." He turned angrily to Sharp-Ear. "I thought you said they weren't fools."

"Calm down, my friend." Silk-Eyes offered her hands to the other elders, and they formed a chain. "We will attempt to communicate with the entity. Her voice is already known to us. We only need to make ours heard."

"'Her'?" Toshi said. "If you say so. Look, what you're proposing is not a bad idea, but it's not the right idea. In the east the Taken One called out for 'her' father. She sent up a signal, and O-Kagachi answered. He appeared and moved much faster than he has before. And I know because I've seen him in action twice. How many times have you seen the great spirit beast manifest?"

Sober silence was the only reply.

Toshi nodded. His voice was calm and rational. "She wants to get out. Help me figure out a way to let her out before she calls O-Kagachi here. Do you understand? He's coming here anyway, but if the entity gets anxious, she will bring him here in a heartbeat. If we give her freedom, she can decide when, where, and if he finds her. She can go to him if she wants."

"With respect, Toshi Umezawa, we would rather understand the consequences of our deeds before we perform them. Lately a great deal of misery has arisen from ill-considered action."

"You're talking about the daimyo," Toshi said loudly. He had finally caught Michiko glancing away from Pearl-Ear and he held her eyes as he spoke. "Konda wronged this being and the entire spirit world when he stole her. When he trapped her like this. That blasphemy is the main reason the spirits became hostile and the direct cause of the Kami War. If we don't redeem that terrible act . . . if we don't right that wrong, we are no better than he who committed it."

Michiko nodded almost imperceptibly before turning back to her sensei.

Sharp-Ear suddenly spoke up beside Toshi, startling him. "The ochimusha has a point," the fox said. The crowd that had gathered muttered in surprise, and Sharp-Ear added, "About the danger, I mean. O-Kagachi followed the entity to Eiganjo and broke the fortress walls. He followed it to Minamo, then to Jukai. We have every reason to expect him to follow it here."

Silk-Eyes dropped the other elders' hands and folded hers into her sleeves. "Are you suggesting we simply bestow some degree of animation upon her and leave her to her fate?"

"No, elder." Sharp-Ear shifted uncomfortably. "But I do think we should explore both courses. While you and the other elders reach out to the entity, others can devise a way to free her from that stone shell."

"A capital idea. Will you agree to lead the inquiry into releasing the entity?"

"I shall, elder."

"Splendid. And we shall proceed as I've outlined. We hope that our efforts will make yours less complicated. There is much the entity could tell us, if we knew how to ask." Silk-Eyes turned to Pearl-Ear and muttered something Toshi couldn't hear. Then the three old foxes bounded easily to the ground and took up kneeling positions around the Taken One, their hands clasped together.

"This audience is complete," Pearl-Ear said loudly. "The elders wish to be alone with the entity, so everyone apart from the guards should withdraw."

Toshi turned to Sharp-Ear. "Am I free to go?"

The little kitsune made a great show of thinking it over. "I suppose so," he said. He carefully took the arrow off his bowstring and tucked it into his quiver. "I also suppose someone should thank you for bringing the entity to the elders. They're probably the only people in the world who wouldn't try to profit from it, you and I included." He bobbed a quick bow to Toshi. "Thank you, ochimusha."

Toshi shook his head. He pointed at Michiko-hime atop the log. "I didn't bring it to the elders. I brought it to her."

Sharp-Ear instantly became more alert, his eyes clear and his muscles tensed. "Really? What for?"

"You know what for. They're bound; they've been bound since birth. They both came into this world at the same time and as a result of Konda's actions. I figured all she'd have to do was touch it and something important would happen. We'd know what to do from there."

"That sounds like your usual plan," Sharp-Ear said. "Rush in, kick things over, and see what breaks."

"What a penetrating wit you have." Toshi sneered. "I suppose I'm not allowed to go near the disk while the elders are staring at it?"

"Of course not."

"Can I talk to the princess?"

"If she'll have you. Even then I'm going to stay within ear-shot."

Toshi cocked his head. "Afraid I'll make off with her again? Not a chance. There's no one worth ransoming her to anymore. Konda doesn't care, and you lot have no money."

"I changed my mind," Sharp-Ear said. "You can't talk to her."

The crowd milled past the platform stump, chattering excitedly. After Pearl-Ear gave instructions to the guards watching Toshi, they lowered their weapons and joined the rest of the soldiers forming a protective cordon around the elders and the Taken One.

Toshi watched until the last soldier was as far from the stump as he was going to get. Then he said to Sharp-Ear, "I can go?"

"You can go."

"And I can talk to the princess? She did say she's still my boss."

"If she'll talk to you and you both stay in plain sight, yes. But don't try anything."

Toshi leveled his bright green eyes at Sharp-Ear and made his most serious and reliable face.

"Trust me," he said.

CHAPTER 21

An hour later Toshi caught up with Michiko by the training lane as the princess moved away from the village.

"Michiko-hime," he called. As the statuesque beauty turned, Toshi noticed the princess's companion Riko attending. Damn. The student girl would just complicate things.

The princess bowed. "Hello, Toshi. I was hoping we'd get a chance to talk." She presented Riko. "You remember my friend Riko from Minamo Academy?"

"Yes." Toshi met the smaller girl's angry eyes. Riko was attractive, in a petite, academic sort of way, but she looked like an akki whelp next to Michiko. Plus, she also clearly hadn't forgiven Toshi for kidnapping Michiko, or punishing Choryu, or one of the myriad other terrible things she'd seen him do.

Toshi bowed to Riko. "A pleasure, as always." Which was the complete opposite of the truth—Riko had been grateful to Toshi when he'd pulled them all out of Minamo, but that was the only time he could recall her not glaring at him with hate in her eyes.

"Would you excuse us, Riko?" Toshi bowed again. "I would like to talk to Michiko-hime in private."

"No," Riko said. She folded her arms, the fingers on her right hand tickling the bow slung over her left shoulder.

"Riko," Michiko said. "As a favor to me."

The student archer looked anxious and Michiko said, "We will stand in the clearing over there. If anything happens or you lose sight of us, you may come running."

Visibly unconvinced, Riko said, "I will be watching you both." She pushed past Toshi and then turned around, folding her arms. Michiko beckoned Toshi to join her and they strolled amiably toward the clearing.

"I appreciate what you tried to do today," she said. "The elders are cautious, perhaps overly so, but they will not let anything bad happen."

"They can't stop this bad thing."

"No. But I agree that they have to try reaching the entity before we decide what to do next."

They approached the clearing. Toshi stopped walking and said, "Do you? Because during the trial back there I could have sworn you agreed with me."

"It wasn't a trial," Michiko said.

"Forgive me. I misspoke. Did you?"

"Did I what?"

"Did you agree with me? That we have a responsibility to set the Taken One free."

The princess hesitated. "Yes. I wish to help atone for my father's crime. It will take years, perhaps decades of hard work, but the first step must be to return what was stolen."

"Can you make them listen to you? What kind of sway to you have around here?"

She laughed a sad, musical laugh. "Not much, I'm afraid. In Eiganjo, I was a prisoner. In Towabara, I am a princess. But here,

I am treated no better than a student, and not a very advanced one at that."

Toshi frowned. "You matter more than that. You are connected to that stone disk somehow. I was just telling Sharp-Ear how you two are sisters, in a way. The entity . . . she kept trying to reach out to me, but I was afraid and didn't know what to do. If you reached out to her, I think she'd respond."

Michiko nodded, her eyes far away. "I did sense something between the entity and me. But I assumed it was just my imagination, a feeling of . . . what we were shown about the night of my birth."

"Also the night of her birth," Toshi said. "There is something between you two. I think if anyone should be trying to reach the Taken One, it should be you."

"I would like to be more involved. I feel a great sense of personal—"

"Then be more involved. Pearl-Ear can deny you nothing. Sharp-Ear would crawl over hot coals to bring you a bowl of rice. And Riko . . . I think she'd do anything twice to see you smile."

Michiko shook her head angrily. "This flattery does nothing to—"

"It's not flattery." Toshi leaned in close, nose-to-nose with the princess. "It's strategy. If you want to do things you know need to be done, you do them. If your room is on fire, you put it out or you leave. You don't ask for permission. You don't wait for approval. You just go.

"I say this village is your room and the Taken One is a very big fire waiting for a spark. Don't let the elders stop you from doing what's right, what needs to be done. All you need is one chance and you can make a difference. Ask Pearl-Ear and

Sharp-Ear to ask the elders. The Taken One has reached out to us, but only you can reach out to her.

"Go," Toshi said. "Go to her and listen. Talk. I've spent more time with her than anyone . . . except your father. I know she wants someone to stand by her. Someone who isn't me, or the daimyo, or anyone else she's met so far. I wasn't good enough." He shrugged. "You might be."

For a moment Michiko seemed younger, more vulnerable, as she had when Toshi had first met her. She opened her mouth to speak.

"For a lowlife, lying thug," Sharp-Ear's voice rang out, cutting off the princess and echoing across the clearing, "you're almost eloquent."

Toshi closed his eyes wearily.

The little foxman tumbled out of the leafy branches high overhead, landing solidly on the tips of his clawed toes. Sharp-Ear leaned under Toshi's chin and peered up into the ochimusha's face, waiting for him to open his eyes. When he did, the kitsune said, "Told you I'd be listening."

"Sensei," Michiko said, "Toshi and I were having a private conversation."

"Business," Toshi corrected. "We were talking business."

"You were talking her into doing something you want her to do."

"No. I was trying to find out what she wants to do."

"And if either of you asked me," Michiko flared, "I would answer, because I am in fact standing here with you."

Sharp-Ear bowed. "Forgive, Michiko-hime."

"If you had asked, Sharp-Ear, or waited for me to answer when Toshi asked, you would know. I do think I should help communicate with the Taken One. Everything Toshi says makes sense."

"I agree." Sharp-Ear bobbed a quick bow. "You are tied to the entity, princess. I do not dispute that. But it could very dangerous to interact with it. You could be like the opposing poles of a magnet and naturally repel each other."

"I am willing to face the danger. For my people, for all Kamigawa, and to expiate my father's sins, I would gladly give my life."

"That is truly noble, Michiko, but rash. You must do as you see fit, but also trust the elders. They are wise beyond human understanding."

"That is very patronizing, Sharp-Ear. It is the quality and the content of a life that creates wisdom, not the duration."

"Again, my apologies. I know you do not need a chaperone or a nursemaid or even a tutor any longer. But you do need good advice. It's something all leaders need. And before you respond to this almost-eloquent fellow, my advice as an actually eloquent fellow is to seek other counsel."

"Like who?" Toshi scoffed. "You?"

"Me," Sharp-Ear said. "And Riko. And above all, Lady Pearl-Ear."

Toshi cocked his head. He could hold his own in an argument against Sharp-Ear, but he could never convince the princess if both brother and sister opposed him. He needed to act quickly.

"The dour frump?" Toshi said. "What do we need her for?"

Sharp-Ear growled darkly. "The dour frump is my sister."

"Oh." Toshi shrugged. "What do we need her for?"

"When people like us are certain we're in the right," Sharp-Ear said, "we need people like her to verify. She's better than us, you see. If she agrees with us, we might actually be in the right. Also, if she agrees, she'll help. And she'll make sure the fewest possible number of people suffer in the process."

Toshi narrowed his eyes, appraising the sly little fox with new respect. "You're on our side, aren't you? You think she should talk to the Taken One now."

"I do. But I also think that everything that comes out of your mouth is suspect. Even when what you say is true, it's not reliable."

Toshi blinked. "Now that's eloquence. But if we agree, why are we arguing?" He turned to Michiko. "In the end, it's ultimately up to you, Princess."

"We are arguing," Sharp-Ear said, "because you seem to be encouraging Michiko to behave like a lowlife ochimusha thief and somehow sneak herself in or the entity out for this attempt at communication. I, on the other hand, am encouraging her to consult with her lifelong friend and mentor, my sister, who is often dour but has never been a frump. If Pearl-Ear agrees, we will petition the elders again. They may yet allow Michiko her chance."

"If Pearl-Ear agrees," Toshi echoed. "She didn't agree back on the big log when we were discussing it. What makes you think she'll agree now?"

"My sister is overawed by the elders, especially in person. But she is far more reasonable and pragmatic on her own. I have convinced her to go along with far more frivolous plans in the past. And, as you said earlier, Pearl-Ear can deny Michiko nothing."

"You're both doing it again," Michiko said coldly. "Talking as if I weren't here."

Toshi said, "Speak up then. What are you waiting for?"

Sharp-Ear bowed. "We are both talkers, the ochimusha and I. But now we will listen. What do you wish to do?"

Michiko looked from Toshi to Sharp-Ear and then back. "I will attempt to communicate with the Taken One," she said. "But I will do so only with Pearl-Ear's support and the elders' full knowledge."

Sharp-Ear grinned triumphantly at Toshi. "Good. Then we're all agreed."

Toshi nodded. "It suits me."

"Splendid." Sharp-Ear clapped his hands and rubbed them vigorously. "Princess, shall we collect Riko and return to the training ground?"

"With all due speed," Michiko said. "I am eager to hear what Pearl-Ear thinks of all this."

* * * * *

"Absolutely not," said Pearl-Ear. "The elders are making steady progress. They expect a breakthrough before dawn."

"Dawn could be too late, sister." Sharp-Ear had led them directly to his sister at the edge of the training ground. They stood on one side of the great fallen log while the elders meditated, chanted, and communed on the other.

Pearl-Ear glared at her brother. "Weren't you supposed to be figuring out how to set the entity free?"

"I am and I have been. Toward that goal I say the ochimusha's notion holds merit. The elders themselves said communication was the first step. Michiko-hime is in a unique position to communicate. If she can reach the entity, we will be a good deal closer to learning what it wants and how we can help."

"But the danger to Michiko . . ."

"I am not afraid," the princess said. "I welcome the chance to do this."

Pearl-Ear stood flummoxed as she tried to formulate another argument.

Sharp-Ear prodded her. "Come on, sister. There is no reason to wait."

"There is no reason to rush."

"There is every reason to rush," Michiko said. "Sensei, you said the elders are expecting a breakthrough. I think I can achieve it. If the elders will let me try, it's possible nothing will happen. I could be hurt. It's also possible the entity will recognize me due to our birth connection and respond more quickly than she has to the elders.

"But the point is we will know right away. The elders' result will be slow in coming and far from sure. This way is better."

Desperate for a supportive face, Pearl-Ear turned to Riko, then Toshi. The student archer seemed overwhelmed by the scope of the discussion, but she had always been a clear and rational thinker. Pearl-Ear could tell by Riko's expression that emotion and logic both had told her to support Michiko's idea.

The ochimusha was another matter. During the audience with the elders he had pressed for direct and swift action, but now he was distracted, tense. Was he truly so afraid of O-Kagachi's sudden arrival? Or was he simply uncomfortable acting in the open, where his actions could be seen and judged?

"Toshi," Pearl-Ear said, "you have been very quiet."

"I think we're all doomed," Toshi said. "I think we've already wasted enough time for O-Kagachi to be arriving any second. Either he or Konda will descend on this village and crush it in order to reclaim the prize." He turned to Michiko. "Sorry, Princess, but that's what I've seen."

Michiko bowed slightly and encouraging Toshi to continue.

"The entity reacts differently to different people. She let me touch her, carry her, even toss her around. She tolerates me, but

I don't think she trusts me. She has no reason to.

"But Michiko is different. I think if she touches the disk, if she speaks to it, it will respond." He shrugged. "That's all."

"But why do you care?" Pearl-Ear said. "You are not a prisoner. You can leave here any time you like."

"I'd never get far enough," Toshi said. "I've been . . . diminished since I saved you at Minamo. I can no longer travel that way I used to. When the fight for that stone disk starts, I'm going to be stuck here with the rest of you. Letting the entity go free is our best hope for avoiding the great serpent and the ghost army, and that's my main goal.

"It'd also be a powerful ally." A mental picture flashed across Toshi's mind, his myojin's mask shattered from a single blow. "I've seen her do amazing things."

Pearl-Ear nodded. Toshi's candor was welcome and, for a change, genuine. "Very well," she said. "I shall petition the elders. If they agree, you may begin immediately. But if and when you do, we will take precautions. The elders and I will be standing by if anything threatens you, Michiko-hime. I will not allow you to be harmed. Is that clear?"

"Yes, sensei."

"Then we are agreed."

Sharp-Ear smoothed the fur around his muzzle. "When will you go to the elders?"

"Now," Pearl-Ear said.

* * * * *

The elders agreed quickly. Toshi suspected they had already reached the limit of what they could do some time ago, and so were happy to have an excuse to regroup. Pearl-Ear made a compelling case, however, so maybe the kitsune elders were simply convinced.

Whatever their reason, Silk-Eyes and the other two solemnly moved back to allow Michiko near the stone disk. Toshi, Riko, Pearl-Ear, and Sharp-Ear all stood behind her as the elders chanted a blessing and an invitation to the Taken One to come forth and be heard.

The princess's face was calm, but her eyes anxious. Toshi tried to imagine what she was thinking, tried to guess which emotion was dominating the others. Fear? Guilt? Pride? Duty?

Toshi decided to offer what little help he could. "Michiko-hime," he said, "you know how to approach her, right?"

The princess glanced back, annoyed. "What do you mean?"

"It's like I told the elder," Toshi said. "She let me touch her and carry her across half of Kamigawa, but she lashed out at anyone else who tried."

"According to you," Sharp-Ear added.

"According to me." He turned to Pearl-Ear and gestured toward Michiko. "May I?"

Pearl-Ear stared at him for a moment and then nodded.

Toshi stepped up to the princess and bowed. "Give me your hands." Michiko stretched out her arms with the palms up. Gently, almost reverently, Toshi took each of Michiko's hands in turn between his. He turned her hands down and spread her fingers wide, his own digits moving gently across her down-turned palms.

"Like this," he said. "Approach slowly and lay your hands on the surface of the disk."

"Should I address her before or after we make contact?"

"I'd say before. I don't know if she ever listened to me, but it's worth a try. When you touch her, you'll feel a shock almost like your hands are being slapped back. I think that's all it will take. Once she recognizes you, she'll be ready to talk. And I think we'll all hear that."

Michiko nodded. "Thank you, Toshi." She finally turned and faced the ochimusha. "And if this doesn't work? If she won't speak to me, or even attacks?"

Toshi grimaced. "Let's just hope for the best right now."

Pearl-Ear stepped forward and said, "The elders are through, Michiko-hime. Whenever you're ready you may begin."

Toshi stepped back from Michiko and stood alongside Sharp-Ear. The little fox nudged him and whispered mockingly.

"Hope for the best?" Sharp-Ear chuckled. "They should hire you to motivate armies before the big battle starts."

"I didn't see you offering any encouragement."

"Michiko," Sharp-Ear called, "don't be afraid. We believe in you."

Toshi snorted derisively. "Oh, that's much better than 'Hope for the best.' You sure showed me up."

"Both of you be silent," Pearl-Ear said. "Go on, Michiko-hime. Our prayers are with you."

The princess strode gracefully forward as the kitsune elders continued their haunting chant. The soft lowing rose in pitch as Michiko stepped up to the disk and knelt before it. She called out to it as the Taken One, and then, as Toshi had instructed, Michiko placed her palms flat against the face of the stone disk below and to either side of the etched serpent.

White light crackled under Michiko's hands, and her back arched. The sheen began to spread across the princess's hands and up her forearms. Smoke rose from the Taken One, and the princess let out a deep, painful moan.

Sharp-Ear and Pearl-Ear shot forward like twin arrows from the same bow. They were twice as fast as Toshi, but he had positioned himself to stop them before they reached the princess.

"Don't touch her!" Toshi sprinted as hard as he could, but the kitsune made him feel like he was standing still. They heard, however, and stopped within arm's reach of the princess and the Taken One, their eyes heavy with concern.

Toshi caught up and circled the princess and the disk so he could see Michiko's face. The princess's eyes had gone murky white and her mouth moved soundlessly. Nearby, the kitsune elders' chant reached its crescendo.

Michiko's teeth snapped shut and she threw back her head. The stone disk vibrated under her palms, and the glow grew painfully bright. Then the princess jerked her head back down and stared directly at Toshi through shrouded eyes.

"Release me," she said, but the voice was not her own.

"Sharp-Ear," Pearl-Ear said, and her brother pounced. He landed on Michiko's shoulders with both feet and both hands, his compact little body just the right weight to push her free without injuring her. Michiko's mouth opened wide as Sharp-Ear forced her back, but her hands stuck to the stone disk. For a moment they hung suspended, Sharp-Ear bearing down with all his weight and strength and Michiko clinging to the Taken One. The disk rattled and shook below them, throwing off steam and light and cacophonous sound. The entire forest began to shake as motion and sound radiated out from the Taken One, engulfing the entire assembly.

Then the connection between the princess and the Taken One broke and Michiko fell back from the disk. Sharp-Ear curled himself around Michiko's shoulders and cushioned her fall with his own body. The strange light winked out when Michiko's hands left the stone disk, and the Taken One stopped rattling and became as lifeless stone once more.

"Michiko," Sharp-Ear and Pearl-Ear said together.

"Please," the princess said. "Let me up, sensei."

Sharp-Ear scrambled to his feet and bowed, offering his hand to Michiko. She ignored it and rose on her own.

"We must do as she says," Michiko said. She turned from Pearl-Ear to the elders to Sharp-Ear and then back. "She's so angry, so frightened. She doesn't understand any of this. Most kami choose to manifest in the physical world. She was forced to. It took her years to comprehend the word 'release' because she's never been contained before." She bowed her head to Pearl-Ear. "We have to help her, sensei."

Pearl-Ear hugged her student, soothing her with a tender hand. "We will, child. We will."

Sharp-Ear exhaled and dusted himself off. "Well, that was both disturbing and partially productive. Michiko-hime was able to reach the Taken One quickly. And she learned something new . . . perhaps not the most useful thing to learn, but it is a start."

Michiko pushed back from Pearl-Ear and raised her hands. "I would like to try again. Please. She has seen me now, heard my voice. I think she will tell us more if I ask."

Pearl-Ear shook her head. "The elders—"

"Wait," said Sharp-Ear. "What is on your hands?"

Toshi quietly stepped back from the stone disk as confusion colored Michiko's face. Before he could turn and run, Sharp-Ear was beside him with a short knife to his throat.

The foxman's voice was cold and menacing. "What have you done, Toshi?"

He smiled down at the kitsune. "What we all agreed to do," he said. "I just sped things up is all."

Michiko stood staring at her palms. Each bore a single crimson kanji. On the left was written the symbol for "sister," on the right, "union." Numbly, the princess looked to the Taken One and saw the same kanji imprinted on the stone disk's face, precisely where her hands had touched.

"You know," Toshi said. "I really thought that would work."

"What?" Sharp-Ear pressed the knife in deeper, raising a thin line of red. "You thought what would work?"

"Well, I used an old fugitive's trick to hide the smell. It's meant to throw off dogs and other scent-trackers, but it worked just as well here." Toshi raised his own hands, slowly so as not to antagonize Sharp-Ear, and showed them his own clean palms.

"Are you telling me that's blood?" Pearl-Ear stepped up to Michiko, who was still standing helplessly with her palms outstretched. The kitsune lowered her head to inspect the kanji. Then she turned and glared at Toshi's hands. When she spoke, her voice was tight and tinged with cold horror.

"Yes," Toshi said brightly. "Mine, in fact."

"But why? Why would you do this?"

"I think we've spent enough time debating why. What difference does it make? It didn't work."

Sharp-Ear growled. "What didn't work? What were you trying to do, besides insert your blasphemous magic into matters beyond your comprehension?"

"They're sisters," Toshi said. "We agreed to bring them together. I tried to encourage things along."

By now several of the kitsune samurai had closed in and surrounded Toshi. Sharp-Ear kept the knife to his throat.

"Sister," Sharp-Ear said, "can I kill him now?"

"No, brother. Bind him, and keep him under watch. We'll have no more of his surprises today. Princess, I recommend—"

Temporarily forgotten, Michiko had gone back to the stone disk. She stood over it, her eyes vacant, and placed her palms over the smeared red kanji on the Taken One's surface.

"Toshi is correct," Michiko said. "This is my sister. And she must be free." Michiko pressed her palms down.

The blast sent Toshi and Sharp-Ear hurtling back into the trunk of a thick century cedar. The fox's knife bit slightly deeper than Toshi was comfortable with, but it was not a serious wound. On the positive side, Sharp-Ear was caught between Toshi and the tree, so the kitsune was crushed almost unconscious.

Toshi climbed off the stunned fox and dashed back to the ritual site. He hadn't seen exactly what had happened, but whatever it was had flung Pearl-Ear, the elders, and even Michiko back from the Taken One. The disk itself had risen three feet off the ground, spinning on its axis and rotating end over end. It rattled furiously as smoke and light poured from its edges. A low hum started from within the stone, growing louder and more intense by the second.

Instinctively, Toshi dived behind the tree that had been holding the disk up. Seconds later, he heard another explosion and a terrible cracking sound. He pressed himself against the tree as a volley of hard, sharp objects embedded themselves in the opposite side.

The entire forest fell silent. Toshi exhaled, gathered his courage, and leaned out from behind his tree.

The stone disk was gone. In its place stood a tall figure shrouded in mist and smoke. It was tall, humanoid, and unrecognizable in the haze.

Good for me, he thought crazily. It had worked after all.

CHAPTER 22

Konda's eyes had not wavered in over a day, so he felt sure he was closing in on his prize once and for all. The closer they got, the more he felt the Taken One's presence and the stronger it called out to him. He kept his moth-riders low, barely touching the treetops as they flew. His handpicked squad of retainers kept pace less than half a day's march behind, moving swiftly without banners or war cries. There was no way the thief could see or hear them coming.

He was still receiving flashes from his troops in eastern Jukai, images and sounds that told him the battle with the soratami was turning to his favor. Most of the orochi had moved on to other skirmishes, but with Konda occupying a healthy share of the soratami armada the snakes were mounting a significant effort to expel the moonfolk. When Eiganjo was restored, Konda would send envoys to the snakes, especially the Kashi-tribe orochi in the far east. His new kingdom would be larger, stronger, and more diverse than ever.

Suddenly, stabbing pain lanced through both Konda's eyes, and he cried out. Had he been in control of his own forward motion, the daimyo would have stumbled and fallen. Though his moth-rider escorts were startled by their lord's distress, they maintained their speed and direction.

His peculiar view of the world changed then, sliding from a series of panoramic glimpses in all directions to a single, focused image of the landscape before him. It took the daimyo a moment to adjust and another to realize what had happened.

Konda ran his hands over his face, confirming what he had feared. His eyes had become normal, fixed in their sockets. Quickly, the Daimyo tested the other gifts he had received from the stone disk. He still felt young and strong, and the skin on his hands still looked no older. He was still a seventy-year-old soldier in a fifty-year-old's body.

Neither had he lost contact with his ghost army. He could still feel their presence and send mental commands that would be obeyed without questions. Indeed, the moth-riders above and the honor guard below continued on as if nothing had changed.

Whatever foul magic the ochimusha was using had somehow partially severed Konda's connection with the Taken One. The daimyo still retained his command and his vigor, but he was no longer able to fix upon the disk.

Unfazed, Konda ignored the searing pain in his eyes and resolved himself. He knew he was close. He knew he was going in the right direction. If the ochimusha had blocked Konda's access to the stone, he was likely to consider himself safe and stay in one place. Konda knew he could find him. When he did, he planned to punish Toshi as long and as painfully as the thief's body could stand.

Grim and determined, Konda urged his moth-riders on.

* * * * *

The Taken One emerged from the smoke and debris with precise, deliberate steps. As the only one upright in the immediate area, Toshi was the first to see her newly chosen form.

Naked and unashamed, she appeared to be a full-grown human woman. Her skin was textured like a snake's scales that formed a cascade of subtle colors that blended into one another. On that supple canvas she carried a band of moody and intense crimson across her shoulders that became a patch of mustard yellow toward the waist, which in turn leeched into a stretch of dusty sage green. Her black hair was also tinted with the barest hints of color, but the hue changed depending on which way the light hit it. Her tresses were cropped short and stood out straight, giving her head the appearance of a lion's mane or a dragon's crest. Her lips were dark, ominous green, and her eyes were vibrant yellow orbs with vertical orange pupils.

As with all spirits from the kakuriyo, this one was surrounded by a cluster of floating facets, minor aspects that attended her like servants. In this case, the Taken One was surrounded by a cloud of miniature stars that glittered as bright and distant as the sky on a clear winter's night. Even in the soft light of the forest at midday, the new arrival's stars sparkled and shone.

The woman fixed her vivid yellow eyes on Toshi as he came around the tree. For a moment Toshi looked the Taken One full in the face, taking in the details and waiting for her to act. As they stared curiously at each other, Toshi realized why the disk-woman seemed so familiar. The eyes and the hair and the skin had distracted him from the elegant cheekbones, the small, perfect nose, and the long, graceful curve of the neck. She was wilder, more imposing, and more alien, but the Taken One looked remarkably similar to Michiko-hime.

"Greetings," Toshi said softly. "Do you remember me?"

The Taken One blinked. She craned her head away from Toshi and then fixed him once more with her hypnotic eyes.

"I am free," she said. Her voice sounded like three voices, a shout, a song, and a whisper all at once.

"You are. We released you according to your wishes. My name is Toshi."

The Taken One did not look interested at all in the concept of names. "Where is this?"

"You are in the utsushiyo, the physical world. Does that mean anything to you?"

The Taken One shook her head. Then she stopped and looked perplexed. "How do I now speak? Why do I now move?"

"Well, you're a powerful spirit," Toshi said. "You would know better than I. But I think it has something to do with her." He pointed to the princess.

Michiko had partially recovered from the Taken One's release. She had risen to her knees and was staring open-mouthed at the fierce reflection of herself.

"Sister," the princess said.

The Taken One spun to face Michiko. She approached the princess like a stalking tiger and stared down into her eyes.

"Sister," she said. The Taken One reached down and took Michiko's hands. Tears welled up in Michiko's eyes as she folded the Taken One in her arms. The two sisters embraced awkwardly at first but then clung to each other as the princess's tears rolled down the Taken One's back.

"Forgive me," Michiko said. "I will never be able to restore what my father took from you."

The Taken One hissed and sprang out of Michiko's arms. "Father," she said. "Where?"

The princess tried to soothe the Taken One with her voice. "He is not here. I do not know where he is."

"She means O-Kagachi," Toshi said. Mentioning the old serpent only made the Taken One more agitated, so Toshi added, "He's not here, either, and we'd like to keep it that way."

The Taken One shook her head angrily. "Father," she said, pointing at herself. "Father," she pointed at Michiko. Then she opened her green lips and hissed.

"I don't like them either." Toshi stepped forward to the two women. "Michiko," he said, "it's important that you find out what the Taken One wants. That way—"

The Taken One hissed again, and Toshi stepped back. "What is it?"

The serpentine woman bared her fangs. "Father called me 'Taken One.'"

"She objects," Michiko said. She reached out to stroke her sister's face, but the newcomer pulled away like an angry cat. "She does not wish to be known by the name my father gave her."

"That's easy to fix. Does she have another?"

Michiko stared at the naked double of herself for a moment. "No," she said. "She never needed one before she was brought here."

"Well, let's keep it simple then. How about 'Kyodai?' It means 'sibling.' "

"Kyodai," Michiko echoed. She stepped in front of her twin and touched herself on the collarbone. "Michiko," she said. Then the princess reached out and touched the other. "Kyodai. Sister."

The serpentine woman stared at Michiko for a moment. Then she nodded and touched her own chest. "Kyodai." The entity smiled for the first time, clearly pleased with her new name.

"Please." Michiko took her outermost layer of kitsune linen from her own shoulders and draped it around Kyodai. "A gift for you, my sister." Kyodai eyed the fabric suspiciously, but with Michiko's help she was able to put the garment on. She was not ready for a formal dinner, but the simple kimono did make her less distracting . . . at least to Toshi.

"So, back to business." Toshi bowed. "Welcome, Kyodai. Michiko and I would like to help you, and we will. But first you have to understand our situation." Here Toshi faltered, for he had no idea how to sum up everything relevant in a way Kyodai would understand.

"Michiko," he said at last, "can you tell her what we're up against?"

"I don't think I have to," the princess said. "She isn't comfortable speaking yet, but I'm sure she knows far more than she can say."

Toshi glanced around the training area. "Does she know why we're the only ones awake?" he said. "I don't mind, but your friends have been asleep for quite a while now."

"You," Kyodai pointed at Toshi. "Me. Michiko. We speak now. Alone. They." She gestured at the sprawled, sleeping bodies of the kitsune villagers. "Later."

Toshi smiled as his stomach went cold. "You're keeping them out?"

Kyodai considered his meaning for a moment and then nodded.

"Very wise," Toshi said. "I commend your judgement. But what I'm getting at is this: Both your fathers are coming here. Konda wants you back as his trophy, and O-Kagachi . . . well, I don't know what he wants. But it definitely involves finding you and wrecking the landscape. What do you want to do? Should we run? Fight? Bargain?"

"Slow down, Toshi. You're just confusing her."

"This is the price of freedom, princess. The burden of making decisions. She has to understand that all of us . . . you, me, her, everyone here is in danger. I don't know if she can die, but I can. You can. We all can, and some of us would like to take steps to avoid it."

"What would you have us do?" Michiko said. "You've been running for weeks and it's changed nothing. Fighting seems equally pointless. We can do very little against the great serpent or my father's army."

"Speak for yourself," Toshi said. "I saw Kyodai slap a major spirit aside with no effort, and that was when she was an inanimate piece of rock. I'm hoping she can do a lot more now that she's got a body." Toshi allowed himself another glimpse of that body, still tantalizing him with flashes of colorful flesh from beneath the sheer kimono. He had always appreciated Michiko's beauty, but it was somehow even more intoxicating on Kyodai.

Michiko crossed her arms firmly. "I would rather the first thing we asked of her wasn't combat."

Thunder boomed high overhead, freezing Toshi where he stood. Tentatively, he lifted his head up and saw the terrible dark bank of clouds that had formed.

"So would I," Toshi said, "but I think we no longer have a choice."

In seconds the sky went from bright and clear to black and ominous. Great flaming eyes winked open across the horizon by the pair, six becoming twelve becoming sixteen. Inflamed by his daughter's sudden release, O-Kagachi at last manifested fully, the great and terrible eight-headed serpent in all his awesome splendor. The tangled mass of heads and serpentine necks filled the entire sky in all directions, blotting out the sun, the clouds, and everything else. The only break in the field of crushing coils was directly at the center, straight up from where Michiko and Kyodai now stood.

The rest of the world literally stopped. On the distant horizon, clouds hardened into sky-bound stones that hung heavy in the air. Falling leaves froze in midflight, birds' wings stopped between beats. The great spirit beast's manifestation seemed to draw all other life and motion from the world, from the sky above to the treetops directly over Toshi's head.

Toshi's knees buckled as all eight of O-Kagachi's heads roared down in brute fury. He experienced overwhelming dread and a sadness so profound it made him feel like a single drop in an ocean of tears. The world wasn't ending, it had ended, and its final destruction was little more than a formality. Toshi steeled himself and swallowed his panic. He couldn't run and he couldn't fight, but he would at least meet his end with his eyes open. Toshi planted his hands on his hips and stared angrily, defiantly up at O-Kagachi.

Come on, he thought. Nothing in either world has ever been able to resist you before. He glanced over at Kyodai. But she is something new.

Then, like some malevolent fog, the great old serpent descended.

Kyodai bared her fangs and hissed angrily at the titanic figure. Michiko stared up in abject awe. All her previous encounters with O-Kagachi had been through visions and dreams, and in those only a few of his heads had appeared. Toshi shared the princess's shock but not her paralysis. He ran to Kyodai and grabbed her by the shoulders.

"Call him off," he said. "You called him to you before, so now you have to send him away. Do it now, or your sister dies."

Kyodai tore her yellow eyes from O-Kagachi and locked them onto Toshi. She opened her mouth and her forked tongue shot out, stopping a hair's breadth away from his face.

"Let go," she whispered.

Michiko found her voice. "Do as she says, Toshi. She will never allow herself to be restrained again."

Toshi held on for an extra second, unblinking as the sharp tips of Kyodai's tongue flickered in front of his face. Then he relaxed his grip and stepped back.

"Forgive me." He bowed. "But what I say is true."

The princess stepped between Toshi and Kyodai. "It is as Toshi says, sister. You would be justified in letting your father destroy me. It would balance what my father did to you. But I do not wish to die. Especially not now."

Kyodai's fierce eyes softened. She extended her hand and took hold of Michiko's.

"Come," Kyodai said. "We will prepare."

The air blurred around the sisters. Toshi blinked rapidly to clear his vision, and when he looked again Michiko and Kyodai were gone.

Overhead, O-Kagachi continued to bear down on him. Scattered around the training area, the kitsune elders, mentors, and soldiers continued to sleep. There was nowhere to run. He couldn't fade away and he couldn't escape into shadows. The Myojin of Night's Reach had completely ignored all of his prayers since he'd arrived in the kitsune settlement, and she certainly wasn't answering them now.

Toshi walked among the fallen foxes, prodding them with his

toe. Some, like Pearl-Ear and her brother, stirred and groaned as if they were about to wake up. None of them did, however, and soon Toshi was back where he started, no closer to a solution but much closer to O-Kagachi. The only good thing he took from his survey was his jitte, which he found tucked in Sharp-Ear's belt.

Furious and frustrated, he slumped heavily to the ground. He sat cross-legged and idly began gouging out small furrows in the dirt with his jitte. Here, at the end, he couldn't even think of a useful symbol to draw. Hidetsugu had once told him it would end like this: Toshi alone, forsaken, and fresh out of tricks as retribution closed in on him. Toshi hadn't given the prediction much credence, and when he did he was certain he'd be much, much older when it came true.

I tried, Toshi thought. The final irony was that he truly had been trying to do the right thing. To release the Taken One, to honor the wishes of Night's Reach . . . he truly had been trying to help others in addition to himself.

O-Kagachi roared again. Toshi tossed his jitte into the air so that the tip stuck in the ground. This, Toshi thought. This is what I get for moral and spiritual diligence.

CHAPTER 23

Michiko felt herself disappear into the world, becoming a part of everything while remaining separate and distinct from it. It was intoxicating but also smothering and constraining. She felt like a fish in a bowl that was exactly as big as she was: the entire world was hers to explore, but her world started and ended with her own body.

See, sister, how I have lived. Kyodai's voice rang in Michiko's head though the princess could not see her. *Before I was taken to your world, I was woven throughout the fabric of both realms like the threads in your clothing. The old serpent embodies everything in the kakuriyo and the utsushiyo. Many of the kami you know seceded from O-Kagachi after they'd been given an identity by the denizens of your world. Your prayers can give the spirits purpose, and that purpose gave them power, identity.*

Michiko's vision darkened. When it cleared, she found herself suspended in a huge, cloudlike void of darkness and unstable shapes. She saw a vast expanse of flickering energy and drifting dust . . . by now a very familiar scene to her. Twice before, powerful spirits had shown her the spirit world, its unfathomable ebb and flow churning in a complex rhythm she would never apprehend.

But the kakuriyo seemed somehow different with Kyodai as her guide. Her sister's presence comforted Michiko, making the strange space more real, more alive, and less overwhelming.

Here, Kyodai said, *there was no "I." There was no Kyodai to separate from the fabric of O-Kagachi. All things in both worlds are part of the old serpent, but none more so than me. For I was forcibly removed from his essence not by the prayers of many but by the arrogance of one. I was never meant to be distinct, never intended to be an individual. Then, I had no motion of my own and no will. I had not even the thoughts required to recognize these essential aspects of existence. I was subordinate, wholly contained.*

"I am so sorry, my sister. That sounds like a hellish existence."

It was not hellish or divine. It simply was. I did not know anything other than what was, so I could not love or hate it. How could I long for the touch of your hand when I did not know you existed? When I did not know I had a hand to touch?

The void shuddered and began to spin. Michiko had seen this vortex form before—the visual effect of Konda's crime.

And then he *came.* Kyodai's voice grew low and malevolent.

The scene before Michiko shifted, taking her from the mysteries of the kakuriyo to a small stone chamber in her father's tower. Konda was there with General Takeno and the daimyo's advisors from Oboro and Minamo. They stood around a flaming brazier that cast eerie blue light across the room. Above the brazier hung a stone disk with a fetal serpent etched across its face.

He stole me from my home, ripped me away from everything I knew and was. He gave me individuality without freedom, that I might recognize my sorry state but remain unable to change it. Here is where the hellishness begins, my sister. Had your father let me be, I would never have known regret, anger, or loneliness. Had he brought me here as a true kami, one to be worshiped with respect and admiration, I would have been another willing participant in the great dramas of the physical plane. I would have showered him with as many blessings as he could conceive, as many as I could bestow. For I would have been alive.

But he did neither of these things. He cast me in stone and left me aware. He made me powerful but denied me choice and action. He created me as an individual entity but used me as a means to his ends.

Michiko found herself constrained again, frozen and immobile. She was looking through a distorting window at her father's face. Awash in blue light, Konda's mad grin and wild eyes were the most frightening things she had ever seen.

This is the face of my enemy. The face of your father. This is what I saw for the twenty long years of my physical existence. I will never allow myself to be imprisoned like this again. Do you understand me, sister?

"I do, Kyodai. He is a great man, but great men do not always make good fathers."

The view from inside the stone disk shimmered. When it cleared, Michiko was once more looking out into the void of the spirit world. Slowly, Kyodai faded into view alongside the princess.

"What of your father?" Michiko asked. "We are agreed Daimyo Konda wishes to imprison you again, to use you for the glory of his nation. We will not let that happen.

"But what of O-Kagachi? What will the old serpent do when he finds you?"

Kyodai looked away, her jaw working nervously in an unconscious imitation of Michiko's own nervous habit. *I fear the worst.*

"Then, like me, you fear he will do more than imprison you,"
Michiko said. "He will devour you. He will consume and digest
your personality until it is once more a mere extension of his. He
will take you back into himself to restore the injury done to this
realm regardless of your wishes. Regardless of the multitude of
injuries he will inflict in the process."

Kyodai's voice was soft, almost melancholy. *I called out for him
when I was afraid. But I am also afraid of him. There is none of
this,* she motioned back and forth between Michiko's mouth and
her own. *No language, none of the sharing of ideas or ourselves.
He is everything and therefore needs nothing. His guardianship is
all that matters, the imposition of boundaries between the realms
of physical and spiritual. Only that drives him. I see now how
terrible he is.*

Michiko looked past Kyodai and took in the whole of the
kakuriyo. From her vantage point she could see the very edges
of the spirit realm, the limits of it scope, the very shape of it.
Though its depths were still immeasurable she felt she could reach
out and take it in her hands like some rare and exotic treasure.
Was this how her father felt? Did he also see the true shape of
the spirit world and dream of holding it, protecting it, shaping it
to his design?

Kyodai was truly her sister, she thought. Their lives shared so
many parallels. Yet they were also strangers, unknown and perhaps
unknowable to each other. Kyodai had taken a body of flesh and
Michiko had seen the cosmos as an ephemeral spirit, but this was
not true understanding. They were only visitors in each other's
worlds, observers of each other's lives. Michiko could never grasp

the perfect nightmare of gaining an identity only to spend twenty years discovering it was that of a helpless, motionless prisoner. Kyodai would never see how Konda's indifference to Michiko was as cruel and painful as his devotion to the stone disk, and how his actions had forever altered the course of her own life. They were two sides of the same mirror, linked, identical, but forever distinct and separate.

Their respective fathers had brought them to this. O-Kagachi existed to embody and enforce the barrier between utsushiyo and kakuriyo. Konda dedicated his life to expanding his realm to include as much space and as many tribes as he could. Each wanted sole authority over the whole of both realms. The only difference was that O-Kagachi wanted to preserve existing boundaries as they were and Konda wanted them to change in his favor.

"We must stop them," Michiko said.

Kyodai turned to face the princess. *I agree. But how?*

"O-Kagachi contains both realms and keeps them separate. My father the daimyo is the same with Eiganjo, ruling it and the surrounding nations alike. They both control the traffic to and from their domains as well as within their own borders. We have all been constrained by those borders, yet we know no alternative. Without the structure our fathers provide, both worlds would be different . . . more chaotic and dangerous, less formal and organized. Without clear lines and borders, spirit and flesh alike would be lost."

Kyodai's fierce eyes became haunted, hopeless. *Then what can we do?*

"We cannot simply escape the guardians who seek us. Nor can we simply destroy the boundaries they exist to enforce. Even if it were possible, the result would be cataclysmic upheaval.

"But we can rewrite those boundaries. Our fathers have defined our worlds for our entire lives, but we can redefine them. This is the way of mortal beings, for the aged to give way to the young. The old must stand aside for the new."

Sharpness crept back into Kyodai's expression. A sly, feral look flickered across her eyes. *Then, my sister, you are saying . . .*

"We can fight," Michiko said. "My father stole and imprisoned you before you truly existed. Your father's outrage gave rise to the Kami War, which took my mother's life and my father's love before I could know either. I will resist both daimyo and serpent to the death before I allow them to cause any more harm."

Kyodai smiled, baring her sharp teeth. *Well said. You know I feel the same. But how will you resist? How can we fight them?*

"I am not wise or strong," Michiko said evenly. "But I am determined. I can handle a bow and arrow. I can strike at my enemies accurately from a great distance. I may not have great power, but I have a strong will."

Kyodai nodded savagely. *I, in turn, do have power,* she said. *Untapped and untested. But with your guidance, with your will . . .* The serpentine woman opened her arms. *Come, my sister. Together we will end this. No matter if we live or die, the world will not go on as it has before.*

Without hesitation, Michiko opened her arms and flowed into Kyodai. Here in the spirit realm, their bodies mingled like a river flowing into the sea, swirling currents of Michiko's will mixing with the rising tide of Kyodai's power. For a moment they were wholly combined yet still discrete, a fusion being with four eyes, two mouths, two fathers, two lives . . . but they shared the same spirit and sought the same goal.

Then the sisters flowed completely together, mingling

mind, body, and spirit into one transcendent whole. Tossed on a crashing wave of memories and sensations that were not and could not have been her own, Michiko abandoned herself to the experience. The last full thought she had before her old mind was swept away was, "I was wrong. We *can* know what it means to be the other."

For the first time in either of their lives, Michiko and Kyodai were at last complete.

* * * * *

Sharp-Ear was the first to reawaken after the sisters had departed, but Pearl-Ear was the first to her feet.

"Hello," Toshi called cheerfully. He was still prodding the dirt with the tip of his jitte. He had inscribed a long, complicated series of the symbols that should have allowed him to escape, but the magic simply wasn't working. He tried some of the most basic kanji he knew, but the power was dead to him, frozen and still like the birds and the falling leaves.

Toshi jerked a thumb up toward the sky where O-Kagachi had already touched the tallest trees. "We'll all be dead soon."

"Merciful spirits," Pearl-Ear said. She dashed forward and grabbed Toshi by the shoulders. "Where is Michiko?"

"And the Taken One," Sharp-Ear added. He was favoring his left leg, and his right arm hung limp by his side.

"Kyodai," Toshi corrected. "She took a name because she doesn't want to be known as an inanimate object anymore." He dropped his jitte and twisted Pearl-Ear's thumbs back, breaking her hold. "Mind your manners, sensei. I'm just as upset as you are."

Sharp-Ear padded up behind Toshi. "Can I kill him now, sister?"

"You have my leave, brother." Without waiting, Pearl-Ear moved over to Silk-Eyes and tried to help the waking elder sit upright.

Toshi threw himself to the side, narrowly missing Sharp-Ear's blade as it whistled past his neck. The ochimusha rolled onto his feet and crouched so that he was at the little kitsune's height, his jitte drawn and ready.

Sharp-Ear struck again, stabbing at Toshi's midsection with the tip of his dagger. Toshi easily parried the blow. Sharp-Ear was slower than he had been—either his heart wasn't in this dirty work or he had sustained more serious injuries than he was letting on.

Toshi watched and waited as Sharp-Ear prepared to thrust again. He was prepared to react to a healthy kitsune's attack in case Sharp-Ear was shamming, but the little fox was no quicker. Toshi easily caught the dagger between the tines of his jitte as it came toward him. With a simple twist of the wrist, he snapped Sharp-Ear's blade off less than an inch from the handle.

Toshi twirled his weapon. "That's what it's made to do, you know," he said.

Sharp-Ear scowled at his ruined weapon. Without saying a word, he dropped the broken knife and drew a second that was just as sharp and still intact.

Toshi sighed, casually meeting Sharp-Ear's eyes. "Go ahead," he said. "There probably isn't a kanji hidden on me that'll reflect your own blade back at you. You're probably safe to do whatever you like." He morosely began prodding the dirt with his jitte. "Probably."

Sharp-Ear sheathed his knife. "I know you're lying," he said. "Then strike."

"But I also know you're crafty. I'm betting you can get away from here if you want to bad enough." He glanced up for a moment. "I'll wait until you try before I cut you. It'll be funnier."

"Good," Toshi said. "We'll all need a good laugh in a few minutes."

"Toshi," Pearl-Ear snapped from where she sat with Silk-Eyes. She must be a teacher, Toshi thought. She's got that iron tone down to a science. "If you are to remain here among the living, tell us, where are Michiko and . . ."

"Kyodai."

"Tell us where Michiko and Kyodai are."

"They rabbited," Toshi said. "She burst out of the stone disk looking just like the princess, only sassier and with a definite air of snake about her. Oh, and she was naked." He looked up at Sharp-Ear. "How's that for amusing, you feisty little fur-ball? They're gone, and we're still here. For once I'm the one who's been left behind."

"It's ironic," Sharp-Ear admitted. "But I wouldn't call it funny."

"Nor I. Anyway." He turned back to Pearl-Ear. "They said they were going to prepare."

Pearl-Ear rose and glided back to Toshi. "Prepare? Prepare what?"

"How should I know? Nobody tells me anything."

The forest around them was now as dark as midnight with O-Kagachi spreading over them like a world-sized umbrella. All of the kitsune stunned by Kyodai's rebirth were now awake, and they wept and prayed in the shadow of the serpent.

"If she's gone," Sharp-Ear said, "why is O-Kagachi still coming here?"

"What am I, a librarian? I barely know why I'm here. When it comes to vast, ancient spirit beasts and their succulent naked daughters, your guess is as good as mine."

Sharp-Ear bristled. "Listen, you."

The air beside Toshi blurred. Instinctively, he took hold of his jitte and rolled backward, away from the source of the distortion. He came to his feet beside Sharp-Ear and they stood shoulder-to-shoulder, waiting.

The same kind of mist and smoke that had accompanied Kyodai's emergence was back, only now there were two indiscriminate figures moving in the haze. The sisters came forward simultaneously.

Michiko and Kyodai were dressed in fine leather armor with hammered metal plates over their torsos, biceps, and thighs. The princess wore hers Eiganjo-style, with full sleeves, woven bamboo epaulets, and a white peaked helmet. She sported a longbow on her shoulder and a leather brace on her bow hand. The square quiver was as broad as her back and filled with gleaming, white-feathered bolts.

Kyodai's new outfit was dusty gray and fit her like a tailored suit. The collar ended high, just above her chin, and her fierce eyes fairly glowed yellow in the dwindling light. She carried no weapon, but she walked with power and confidence. Both sisters were now accompanied by the cloud of stars that attended Kyodai when she first emerged.

Michiko said, "Hello. We have come to end this."

Toshi smiled a sickly grin. He poked a thumb up at the sky. "Be my guest."

Kyodai looked up at O-Kagachi, who was steadily crushing the tops of the trees as he descended. Without taking her eyes off the serpent, she extended her hand to Michiko. When the princess took it, Kyodai tossed back her head and hissed, raising the hair on Toshi's arm.

"Father," Kyodai said. "At last we meet." She dropped Michiko's hand and spread her arms up to the sky. "Embrace me, O-Kagachi. I have waited so very long."

Michiko drew an arrow and nocked it onto her bow.

"Michiko," Pearl-Ear said. "What have you done?"

The princess lowered her bow. "Nothing yet, sensei." She bowed. "Wait and watch."

CHAPTER 24

O-Kagachi was barely a hundred feet above the forest floor when the sisters soared up to meet him. With this, Toshi had reached the limit of his astonishment. Anything else he saw today would necessarily fail to amaze him, as he simply had no more surprise left.

The stars around them flashed. Surrounded by individual nimbuses of harsh white light, Michiko and Kyodai spiraled up and around each other in a fluid double spiral, circling mirror images of each other. Despite their speed, ferocity, and confidence, the women seemed small and insignificant against the mighty serpent's coils. It was like they were rising to battle the sky itself after the sky had sprouted teeth and claws to receive them.

Toshi noted that Kyodai's transformation seemed to have baffled O-Kagachi's unerring sense of the Taken One's location. Either that or he simply did not recognize the fierce warrior-maiden who now confronted him. If he did, he continued on to meet her as he would any other foe. Toshi had hoped there would be some sign, some form of acknowledgment between the two powerful spirits, but his hopes were quickly dashed. This did not truly surprise him; family relationships were often difficult.

Michiko broke formation first, soaring wide under O-Kagachi's lowest head. As she'd intended, the head oriented on her and snapped its massive jaws. Michiko was too quick, however, easily zipping out of range of those gargantuan fangs.

As the rest of his coils pressed ever downward, O-Kagachi's head roared after the princess. Powered by the great roiling muscles in his neck, the serpent's jaws overtook Michiko in a heartbeat. She disappeared behind the massive, square head, but dropped below the serpent's strike by letting herself fall rather than trying to fly out of danger. The moment she had cleared O-Kagachi's bottom jaw, Michiko swooped back along its neck, aiming her bow at another head over the edge of the forest.

Kyodai rose like a rocket, following one of the serpent's necks to the uppermost head. Two other heads harried her as she climbed, snapping with their jaws and trying to batter her from the sky with teeth clenched tight. She weaved and dodged around the central neck, narrowly avoiding her attackers. They could not catch her, could not harm her, could not stop her. She was a beautiful song of battle come to life in the skies over Jukai.

Suddenly, O-Kagachi flexed the great sinews in the neck Kyodai was ascending. It was barely a nudge from where Toshi was sitting, but from a giant even a nudge is devastating. Kyodai was hurled violently away, glowing as she soared back to the ground like a shooting star.

Michiko was just stretching her bow when Kyodai was struck from the sky. The princess let fly with her arrow and changed course so that she streaked to intercept her sister before Kyodai hit the ground. Judging by her speed, Toshi knew she'd make it in time.

The arrow was just as strange as the warrior who'd fired it. The bolt started normally as it sped straight and true toward a thick rope of O-Kagachi's coils. Halfway to its mark, the arrow burst into brilliant, sparkling light that cast a red tint over the serpent's mammoth scales. The wooden shaft and white feathers were no longer visible—Michiko's arrow had become a flashing bolt of pure scarlet power.

The red missile tore through O-Kagachi's hide and disappeared below the serpent's scales. A single gout of thick, black liquid jetted out. What flowed through O-Kagachi's veins was not blood, but a strange miasma of dark humors. To Toshi, the muck seemed like jagged shards of the void suspended in a torrent of shadow. The thick cloud dispersed quickly as it flowed away from the serpent, but the splinters of void lingered in the sky.

The wound then swelled and burst as the magical bolt that caused it exploded.

O-Kagachi howled and thrashed, but Toshi could see that it was not gravely hurt. Michiko's attack had blown a man-sized hole in the serpent's neck, but it was barely a pinprick to such a massive beast.

Toshi looked back to the sisters and saw that Michiko had indeed stopped Kyodai's fall. The two warrior-maidens clasped hands and streaked toward the closest head. They left a brilliant line of white in their wake that slowly crumbled to powder and fell like snow. They changed course once the other heads began to close on them, rolled, and then punched through the tough scales on the serpentine neck below them.

Time seemed to slow as the sisters disappeared into O-Kagachi's body. It was one thing to see a bolt of magic sink under the great brute's hide, but this was the sisters themselves. Toshi stared at the entry wound Michiko and Kyodai had made going in, willing them to come back out. Any second now, he told himself. Any second now.

Toshi discovered a new vein of surprise when the sisters burst free from the opposite side of O-Kagachi's thick neck. Huge chunks of muscle and meat blew out with them, along with a great wash of the nauseating mist of darkness and void. Though the muck came Michiko and Kyodai, still unmarred, pristine, and on the offensive.

This time O-Kagachi did roar, and the dragon made a much more terrible sound when it was pained than it did when angry. At last the old serpent broke off his descent and turned his full attention on the fast-moving insects that continued to sting and annoy him.

All eight of the serpent's heads now turned and joined against the sisters. Driven and pursued from all directions, Michiko and Kyodai were forced to separate. It seemed impossible that they would be able to stay away from so many fast-moving threats—O-Kagachi was so large there was hardly anywhere else to be but in his way.

But the sisters moved in flawless unison to use the serpent's size against him. They were both small and fast enough to dodge his strikes out in the open, but they were even more effective in close quarters. Together they circled around his necks and zipped between his coils so that he could not strike at them without hitting himself. O-Kagachi was too old to do himself serious injury this way, but Toshi did see heads slamming solidly into coils and other heads as the serpent tried to crush these annoyances against his own body.

From the confusion of scales and coils, two of O-Kagachi's heads struggled free. They both extended toward the central mass of the serpent, where Michiko and Kyodai buzzed around his body like bees around a hive. Michiko was managing her bow well as she flew, sending bolt after bolt of red fire into O-Kagachi's hide. Kyodai was likewise attacking whenever her path took her close to the serpent's skin, though Toshi could not see the method she was using. It was most likely her bare hands, or perhaps her teeth, for each time she skimmed the surface of O-Kagachi's scales she left a wake of scintillating stars and long, ragged rents in his flesh.

While the sisters continued to nettle him, the wily old serpent struck. He lashed out at both women with the heads he had worked free, one lagging a second behind the other. Each sister dodged, but O-Kagachi changed the lagging head's course and intercepted Michiko as the princess safely avoided the first strike.

It was a glancing blow but enough to shatter Michiko's bow and send the princess soaring straight up. In a second she was gone from sight, hurled so high that Toshi wondered if she'd ever come down.

Michiko's injury had an effect on Kyodai, though Toshi couldn't tell if she felt the same blow as the princess or if she was simply shocked by brutality of it. Whatever the reason, Kyodai paused for a split second too long as she tried to follow Michiko's upward flight. O-Kagachi hooked one of his necks below Kyodai and rose up with his jaws spread wide. Kyodai disappeared behind those terrible teeth and vanished into the serpent's snapping maw.

Toshi stood completely stunned as the last, thinnest thread of hope snapped. The sisters had never posed a serious threat to O-Kagachi, but they had stood against him longer than anything else could have. While they were alive and active, Toshi could contemplate seeing another day. Now that Kyodai was being digested and Michiko was halfway to the moon, there was nothing to stop

O-Kagachi from razing all of Kamigawa, starting with the patch Toshi currently occupied.

His worst fears were realized almost instantly. The head that swallowed Kyodai straightened, leveled, and then plunged down toward the forest. The rest of the serpent's heads sorted themselves out from each other and the larger mass of coils, spreading out to surround the kitsune village once more. The battle must have quickened O-Kagachi's blood, for he was descending disturbingly fast.

But the lead head that had swallowed Kyodai shuddered and stopped on its way to the forest. It jerked spasmodically, rolling from side to side, even shaking vigorously like a wet dog. Close as it was, Toshi could see the broad, winglike fins behind the serpent's skull and the terrible vacant glare of its star-sized eyes.

The head twitched one last time and then burst open at the jaw. Kyodai fought her way clear, surrounded by more stars than ever. Toshi could hear her feral screams echoing across the sky. She left the serpent's jaw hanging loose from one side of his mouth as his tongue lolled grotesquely across his throat.

A shiver of rage and pain flowed across O-Kagachi's entire body. The maimed head danced and thrashed upon its long neck as the others all opened wide and roared. Even as he bellowed his injury to the world, O-Kagachi was recovering, orienting on Kyodai and beginning to stalk.

Kyodai did not wait. She flashed upward, shooting into the sky after Michiko. Toshi almost called after her, but he needn't have worried. Now that he'd been wounded, O-Kagachi was focusing exclusively on his daughter. The old serpent wouldn't spare the forest a glance until he had avenged that injury and prevented any chance of a sequel.

Ponderously he rose to give chase, but a moment later Kyodai returned with Michiko in her arms. The princess seemed limp and unconscious, but Kyodai hovered with her burden, defiantly staring into the eyes of O-Kagachi. For a splendid, terrible moment the combatants held this pose, a single one of O-Kagachi's heads glaring fixedly at the sisters as Kyodai glared back. What exchanged between these two incredible beings was beyond Toshi, but it was clear that if O-Kagachi did not recognize his daughter before, he did now—as his mortal enemy.

Kyodai let out an inhuman scream and hurled Michiko skyward, clear of the coming charge. She rushed forward to meet O-Kagachi's wide-open jaws, borne forward on a powerful storm of muscle and malice.

Toshi wanted to see the impact, but his eyes were drawn to the tumbling figure of Michiko-hime. He was enough of a faker and a trickster to recognize a ploy when he saw it. Kyodai had just abandoned the battle to recover her sister, so tossing her away in a fit of anger either meant Kyodai had lost her temper and her wits . . . or that she was up to something.

He was rewarded when Michiko snapped back to full consciousness at precisely the moment when Kyodai and O-Kagachi plowed into each other. The former Taken One punched into O-Kagachi's face like it was made of soft dough, and the serpent's neck was compressed back on itself behind the head. The fierce woman took the worst of it, as O-Kagachi's mass was unfathomably larger than hers. She broke two of his teeth and drew blood from his nose, but Kyodai herself was propelled backward at tremendous speed.

Toshi saw that everywhere the sisters had struck was covered in stars. O-Kagachi's broken jaw, the slashes on his necks, and the gaping holes in his hide were all wreathed pieces of light and void alike, but the stars were prevailing. Like the scab that forms over a healing wound, the stars seemed to patch and protect the damage done by the sisters. Was this part of their plan?

Half-mesmerized, Toshi shook his gaze free and quickly looked back to Michiko. The princess hung suspended by her nimbus of white with her bow arm extended. The gauzy star-fire around her flowed into her open hand, thickened, then solidified. The mist sparkled, and then Michiko was holding a new bow made of white wood. She wasted no time in putting the new weapon to use, drawing an arrow and firing it in one smooth motion.

This time the arrow converted into a gleaming bolt of white energy. The glowing missile slammed into the top of the head Kyodai had just immobilized. Instead of tearing the serpent's skin or burrowing into the meat below, the bolt seemed to spread out along the surface of O-Kagachi's scales. The growing white stain stiffened and calcified the serpent's body as it went—Toshi could hear the scales creaking and hardening even from where he stood.

In seconds the entire head and most of the surrounding neck had been covered in a sheath of stone. Toshi saw the muscles below the petrifying mass straining to keep the head aloft before they were engulfed by the shroud of white. Undaunted by the fate of their fellow, the serpent's other heads now surged forward to attack Michiko.

Kyodai returned before they could strike, flashing like a lightning bolt into the calcified head. She was a screeching bird of prey as she flew once more into the face of the serpent.

The impact sounded like an entire mountain shattering. Great plumes of white dust shot out from a cloud of force-driven debris.

Within the cloud of grit and dust, millions of distant stars flickered. Every one of the serpent's other heads shot straight out and howled, filling the air with an indescribable wail of pain and fury.

Toshi picked himself up off the ground. For some deep, instinctual reason he felt he was unworthy to look at the aftermath of the sisters' attack. It was like a kind of blasphemy, seeing something mortal eyes were not meant to see. Then he looked anyway.

The sky above the battle was filling with fading pieces of void and an ever-brighter field of stars. Below this curtain of darkness and light, O-Kagachi was now a seven-headed serpent, the eighth now little more than a ragged stump at the end of a long, flailing neck. Michiko's arrow hadn't just immobilized the serpent's head in stone, it had wholly converted it to stone. As Konda had done to Kyodai, Michiko did to O-Kagachi. The sisters had no intention of putting their stone idol on a pedestal and worshipping it, however.

Livid with rage and pain, O-Kagachi flailed at the sisters, throwing his heads at them like a barroom drunk throws punches. Michiko and Kyodai easily avoided these enraged, clumsy attacks. They drew one head away from the rest, and when it was isolated, Michiko rose over it while Kyodai drew back. Michiko fired another white arrow, which O-Kagachi almost dodged, but the bolt still caught him behind the ear.

The process was even quicker this time. The calcifying stain spread across the serpent's face and across his skull, working its way down the massive neck. O-Kagachi struggled to move the stricken head and to bring his other coils up to block Kyodai's killing stroke. The yellow-eyed maiden was too fast and too fierce, dipping down and shattering this head from below.

The sisters established their perfect rhythm on the next head:

isolate, immobilize, and shatter. The headless necks all hung lifeless, weighing O-Kagachi down and disrupting the movements of the survivors. The longer he struggled with his injuries, the wilder and less focused he became.

The serpent truly panicked after they destroyed his fourth head. Effectively halved, O-Kagachi was still a formidable threat—he had battered down the walls of Eiganjo with only three heads, after all. But Eiganjo had only men, moths, and magic to send against him. Michiko and Kyodai were unlike anything he had encountered before, a brand-new fusion of flesh and spirit. If O-Kagachi hadn't been frothing with pain and rage, Toshi expected he would have been raging over the sisters' very existence. He was the great spirit of all things—how could something unknown to him exist, much less cripple him?

The fifth head fell to the sisters, and then the sixth. The sky above the serpent was now covered in an unbroken sheet of glittering starlight. A cheer went up among the kitsune around him, but Toshi was not yet ready to celebrate.

Almost on cue, the sisters stopped their attack and streaked toward the ground. They regrouped between O-Kagachi and the observers in the forest. Toshi saw them talking and nodding, pointing to the last two heads.

Don't get fancy, he thought. Do your thing on these last two before O-Kagachi surprises you.

But the sisters did not hear or heed his heartfelt advice. Instead, they split and each went straight to one of the remaining heads. O-Kagachi hadn't been able to catch them when he was whole, and now it seemed all he could do was snap, roar, and hate.

The sisters landed simultaneously. Each stood proud and strong on top of a flat, boxlike skull. They faced each other and nodded, and Michiko drew her bow. She fired an arrow at Kyodai, allowing for the vigorous thrashing of the serpent's coils. Halfway to its mark the arrow changed into a streak of vivid blue. The azure line raced back toward Michiko at precisely the same speed as it hurtled toward Kyodai so that it touched both sisters at the same time.

At that precise instant, Michiko and Kyodai both turned and caught the incoming blue bolt with both hands. The sky, the air, everything in Toshi's field of vision was swallowed by a sapphire wave of light and force. Blind, he staggered and stumbled against a cedar tree. He turned toward the last place he had seen the sisters and waited for his vision to clear.

Spots danced before his eyes and the blue sheen blurred details, but Toshi saw. As light flickered in the sky and behind his eyelids, Toshi watched, the sisters, now gigantic, grappling on even terms with O-Kagachi's two remaining heads. Kyodai had her quarry clamped under her arm like some great, playful dog. Michiko was keeping the serpent's other jaws closed with both hands, straddling the neck like a powerful horse.

Then, faster than he could register, the sisters and O-Kagachi all shrank from the size of giants who filled the sky to that of average, full-grown humans. It happened as fast as snow melting on a hot griddle, a smooth but dramatic change. One moment they were grappling in the sky like gods and the next they were back on the ground, no larger than they had been before the old serpent came.

O-Kagachi had been reduced far more than the sisters. The great old serpent was still in their clutches, struggling with all his might as his hardened and shattered necks flopped appallingly on the ground. Each of his final two heads was now only a square foot in size, easily controlled by the vivacious warriors who had bested him.

Pearl-Ear stepped forward, Michiko's name on her lips, but the princess called, "No, sensei. We are not yet finished."

Michiko and Kyodai looked at each other. They nodded and lifted the serpent's struggling heads up to eye level.

"This is the way of mortal beings," Michiko intoned. "The aged give way to the young."

"The old must stand aside for the new," Kyodai replied.

The air between them blurred, and when it cleared, O-Kagachi was no larger than a soldier's pack, each wriggling head as long and as broad as a garden snake.

The sisters exchanged one final glance, then as one opened their mouths and bit the final heads off O-Kagachi. With foul black mist and blood streaming from their mouths, they simultaneously chewed, swallowed, and tossed the headless stumps aside.

Michiko turned to Pearl-Ear, wiping her face on the back of her leather gauntlet. "Now," she said grimly, "it's finished."

Kyodai's serpentine eyes glittered as they reflected the starlight around her. "Not quite," she said.

CHAPTER 25

Daimyo Konda redoubled his efforts when he saw the great serpent appear suddenly in the sky. It was troubling, as O-Kaga-chi had never manifested so quickly or completely, but Konda was confident in his eventual success. Anything less than victory was beneath him, unworthy of his destiny. But just to be safe, he summoned the rest of his ghost army to him, ordering them to break off their attack on the soratami and come west with all due speed.

There was no reply from his soldiers in east Jukai. Cold, painful doubt spread throughout Konda's body—had his connection to his army been severed, or had the army itself been destroyed? O-Kagachi's arrival in the utsushiyo always came with unexpected consequences. It pained him to turn away from his loyal retainers, but he could not afford any more distractions at this crucial juncture.

One benefit of the serpent's arrival was that it verified the Taken One's location. Konda urged his escorts to fly faster and lower, his hand trembling on his sword. Soon he would prove that his was the dominant force in Kamigawa.

As he closed in on the serpent's position, something strange happened. There was a storm of arcane blue light, and then Konda saw two women in the sky alongside the old serpent. After that, O-Kagachi vanished from sight.

The daimyo's heart fell. The only possible reasons he could think of for the great serpent's departure were that the thief had slipped away with the Taken One once more, or that O-Kagachi had finally claimed the prize. Nothing else could explain it.

Though his confidence faltered, Konda continued on. He had to know one way or the other. If O-Kagachi had won the race, Konda must return to Eiganjo and develop the means to storm the kakuriyo once more. If the chase was still on, Konda wanted to be sure he reached the prize before the great spirit guardian.

At last, Konda guided his escorts down through the canopy. His spectral moths wove easily through the thick forest until they came upon a long, narrow alley that had been cleared of trees. Konda briefly wondered what tribe had been so industrious. As far as he knew no one inhabited this stretch of Jukai.

Just off the artificial clearing sat two kitsune and a human. They did not seem frightened of Konda's strange and otherworldly escorts, so the daimyo directed them to set him down near the trio. As the moths rose back into the sky, they seemed to fade away into the strange-colored sky. Is it finally over? Konda wondered. Have I finally achieved my goal? For he knew that his army would never abandon him unless the day was already won.

One of the seated kitsune rose to greet him, but the other and the human remained seated with their backs to Konda. It was difficult to expect everyone to recognize him on sight, especially this far from Eiganjo, but the daimyo was still annoyed. He prepared to introduce himself. They would fall over themselves to bow at his feet once they knew who he was.

"Greetings, Daimyo Konda. We have been expecting you."

Konda squinted in the late-afternoon sun. "Lady Pearl-Ear?" he said.

Pearl-Ear bowed. "At your service. Or rather, formerly at your service. I was more recently your prisoner than a member of your court."

"You endangered my daughter," Konda snapped. "What is going on here, Lady? Where is the Taken One?"

"Were it up to you, Daimyo, I would not even know what you were talking about. But I do. And you will not like the answer."

"Already I do not like your tone," Konda observed. "And I suggest you demonstrate an appropriate level of respect before I restore your status as prisoner."

"She is showing you appropriate respect, old man." The human rose to his feet with his back still to Konda. "How you feel about it is your problem."

"Turn, sir," Konda said angrily. "I would see the face of folly before I chop it off at the neck."

The man turned. Konda immediately recognized the thief Toshi Umezawa and drew his sword. "Finally. You will tell me what you have done with my property or I will have you cut to death by inches."

Now the other kitsune rose. His face was unknown to Konda, but he spoke with breathtaking familiarity.

"Get in line," the little foxman said. "And for the record, she's nobody's property any more."

Konda looked at Pearl-Ear. "Are you and this fellow in league with the ochimusha?"

"Not precisely, Daimyo. But we are his allies for the moment."

"Actually," the little fox said, "we hate him almost as much as you do."

The thief shrugged and smiled . . . actually smiled in the face of the daimyo's sword. "I don't make a very good first impression," he admitted. "But ask around. I'll grow on you."

Konda continued to glare. Magic was at work here. A woodland spell or a cursed spring: something had obviously deranged their senses. "You will surrender to my soldiers and come quietly with me to the tower," Konda said. "Or I will crush you all where you stand."

The ochimusha cocked his head. "All of us? Are you sure?"

"Father."

Konda spun at the sound of Michiko-hime's voice. What was she doing here? Why was she dressed in warrior's armor? What were those twinkling lights surrounding her?

"Michiko," he said. "Where have you been? Why are you here?" He turned to Pearl-Ear and the others and shouted, "Where is my prize?"

"Your prize is here, Father." Michiko spoke softly, almost sadly. "Though for the twenty years you clung to it, you never once understood its true value. Was it worth the price you paid? Was it worth two decades of war? Was it worth offending the entire spirit world and endangering the physical one? Was it worth the life of my mother and thousands more?"

Konda glowered. "You may not speak to me this way, Michiko."

"I may do however I like, Father. I am no longer your princess. Your prize is here. You may claim it any time. I believe she is as eager to see you as you are to reclaim her. Perhaps more so.

"I never understood the magnitude of your crime, Father, and when I did I despaired. You were never worthy of the prize you stole, Daimyo Konda. But I see now that in the end, you do deserve it." Michiko turned and began to walk away.

"Come back here, child. How dare you!"

"Daimyo Konda." The strange triple voice brought a chill to Konda's chest. Slowly, he turned and faced the speaker.

She was so like his daughter that he was momentarily confused. The hair, the eyes, the lips, and the clothes were all too strange and wanton for Michiko, but the new arrival could have been the princess's sister. She was unsettling however, with her serpent's eyes and a shroud of stars.

"Who are you?" There was something else familiar about her as well. Not just the resemblance to Michiko, but the sensation he got from looking at her. It felt comfortable, as if he'd seen her a thousand times.

"I have chosen the name Kyodai. But you knew me by the name you gave me."

The chill in Konda's chest expanded. "Then you are . . . are you . . . ."

"I am she who you took from the kakuriyo twenty years ago. You brought me to this world to make you immortal, to make you invincible. To make sure the name 'Konda' would never fade from the memory of Kamigawa. Rejoice, Daimyo. Your goals are all about to be realized."

Kyodai opened her mouth and bared her sharp serpent's fangs. Konda had time to utter one final word, one last plea before the Taken One struck.

"Please," he said.

Kyodai's tongue lashed out, stretching across the distance separating her from Konda. The daimyo barely saw the sharpened tips as they shot toward his face and punctured both eyes.

Konda screamed and staggered back. He clapped his hands over his face and stumbled to one knee. He tried to speak, but his tongue had become like a block of ice. His throat closed and he felt his joints stiffening. His hands grew rough and hard against the skin of his face, and it took all of his strength to pull them down to his sides. He lost all feeling in his legs, though he could still twist and jerk from the waist up. Slowly, he lost this last iota of mobility, and his body became frozen and inert.

Strangely, Konda found he could still see. He was completely immobile, paralyzed and speechless, but he could see and hear perfectly well. Apart from a strange, fish bowl distortion across his field of vision, his view of the clearing had not changed.

Kyodai strolled toward him, her face filling his view. "Behold," she said, "the enduring legacy of Daimyo Konda. His name and his face will never be forgotten, for they shall be preserved here for all time."

The fierce woman's face turned away. Konda heard her say, "Of course, they'll have to be very, very patient to see all of him." When she turned back around, Kyodai's black, vertical pupils almost eclipsed her yellow eyes. Her lips were drawn back in a feral snarl, and she was hissing in pure hatred.

Kyodai lunged forward and drove her fist through Konda's petrified face, shattering his head and the upper half of his chest. There was a momentary pause, and then she struck again, crushing the rest of his body to gravel and dust.

Konda did not die. Instead, the countless pieces of his eyes continued to relay visual images to his shattered brain. He saw not a single picture of the forest and the woman who destroyed him, but a million bits of color and texture, all overlapping and disjointed so that there was no way to clarify the image.

"I know you can hear me," Kyodai said. She was correct, though now her unsettling triple voice was a nightmarish chorus of disorganized and painful noise. "Your daughter has asked me to return in twenty years to see if I feel the scales have been balanced. For her sake, I have agreed."

The kaleidoscope images of Kyodai all leaned down over the debris that had been Konda. The mass of echoing voices whispered savagely, almost spitting the words. "They will never be balanced. I will return, Daimyo Konda. But I will never forgive you."

Kyodai rose and turned away. Konda tried to scream, to release the rage and horror building up within him.

Instead, the pieces of the daimyo's broken body remained as silent as stone.

* * * * *

Toshi bowed as Kyodai approached him. "If you have something similar in store for me," he said, "I prefer to get it over with quickly."

Kyodai returned his bow. "I have no plans to punish you, Toshi Umezawa. We are connected by blood, you, Michiko, and I. I know you better than anyone, and not only because your blood opened my way to freedom. I was with you in Minamo, and in the wilds of eastern Jukai. You are no better or worse than other men, but your actions were helpful to me. You saved me from the tower when no one else could. You kept me from the daimyo and O-Kagachi alike. For that, I am grateful."

Michiko suddenly appeared alongside Kyodai in a sparkling sheet of purple light. "It has been done?"

Kyodai nodded. "It has."

Toshi noticed Pearl-Ear and Sharp-Ear standing nearby. Since he had nothing else to say, he asked the question that was clearly on their minds. "What will you two do now?"

Michiko answered. "We have replaced O-Kagachi as the guardian between worlds," she said. "It will take some time for the effects of this to be felt. The Kami War will continue for a while, but we will soon show the spirit world that there is no more reason to fight."

Kyodai spoke up. "The nature of spirit worship will also change, over time. Michiko and I are far more interested in a blending of the two realms, in sharing each's assets with the other. This too will take time. There will always be spirits and those who pray to them. We will not change that. But the power of the spirit world, the magic their blessings create, these things will be far more accessible to the people of the utsushiyo."

"There is one more enemy you must overcome," Toshi said. "Mochi, the Smiling Kami of the Crescent Moon."

Kyodai looked perplexed, but Michiko nodded. "He is a mischievous moon spirit," she explained. "He facilitated and encouraged my father's crime so that his people, the soratami, could profit from it."

Kyodai's yellow eyes narrowed. "And where is this moon kami?"

"I am here, Lady." The boyish voice spoke from a cloud of glittering blue dust. A sharp, glowing white smile appeared in the center of the cloud, and the dust coalesced into the moon spirit's familiar chubby shape.

"Hail to thee, newly crowned rulers of both worlds. I offer fealty and service from the Smiling Kami of the Crescent Moon."

"That's Mochi," Toshi said. "He's prone to flowery speeches."

"And Toshi is prone to suspicious accusations. I am not a harmful spirit, O sisters. I am playful and duplicitous, but I have never wished you ill or done you harm. Not by action or omission."

"But you did encourage Konda to raid the spirit world."

"That was through ignorance and curiosity. I had no idea he would capture a living spirit. I never expected him to seal you up in a room for twenty years. Michiko can tell you: I have helped her several times, always at some risk to myself."

"My sister has a kindly disposition," Kyodai said. "But she and Toshi both view you with suspicion."

"I am playful and duplicitous," Mochi said again, displaying his dazzling moon-white teeth. "If you know Toshi at all, you'll know he actually admires me on some levels. He just doesn't like the competition."

"I do know Toshi," Kyodai said. "And there is more truth in his blood than there is on his lips."

Mochi's smile softened. "I'm sorry, Lady. I don't understand."

"Toshi has a blood debt against you," Kyodai said. "I have tasted it."

"No longer," Mochi said quickly. "The oath has been dissolved."

"Oath?" Kyodai said. "I know nothing of oaths. But I have come to understand reckonings." She turned to the ochimusha. "You have not asked for any sort of reward, Toshi. Not even after I thanked you for all your help. I believe I know what would make you happy. Would you like me to try?"

"Lady." Mochi's smile had grown strained. "Please don't jest."

Toshi looked at the moon spirit. He thought back to all the trouble he'd had with the soratami and their agents. Many who had suffered and died along the way could trace the cause back to the little blue kami with the brilliant smile.

"Go ahead," Toshi said. "Try."

Kyodai cupped her hands and gazed deeply into them. She was muttering something under her breath. Nearby, Mochi tensed and strained, but he didn't move.

"Trying to flee?" Toshi called. "It didn't help Uyo. I'm betting it won't help now."

A small curl of smoke rose from Kyodai's hands. The smoke curved into a circle as it rose, forming a tiny vortex. The inverted cone grew taller and wider at the open end, eventually curving toward Mochi. It stopped a few feet from the little blue kami, but the mouth continued to widen until it was taller and broader than Mochi himself.

A familiar, terrifying chuckle rose from the center of the vortex. Toshi felt a combination of giddy anticipation and mortal dread. If that was were it sounded like . . .

Hidetsugu's leering face appeared in the cone of black smoke. His eyes were whole and they glittered in cruel amusement. Instinctively, Toshi stepped back, but the o-bakemono chided him before his heel left the ground.

"I see you, blood brother." The ogre blinked his restored eyes. "You have nothing to fear. In fact, I owe you a huge debt."

Toshi relaxed somewhat as Hidetsugu turned back to Mochi. "Speaking of debts . . ."

The vortex was an unstable window to wherever Hidetsugu was. Though his head originally filled the cone, the smoke swirled, and cinders flew across the opening until the ogre's entire body was visible. Hidetsugu wore a black sleeveless robe tied loosely around his waist.

"We will kill you," the ogre recited. "We will burn your fields, steal your treasure, destroy your house, and enslave your children.

We will murder your spouse, poison your pets, and pass water on the graves of your ancestors. We will do all this, and the only way to avoid it is if we cannot find you."

The ogre turned to Toshi and they both said in unison, "We've already found you."

Mochi continued to smile. "No," he said gently. "Please, Lady. No."

Hidetsugu undid his robe and grabbed the lapels. To Toshi, he said, "For Kobo."

Toshi nodded. "For Kobo."

Mochi screamed as Hidetsugu opened his vest. Instead of the burly mass of rippling muscles and scar tissue, his chest was a seething mass of black, disembodied jaws. Laughing uproariously, Hidetsugu spread his arms, allowing the horde of hungry mouths to stream out of the smoke vortex and swarm over the moon kami. His soft blue flesh tore beneath their fangs, and he screamed again, bleeding moonlight from a thousand jagged wounds.

Sharp-Ear, Pearl-Ear, and Michiko turned away. Toshi and Kyodai continued to watch. The savage nightmare lasted only a few seconds, but they were seconds Toshi would remember forever . . . sometimes with callous glee and sometimes with cold terror.

When they were done, the oni mouths left no trace of Mochi at all. They consumed the last speck of blood-spattered dirt and swarmed back into the vortex to re-enter Hidetsugu's body.

"At last we are through, Toshi Umezawa." Hidetsugu retied his belt. "The hyozan's final reckoning is complete." He bowed. "And to you, sisters," he said, "you are always welcome in the halls of Chaos. Come visit me if you require a . . . different perspective."

Kyodai bowed. She parted her hands, and the vortex of smoke dissipated into the air.

Toshi stepped up to the sisters. "If you do not need me any more," he said, "I will be on my way."

Kyodai bowed to him as she had to Hidetsugu. "Farewell, Toshi Umezawa. The world is a far more interesting place with you in it. We will surely meet again."

Toshi turned to Michiko and winked. "Boss."

Michiko nodded. "Umezawa-san."

Sharp-Ear and Pearl-Ear both seemed dazed, but they were glaring at Toshi. He bowed, a malicious grin on his lips.

Eager to depart before the kitsune began making speeches, Toshi waved, spun his jitte around his index finger, and hiked off into the woods.

* * * * *

Half a day's hike from the kitsune village, Toshi walked into an ambush. He was exhausted, and his head was spinning from the day's events, so he didn't feel too ashamed of being caught. He wasn't overly fond of the sharp, silver spike that angled up through his ribs, but at least he wasn't ashamed of being caught.

His attacker pounced from behind a tree. All Toshi saw was a flash of metal before the searing, icy pain shot through his lungs. Whoever she was, she was fast and determined, and she didn't make a sound. She stood with her weapon in Toshi's chest, glaring at him until he fell backward to the ground. She held onto the spike so that it scraped painfully against his ribs as it pulled free.

She was clearly a soratami. Even if her pale skin and slight build didn't give her away, she was wearing a bizarre metal mask in the shape of the crescent moon. Had Mochi come with followers? Was he sneaky enough to bring a secondary force to avenge his own death?

Toshi tried to crawl away, but the slightest breath caused searing agony. His lungs felt packed with broken glass. The moonmaiden's single visible eye held him contemptuously as his blood dripped from her weapon.

"So," he managed. "What's this all about?"

Slowly, the soratami reached around and undid the strap that held her mask in place. The metallic silver fell to the forest floor, and she looked at him, watching him bleed and waiting for him to recognize her.

Not that it should have been hard. Her nose was badly broken, bent in one direction from top to middle and in the other from middle to tip. She also had a series of deep, livid scars angling down one side of her face that stretched to her throat and on under her collar. Whatever had created those scars had also taken her eye.

"Sorry," Toshi said. "Don't know who you are. What'd I ever do to you?"

"I am Chiyo of the soratami," she said. "You desecrated the streets of Oboro. You beat me bloody and set your oni dog on me." She ran her fingers over her missing eye. "You murdered my mentor and my patron spirit."

"Oh, that," Toshi said. He gritted his teeth against the pain in his chest. "So . . . anything to say before you kill me?"

"I have already killed you. Now I am going to stand here and watch you die."

"I can . . . I can think of better ways to spend five minutes."

"I cannot. And you'll be very lucky indeed if you only last five minutes. I was very precise. You should last at least thirty."

"Oh, good. Time for a . . . pleasant little chat."

"Say as much as you like, lowlife. I've seen how your mouth never stops moving. The more you talk, the more it hurts. I planned this very carefully."

"How . . . how do you like the results so far?"

"Very satisfying. So far."

Toshi.

Toshi perked up at the sound of a voice in his head, but even that sent fresh pain grinding through his torso.

I am almost ready to forgive you, Toshi. Night's voice was calm, casual. *Almost. Are you ready to be forgiven?*

"I am." Toshi spoke aloud because it was becoming difficult to think.

Chiyo sneered, unaware of the far more important conversation Toshi was having. "Not for long."

Good. Now. I can save you, of course. I can take you away from here. I can even smite the vengeful soratami for you. All you have to do is ask.

"Smite," Toshi said. "Smite away."

"I've done all I need to," Chiyo said.

Forgive me, my former acolyte, I misspoke. All you have to do is ask . . . and declare yourself mine once more.

"I am yours," Toshi winced.

Again. Say it properly.

"I am yours, O Night."

Excellent. Now. Extend your hand.

The pain was blinding, but Toshi managed to lift his arm.

"Oh, yes," Chiyo said. "Beg. That would be a most unexpected bonus."

Sneering through her ruined face, Chiyo leaned forward to

catch Toshi's dying plea. She was not so foolish or triumphant as to come within reach, but she did come closer.

A stream of solid darkness flowed from Toshi's outstretched hand to Chiyo's face. It hardened around her features in an instant, cutting off sight, sound, and air. She staggered by Toshi twice, wildly slashing with her silver spike, but she never made contact.

It was something of a fair trade: the pain in Toshi's chest continued to mount, but he did get to watch Chiyo slow, stop, and ultimately fall to the forest floor.

"Thank you . . . O Night. I'll take even a small, cheap victory . . . when it's offered."

Toshi, my loyal acolyte. I promised I'd save you, didn't I?

"Yes. But I figured that was part . . . part of the joke."

This is no joke, Toshi. Night's voice grew loud, though her tone remained maddeningly calm. *And besides . . . you don't actually think I'm through with you yet . . . do you?*

Toshi grunted. "I had . . . I had hoped."

With a laugh that sounded like glass breaking on tombstones, the Myojin of Night's Reach enveloped Toshi in a curtain of pure darkness.

Toshi regained consciousness on a high cliff overlooking the sea. He groaned and rolled onto his back, checking his chest with his fingers. The wound was gone, but some of the pain remained. It would be a while before he got his full wind back.

Gingerly, he crawled to his knees and then stood. He didn't recognize the coastline. In fact, he didn't recognize the ocean. He was used to dark, brackish water that barely crested above three feet. These waves were a light blue-green and huge—the smallest swell was taller than Toshi himself.

Out to sea, he saw two huge spires of rock. They looked too perfect to be natural, but who could have constructed them? And what purpose did they serve so far away?

He was ravenously hungry, but the only edible thing he saw was a twig-sized sapling that might someday be a fruit tree. He carefully approached the edge of the rocky cliff. It was a sheer drop of over one hundred feet to the pebbled beach below. If he wanted fish, he'd have to navigate down the treacherous cliff face, and his ribs were in no shape to do that.

Toshi inhaled and then coughed. The air here didn't smell or taste right. He began to have serious concerns about where

Night had deposited him.

Toshi. Then the myojin's voice came to him, soft and muted as if she were far, far away. *You're awake. Excellent. Let me ask you . . . did you ever wonder why I wanted you to protect the Taken One?*

"Where am I, O Night?"

It's rude to answer a question with a question, Toshi.

Toshi sighed. "No. I didn't give it much thought, actually. I supposed it was because you liked the way things were, and if Konda or O-Kagachi got it back, things would change."

You were partially correct, but there was another, far more interesting reason.

"It sounds interesting. I am interested. But must I guess this other reason, or will you tell me?"

When Konda acquired the Taken One, he changed the fundamental balance in Kamigawa. He broke through the barrier that separates the real world from the spirit world. O-Kagachi embodied that barrier. Konda's act was a direct attack upon him.

"I understand."

In fact, Konda's crime allowed me to see the barrier from a whole new perspective. When the serpent turned his attention to finding and reclaiming what was stolen, the barrier between worlds was further weakened. And without his being wholly dedicated to protecting it, I found I could traverse not only the boundary between physical and spiritual, but the boundary between Kamigawa and other worlds. Strange, new worlds with different rules, different paths to power. While O-Kagachi was not watching, I was able to visit these worlds. What do you think I found there?

Toshi did not like where this was going. "Uhh," he said.

"Treasure? Enlightenment? New purpose?"

All of those things and more. I found that just as I am worshiped on Kamigawa, so I am on other worlds. They call me by different names and they practice different rites, but every new world I saw ascribed some deeper significance to the darkness that fills half their lives. This knowledge was very . . . stimulating to me.

Toshi nodded. "So you wanted me to keep O-Kagachi running so you'd have more time to get to know your new followers."

In a sense, yes. I even harbored notions of making you my chief acolyte on Kamigawa so that I could explore other realms on my own. That was of course before you brought the Taken One to my honden and she treated me so roughly.

"I tried to explain—"

Hush, my acolyte. That is all in the past. What matters now is the future of Kamigawa, a future for which you helped lay the foundation. The sisters mean to change the way magic functions. They will succeed, in time.

"But that isn't my—"

And when they succeed, I will have to relearn the blessings I can bestow. I will have to grow and adapt and change.

"Change is good," Toshi said. "Change is life."

In this case, change is an inconvenience. I preferred Kamigawa as it was, Toshi. And I can never have that again. So, for your part in all this, I am rewarding you thusly: you are no longer in Kamigawa, but in a new world that I recently discovered.

"New . . . as in empty?"

Not at all. There are billions of people here.

"Billions?"

And billions of other sentient creatures. Magic here is quite different from what you're used to. I thought it appropriate that you should be in the same position you put me in. There is great power here, Toshi, amazing reserves of magical energy. But you cannot access them by prayer or by kanji. Just as I will have to learn a new way, so must you.

"So," Toshi said, "I'm banished."

Not banished. Planted. You are a seed, Toshi, and it is my sincere hope that you flower. Every nation should cultivate an Umezawa to keep things from becoming static. To keep those in power from taking it for granted. The landmass you are currently standing on is ruled by a powerful queen who styles herself a goddess. You are my gift to her, to this entire world. A bold and clever man like you will go far . . . or, he will be killed by someone more powerful and treacherous in the first year. I can't imagine someone more powerful and treacherous than you on Kamigawa. But this is not Kamigawa.

"I'm starting to appreciate that."

Before I leave you to your new life, I have one final gift. It would be unfair of me deposit you here with nothing but your natural advantages. I hope you can use this to define yourself, to set yourself apart from the common man.

Goodbye, Toshi Umezawa. Perhaps I shall return to check on your progress someday. When I do, I am sure you will have justified my faith in you.

Toshi decided to say nothing as Night's presence left him alone on the alien shore. There was no point in antagonizing her. If he left the impression, of being a good little acolyte who took his punishment like a man, she might even remember him fondly. She might find a use for him back on Kamigawa.

No sooner had Night departed than Toshi's vision began to fade. The image of the sea, and the spires, and the fledgling fruit tree were the last things he saw before darkness obscured all. He turned his face toward the sun and felt its warmth, but he saw nothing but a curtain of unending black.

"Blind," Toshi said. "Great." But he felt surprisingly calm. He turned in place until he felt the sea breeze on his back, and then he walked carefully away from the cliff.

He scratched a few kanji into the sandy soil with his finger, but nothing happened. Blind, abandoned, and powerless. He might as well just turn about and run off the cliff at top speed.

The wind shifted then, and the inland breeze caried the rich, loamy scent of a swamp. Not a rotten, toxic cesspool like Numai, but a sweet scent. It was the scent of swamp grass and thick moss, of ferns and clean mulch. In Numai, things rotted without ever rotting away. This new swamp smelled of decay, but it was the decay that broke down dead things into the raw materials living things needed. This swamp was alive, vibrant, part of a larger cycle that fed the entire landscape.

Toshi smiled. This was clearly the new power Night's Reach had talked about. All he had to do was find his way there and figure out how to tap into it. He might fall in a hole or get bitten by a rabid wolf on the way, but it was a far better plan than running blind off a cliff.

Toshi tilted his head back and sniffed deeply, fixing the healthy swamp smell in his mind so he could stay oriented on it. This wasn't so daunting a task. First, find the swamp. Then, find a way to use the power there. Then, settle in and build a life that doesn't revolve around rats, looting, and reckoner gangs.

Toshi took one step toward the swamp. He didn't stumble, didn't fall, and didn't plunge his foot into a hornet's nest.

So far, he thought, so good.

THE
KAMIGAWA CYCLE
CONCLUDES!

WRITTEN BY SCOTT McGOUGH,
AUTHOR OF THE MAGIC LEGENDS CYCLE TWO

OUTLAW: CHAMPIONS OF KAMIGAWA
Book One

In a world of mysticism and honor, a war is brewing. Spirits
launch attacks against humans as, in the shadows, a terror lurks
just beyond sight. Michiko, the daughter of the warlord Konda,
must brave the dangers outside her father's fortress and stop the
war that is about to sweep the land.

HERETIC: BETRAYERS OF KAMIGAWA
Book Two

Now in the employ of Princess Michiko, Toshi Umezawa tries
to honor his commitments while pursuing his own ends. As the
Kami War threatens to engulf Kamigawa, a spirit beast menaces
the world. At the center of the battle is the Daimyo whose sinister
crime gnaws at the world's heart.

GUARDIAN: SAVIORS OF KAMIGAWA
Book Three

Guardian brings to a close the explorations and adventures in the
new and mysterious area of MAGIC: THE GATHERING first introduced
in *Outlaw*. This novel previews the newest trading card game
expansion set to be released in 2005.

DIVE INTO THE WORLD OF MAGIC!

PLAY MAGIC: THE GATHERING

NEW EXPANSION SETS

Betrayers of kamigawa

SAVIORS
of kamigawa

MagictheGathering.com